THE CHICKEN SOUP MURDER

for Mike

THE CHICKEN SOUP MURDER

MARIA DONOVAN

Seren is the book imprint of
Poetry Wales Press Ltd
57 Nolton Street, Bridgend, Wales, CF31 3AE
www.serenbooks.com
Facebook: facebook.com/SerenBooks
Twitter: @SerenBooks

The right of Maria Donovan to be identified as
the author of this work has been asserted in accordance
with the Copyright, Designs and Patents Act, 1988.

ISBNs
Paperback – 978-1-78172-398-2
Ebook – 978-1-78172-399-9
Kindle – 978-1-78172-400-2

A CIP record for this title is available from the British Library.

The publisher acknowledges the financial assistance of the Welsh Books
Council.

Cover Illustration: © www.123rf.com by Oleksandr Melnyk.

Printed in Bembo by TJ International, Cornwall.

Contents

I	Through the Dog Flap	7
II	Friends of the Dead	73
III	On the Run	179
	Acknowledgements	256

I

THROUGH THE DOG FLAP

The day before the murder, George Bull tried to poison me with a cheese sandwich.

Break time: he got me in a headlock in the playground, patted my face like he was being friendly, smiled for the cameras and said, 'Why don't you and me have a picnic?' George Bull: he's George to the teachers, Georgie to his dad, but to me he is just Bully. He let me nod, and breathe, and walked me off to a corner of the field.

Up on the hillside the girls were playing houses, marking out rooms on the ground with lines of cut grass left by the big mower. Janey and I used to do that, when she wasn't playing football. But she had left me behind and gone to Big School. I felt Bully's arm round my neck and remembered that I mustn't call it Big School.

He let me go and got a tea-towel out of his bag to use as a tiny tablecloth, like we were going to have a nice time. It had a scene of Dartmoor on it and I knew it was the one our neighbour Irma used to keep pinned to the wall. She was my nan's best friend, until Bully and his dad moved in with her. I hadn't been inside her kitchen for a while. I looked at the ponies and pixies and remembered what my nan said, that there ought to be a chain gang and a view of the prison.

'Right then, Nanny's boy,' said Bully. He took my lunchbox and sniffed my sausage sarnies. 'Mmm. Here…' pushing a packet of sandwiches in my face '…you have some proper food for a change.'

'What is it?'

'Cheese.'

He knows I can't eat cheese. It makes me ill. OK. I'm not allergic − I won't stop breathing: I will maybe get a bad headache and throw up. It won't kill me. Only – last time he was punching me, Bully kept saying it was wrong to be intolerant, so I'm not using that word again.

'Get it ett,' he said and dug his dirty fingernails into my nan's homemade bread. Nan had slicked up the sandwich with mayonnaise and ketchup, the way I like it. He chewed with his gob open so I could see the mess, pink and brown, going round in his food-mixer mouth. He ripped open a packet of crisps. I love crisps but I knew he wouldn't give me any. Eating them, he made as much noise as a giant crunching bones. My tummy rumbled.

'What sort of cheese is it?' I said, opening one of the sandwiches and peering inside. 'Because I can eat sheep's cheese. Or goat's cheese. In moderation.'

'"In moderation!"' he said, exploding wet crumbs. 'You are asking for it, Harry Potter.'

I've only got the haircut (thanks, Nan!) not the glasses or the magical powers. Sometimes though I shut my eyes and wish. I wish Bully would just disappear. I dream of him and his dad leaving. I want to believe that good things are possible. Some day I will find out that life is only pretending to be shit: here is your wonderful surprise.

Even saying the word 'shit' in my mind made me feel uneasy. Nan wouldn't like it.

'I don't want to do the test tomorrow,' said Bully. 'Are you ready?'

'No.'

We have been doing SATs all week. Science next. Stuff like Interdependence and Adaptation. Even though I like science, I'm scared I'll get it all wrong.

How can you feel sick and hungry at the same time? I wished I was a Producer, like a tree, so I could feed on sunshine, air and water. But I am a Consumer. I have to eat. I wished I could eat grass. What do you always find at the start of a food chain or web? A green plant. A cow eats grass and out comes milk. But leopards and lions don't try to suck on a cow or a goat. They just eat them up. That is an Irreversible Change.

'I said,' said Bully, 'what did you get for that third question in Maths...?'

Nan says bad things come in threes. First Janey's dad died. Then Irma's dog. And then Irma got a boyfriend. But even though that's bad, it's not like someone dying.

It was going to be a long hungry afternoon. Unless, maybe, if I wished hard enough – this time the cheese wouldn't do me any harm. I took a nibble – and felt the inside of my mouth sting.

I had a nice life before the Bulls moved in next door. I liked our little town near the sea with its magic hills. I liked where we lived in our pebble-dashed semis in a long arc. I liked our neighbours. They were our friends, our family. Irma's house was the other half of the one I shared with Nan. On the other side of Irma's was the house where Janey lived with her mum and dad and little sister. Their house was the same as ours: Irma's was like being in a mirror. Three happy homes each with a long garden. Out the front we had a big green to play on that we called The Middle because Janey's dad liked cricket.

The first thing I ever remember was being in Irma's garden, sitting close to the fence, curling my fingers through the green wire. On the other side was Janey, wispy hair and snubby nose, sitting in her garden on her padded bottom, looking back at me. She curled her fingers round mine and gripped so hard it made me shout. She grinned.

Janey's birthday is in April and mine in October so she started school before me. Sometimes her mum looked after me, and I would curl up in an armchair on rainy afternoons and doze and dream, waiting for Janey to come back in her uniform, smelling of pencils. I was happy when I first started school, because I knew Janey would be there. We walked there together and she didn't let anyone tease her about hanging out with a boy in the Infants. After that, because our school was so small, we were sometimes in the same class anyway, even though we weren't in the same year. When we came home we had to change and then we could eat something and play. We made an obstacle course that took in all three gardens. When we got tired of just racing each other, one of us would take a mouthful of water and try to go round the course without spitting or swallowing. The other one had to make you laugh (no tickling), mostly by pulling faces or jumping out and shouting 'Boo!' or doing a posh-voice cricket commentary, a bad impression of Henry Blofeld's: 'And there's no run!'

Irma always let us play in her garden. We could get through the fence from my side and didn't have to ask.

Once, I climbed into her apple tree and couldn't get down. I sat there on the branch until she came out and found me. When I saw her hands reaching up for me, I stopped being scared: it was funny because I could look down at her – and I thought: this is what it will be like when I'm grown up.

Irma gave us biscuits and elderflower cordial and she brewed elderflower champagne and weird fruity wine to share with Nan. They were always having what they called 'a laugh and a joke'. We were always listening, sieving out the words we would remember.

The days went on. We never thought about them stopping. There would always be a tomorrow.

And there was always someone around when we came home: Irma or Nan or Janey's mum or dad. Irma was the one who was home the most because she finished early. She had a bit of money from somewhere, Nan said, and only worked to not be too lonely. She looked after us, and Janey's dad did jobs for her and mowed the lawn. Nan would take her shopping or use her staff discount at the DIY store where she worked to get things Irma needed for the house. Nan took over all the DIY when Janey's dad died. She tried to show Irma what to do so she could look after herself, but it was no good. Irma didn't have a clue.

Sometimes Nan would invite Irma out for a meal to say thanks for looking after me, and I'd sit between them at the table, or we'd go for an outing in the car with me sitting in the back. We used to all go round to Janey's mum and dad's for a barbecue. You could knock on anyone's door, open it, call out hello and just walk in. Sometimes I used to climb through the dog flap in Irma's kitchen door and help myself to biscuits. If she came home and found me sitting at the table she didn't mind. When the dog died she still kept the dog flap and though Janey said it was for the dog's ghost, so he could come and go, I knew it was for me.

Sometimes people were nice to me because I didn't have a mum and dad. Sometimes they were nasty, like it was my fault. When Melissa was born (Janey's little sister), they let me have a turn at holding her because I would never have a brother or a sister of my own. And Janey's dad played games with us: football in winter and cricket in summer. Janey was always better than me and I didn't mind. Her dad used to take her training in the evenings and to matches on Saturday mornings. Sometimes I went to watch. When she won a trophy, we were all there: Nan and Irma, Janey's mum and dad, Melly – and me. We were, Nan said, 'A unit.'

Then Janey's dad got tired: too tired to take her to football. And he found out he was ill. Janey said, 'My dad's got cancer.' I wanted to give her a big hug like we did when we were small, but by then she was eleven and I thought she might punch me. She looked like she wanted to punch something.

Nan said, 'Janey's dad can fight it. There are so many cures these days.'

Janey's mum said, 'Fat lot *she* knows.'

He watched Janey play a match for the last time. Her mum had to drive so Melly went too. And me. Janey tried so hard to score a goal for him. But it didn't happen that day and she came off the field with her head down. He said she could get into a better team, if that was what she wanted.

In the summer holidays, Janey's mum said, 'Can you please play quietly?' She had stopped working by then. They had made plans to have all kinds of outings: he wanted to go and see a test match – maybe at Lord's or the Oval, because he'd never been, but by then it was too much and it was too far and it was too late.

That was the summer Janey changed schools. Irma and I went to sit with Janey's dad one afternoon, while Janey's mum took her to get her new school uniform. He had been teaching me to play chess so we got out the board. He was good at explaining all the pieces and what they could do but his voice wore away like it was being sandpapered. We stopped the game when Janey got home. I felt bad because he was too tired to be interested in her new uniform.

The next day, Janey put on the uniform and he got dressed and they had a picture together. Then he put on his pyjamas again and that was the last time he wore proper clothes.

We had one last barbecue. Usually when we were all together, people were buzzing, trying to catch whatever joke was hanging in the air. But now it seemed like it was only Janey's dad who made jokes and his voice was so breathless you had to lean in and listen hard to hear what he was saying. Janey's mum couldn't sit down. She was busy all the time, getting us drinks and food. Even when she stood still her eyes were going left and right like she was looking for something. Nan looked after the barbecue way down at the bottom of the garden because the smell of food made Janey's dad feel sick. Janey and I quietly kicked a ball between us, ready to listen. She was serious, watchful, except when her dad looked at her and then her face opened into a big smile.

A piece of chicken and some salad appeared in front of Janey's dad as if by magic. He didn't eat it all. I ate three sausages standing in the kitchen where nobody could see me.

Sometimes I wanted to cry about it: sometimes I wanted to shout or run to break the tight feeling – but everyone else was being normal so I had to be normal too.

By the time we started back to school, Janey's dad was dead.

Maybe it was all the talk about living life while you can – anyway, Irma got a boyfriend. Nan didn't like him. She slapped herself on the forehead and said, 'But it was my fault they met!'

Nan and Irma had been saying they wanted to make the best of the time they had left (as if they hadn't been happy before). They went looking about for things they could do. First they tried amateur dramatics. Irma loved it but Nan stopped going after the first time. ('Your trouble, Zene,' said Irma, 'is that you can't forget yourself.') Then Nan wanted to take a self-defence class and Irma went along to try that, too. The instructor was this policeman: PC Shawn Bull. He took what Nan called 'a shine' to Irma. At first Nan thought it was funny. 'I saw his eyes light up when he saw you,' she said.

'Did they?' said Irma, smirking and coiling a lock of grey hair round her finger.

Nan soon decided she didn't like doing self-defence. 'It just makes you think about being attacked all the time.'

Irma went without her. 'He's got a son your age,' she said to me, excited. 'I think he's just started at your school.' I had never seen her so cheerful. But there was only one new boy in my class.

'Oh,' I said. 'You mean George Bull.'

'Yes,' she said. 'Do you know him?'

'He hits me,' I said.

'Oh, I'm sure he doesn't hate you,' said Irma, deliberately mishearing. 'I've met him. He's been through a lot, but he's a very nice little lad.'

'Not to me he isn't.'

Nan was watching Irma.

'Boys will be boys,' Irma said and laughed. 'We'll have to see if we can get the two of you to be friends.'

Nan said to me afterwards, 'Keep out of that little bully's way if you can. We don't want his dad finding out about you-know-who and you-know-what and you-know-where.'

'Bit late for that,' I said. After all, I'd been telling the others at school that my parents were International Jewel Thieves since I was five. It was the best reason I could think of for why they were in prison. I couldn't change my story now.

Shawn Bull always looked at me like I had done something wrong or was going to in a minute. Nan said he was an un-pc PC because he saw Janey in her football shorts and called her 'Sporty Spice'. One day, when we were all still trying to be friends, Irma said, 'Won't it be nice for Michael to have George in the same class? He's missed Janey since she went up to Big School.' Shawn Bull winked and said, 'That's older women for you.' And Irma, who was like a grey-haired girl with her bob and her long pink skirt, went all giggly and blushed until Nan looked like she wanted to be sick.

Nan thought there was something not quite right about the Bulls. She tried to warn Irma. 'What are you doing with a man who's ten years younger than you? Don't you see he just looks at you and sees a nice house with the mortgage paid off, someone to look after his horrible little boy, and early retirement?'

'You're jealous,' said Irma, 'which is too bad, because Shawn and George are moving in.'

After that we couldn't play in Irma's garden any more. Shawn

Bull did the DIY for Irma instead of Nan. He mowed the lawn and dug the garden and complained because Janey's mum let the brambles grow on her side and they were looping over their fence. Irma used to pick the berries – free fruit – and didn't mind. But she didn't tell PC Shawn Bull that. She stayed quiet.

Nan said we'd better try to get on with them, after all, so I let Bully come round and play at mine – only he laughed at my farmyard animals wallpaper and snatched Ted off my bed and punched him in the guts. I screamed and Nan sent Bully home.

Ted is the only thing I have that was my dad's. It was the bear Nan bought him when he was a little boy. Before he met my mum and 'went to the bad'. I'm not really sure what bad they went to. Nan won't talk about it.

She said to Irma, 'How can you let your boyfriend's son bully Michael?'

Irma said, 'Maybe it's time Michael grew out of geese and cows and donkeys on the walls.' She said Nan should use her staff discount and redecorate. But maybe Irma did say something to Bully or his dad. I don't know – Bully didn't stop hurting me. He just made sure he didn't leave any marks.

He tried to make friends with Janey. She didn't want to know. He tried making fun of her. She ignored him. He saw us playing football and said to me, 'Have you done her yet?'

I was going to say, 'Done her what?' when Janey jumped in.

She said, 'Michael's not my boyfriend.'

No. I was not her boyfriend. I wasn't even the boy next door: I was just the boy next door but one.

By going home time my nose was blocked up, my head thumping. I felt sick and the inside of my mouth was sore; nasty trickles of salty mucus kept sliding down the back of my throat. I just wanted to get home, draw the curtains and lie down on my own bed. Most days I tried to get home fast but that day the headache slowed me down.

I was almost in sight of The Middle when I heard Bully galumphing up behind me. His arm snaked round my throat and all the weight of him fell on my back, pushing me down so that my head went bang bang bang and I thought I'd throw up over my own shoes. Suddenly there was a *'Boof'* sound and a grunt from Bully and I could breathe again. I scrambled up and put my hand over my mouth to stop from being sick, and there was Bully rubbing the back of his head and Janey strolling up to collect her ball.

'So sorry,' she said. 'I was just practising free kicks.'

'You're rubbish, Hunt,' said Bully, half-heartedly. Some of the boys liked to say 'Hunt' as if they were clearing their throats, but he didn't even try.

She gave him half a smile and lifted the ball with her foot so that it popped up into her hands and stuck there. She pushed the ball at his face but didn't let go. He flinched and put up his hand. I rolled my eyes at her: it's me that will get it tomorrow.

Janey and I walked to her house, Bully lagging behind. I could feel him throwing daggers. They stuck in my back and trembled there. I thought of him climbing up this ladder of knives, the thin steel bending under his weight, the terrible pain in my back, the vertebrae pinging out of my spine. Oh why, Janey? Why did you have to make things worse?

'So. You OK?' said Janey.

'I ate some cheese,' I said, glumly.

'That was silly of you.'

'I didn't *want* to.'

We reached her house. Bully was still right behind us. 'Come in a minute,' said Janey. 'Mum can give you one of her horrible herbals.' We went in. We heard Bully kicking Irma's gate open.

In the living room of Janey's house, Melly was sucking her thumb, cuddled up against her mum and watching a cartoon with the sound off. She crinkled her eyes at me. Janey's mum was folding washing with one hand and listening to *Test Match Special*.

'Hi, Smelly,' said Janey, messing her sister's hair.

'Football again?' said Janey's mum. 'It's summer, Janey. Why aren't you playing cricket?' She was wearing the same dark blue silk wrapper with big orange flowers she'd had on since the funeral. Dirty clothes lay rumpled on the floor and piles of clean stuff covered the chairs. She was careful with some things: up on a shelf next to a photo of Janey's dad was the chessboard, just as we had left it when we were playing our last game. Janey's mum had put it there so the pieces wouldn't get knocked over, but it was getting all dusty.

Janey perched on the arm of the sofa. I just stood there, first on one leg, then the other. Janey's mum is very pretty. She has dark hair that curls round her face even when she doesn't brush it, and very dark eyes. She looks good even when she doesn't wear make up. Even when her eyes are red. 'Well,' said Janey's mum. 'How was school?'

'OK,' we both muttered.

I see Janey is checking her mum for stains, although they don't show much on the dark material.

'How are they doing?' I said. I hadn't heard the cricket score all day.

'West Indies are batting,' said Janey's mum. 'Chanderpaul's in, but they're missing Chris Gayle.'

'*You're* missing Chris Gayle,' said Janey. Teasing her mum was one of her tactics; she said she wanted her mum to know it was OK to like someone (especially a tall international cricketer like Chris Gayle, who wasn't likely to come round their house). Nan said it was hard to know sometimes who was the mother and who was the daughter. 'Twelve going on twenty-one,' is what she said about Janey.

A deep West Indian voice flowed out of the radio. There's

no Sky Sports here any more. 'Oh,' said Janey's mum. 'Ssh. That's Viv Richards, summarising. Sir Vivian.' She sighed. 'I could listen to him all day.' We listened. Viv Richards has a wheezy laugh. It made Janey's mum smile.

'Mum,' said Janey. 'What if we could get tickets. We could go on Saturday.'

'Oh no, it's far too expensive!' said Janey's mum.

'No it isn't. It's like, instead of a holiday or something.'

'Anyway, you've got homework.' She seemed to see me properly then. 'You'll be going up to Big School next year, won't you, Michael? Are you all right? You look quite pale.'

'He ate some cheese,' said Janey. 'And you said, "Big School".'

'Do you want one of my remedies?' Janey's mum put the clothes she'd folded on top of one of the piles. She didn't put it on straight. I knew it would soon fall over and the clothes would slide to the floor and get mixed up with all the dirty ones, and trodden on and dusty, until she picked them up and washed them again. I'd seen it happen before, but there was nothing I could do about it. Janey pretended not to notice.

'I'm all right,' I said. 'I'd better go home. Bye, Melly.' Melly frowned at me and took her thumb out of her mouth as if she was going to tell me off for something, then thought better of it and stuck the thumb back in. She rubbed her cheek against her mum's arm: it was one of her not-speaking days. Make the most of it, said Janey's eyebrows.

Janey walked me to my own gate. Bully was lurking in the bushes but he pulled back because there was Irma coming home. We met her by the For Sale sign sticking out of her front garden. She was wearing her pink cardigan with ruffles and a pink hair band to match, a wide skirt almost down to her ankles in grey the same colour as her hair. When she saw Janey and me she hunched up her whole body in delight and squeezed her eyes shut. She didn't see Bully. She did a little dance right there on the pavement, sticking out her elbows, and burst out singing: '"Hallo! Hallo! Who's your lady friend? Who's the little girlie by your side?"' She saw our faces and stopped. 'Oh Janey,' she said, looking concerned. 'How's your mum?'

'She's fine,' said Janey. Irma didn't know that Janey was cross with her for saying her mum had gone 'a bit Miss Havisham' – because of the dressing gown. I only told Janey because I didn't know what it meant. I wished I hadn't said anything.

'Of course she is,' said Irma, all sympathetic. 'Or – she will be...' I could hear Janey's teeth grinding. Then Irma added, brightly. 'Well. I've just heard from the estate agent. The Sold sign will be going up tomorrow.' She seemed really happy about it.

'Sorry,' I said.

Her face fell. 'Oh, it's not your fault, Michael.'

'No, I mean, sorry, I've got to go. I feel funny.'

Irma was going to make a joke and then Janey said, '*Some*body made him eat cheese.'

'Oh dear, dear,' said Irma, looking nervous. 'Is your grandmother not home? No?' She tutted. 'Well, you just come round to see me if you need anything.'

'Why would he do that?' said Janey, pushing open the gate.

'Manners, young lady!' said Irma.

'Pish,' said Janey. 'Manners?! I suppose it's good manners to make someone eat stuff that's bad for them?!'

'What do you mean?'

'Ask that nice little boy who lives with you now.'

Irma looked guilty, but she tossed her head like a bull, throwing Janey's words over her shoulder. 'You are being very rude, young lady, and there's no need for it. I shall speak to your mother.'

'Go on then,' said Janey. 'Like I care.'

'Don't care was made to care!' snapped Irma, red in the face.

Janey rolled her eyes and marched me down the path to my own door. 'Do you want me to stay?' she said. 'Are you going to throw up?'

'Err, thanks,' I said. 'I'll be all right.'

'OK,' she said.

When she'd gone I locked the door and got the bucket and went up to my room to close the curtains and lie down with a cold damp flannel on my forehead and a towel over my chest. Nan always puts Dettol in the bottom of the bucket and the smell of it is like being ill: you *will* throw up. Sometimes the best thing is to lie still and hope the hammering stops. A while later I heard Nan calling, 'Woo-hoo! Michael!'

I didn't call back. It would have hurt too much and anyway I wanted her to come and find me. I heard her unpacking shopping in the kitchen. Then the front doorbell and Irma in the hallway asking, 'Is Michael all right?' and Nan saying, 'Fine. You had any more nasty bangs lately?'

I listened hard.

'Only he didn't look so well when he came home,' Irma was saying.

'Thank you so much for your concern.'

'There's no need to be sarcastic, Zene.'

'I'm not. I always sound sarcastic. You know that.'

'Oh. Well. Anyway.'

After that I couldn't hear them because they went into the kitchen. I listened but their voices just went wow-wow-wow.

When Irma started going out with PC Bull she was always asking Nan's advice. Nan even said it was OK for Irma to have 'a bit of fun'. She got Irma laughing. Irma said if Shawn Bull were a toy boy he'd have to be Action Man. Nan said with his bald head and fat neck try the Hood from *Thunderbirds*. One minute they were screaming with laughter and then they were just screaming. Irma didn't like Nan's jokes any more. She said Nan ought to respect her choices. For ages they were careful how they spoke to each other: polite, with long silences. Nan told Irma she was in danger and a fool; Irma said Nan was jealous.

Nan was upset about it, but what could she do? Irma just wouldn't believe that her new boyfriend was trying to kill her.

When the Bulls moved in next door and Irma decided she didn't need Nan's help, she said, 'Zena, I've got a man to do things for me now.'

Irma looked taller and she smiled a lot. Even when she started having little accidents, she told Nan about them with a laugh. A light bulb Shawn Bull had changed for her fell out of its socket and smashed into her breakfast cereal. The stepladder collapsed when she was cleaning windows.

'I thought you had a man to do things for you,' Nan said.

'Oh, I can still clean a window!' said Irma. 'Shawn's retiling the kitchen.' She said come and have a look. We both went.

'Very nice,' said Nan. 'But that socket looks dodgy. It's just hanging off the wall.'

'It's fine,' said Irma. 'Shawn knows what he's doing.'

One day Irma went to take the lid off the pot she had simmering on the stove and Bang! She got an electric shock. Turns out the wires in the socket were touching and the cooker wasn't earthed. Irma was still laughing about it. 'I said to Shawn, "You're trying to bump me off!"'

Nan is a First Aider at work. She said, 'Irma. It could have been serious. It could have stopped your breathing or your heart or...'

'I did feel a flutter,' said Irma, 'but that's all.'

'If it had made your heart fibrillate...'

'What's fibrillate?' I asked.

Nan said that it's when the heart goes haywire, all the cells contracting at different times. Instead of pumping blood, Irma's heart would be useless, shaking like a jelly.

Irma said, 'Oh pish. It was nothing.' She showed her hands: not even a bruise or a burn. Nothing to show – though I wondered if some of her nerve-endings had been fried. Nan kept saying she wasn't quite the same old Irma.

'You've had a lucky escape,' said Nan. 'I wouldn't use that cooker again if I were you. Are you sure he didn't leave it like that on purpose?'

'I wish I hadn't told you now,' said Irma. 'Please stop going on about it.'

Still, Nan couldn't help being worried about her friend. She even spoke to Shawn Bull and told him to be more careful.

He said, 'You're the one who should be careful. I know all about you.'

Irma was there when he said it. She did look shifty.

Another time, Nan said, 'I would never have thought that a woman could be so blind and change so much just because she has a new man in her bed.'

After that there was hardly ever a laugh and a joke between them; they looked at each other with narrowed eyes.

Nan said, 'Michael, if you ever hear screaming coming from next door, don't go round: just dial 999 and ask for an ambulance.'

Not long after that, Irma put her house up for sale.

From up in my room I heard them go into the hallway again. Nan said, 'I wish you hadn't, Irma. All these years. I thought you knew how to keep a secret. I never thought you'd do that to me.'

'When you're with someone, Zena,' said Irma, 'really *with* someone, it's hard to have secrets. And anyway, like Shawn says: if you haven't done anything wrong there's nothing to worry about, nothing to hide.'

'So – when are you moving?'

'It won't be for a few weeks yet. I'm still here if you need any help.'

'Same to you,' said Nan.

'With Michael, I mean,' said Irma. 'I'm free tomorrow. Got to use up all those holidays before I leave work.' She laughed but Nan didn't join in.

Irma left and Nan came upstairs. Gently, she pushed open my door. I shut my eyes. 'Michael?' she said, softly.

'Mmm?'

'Are you all right? What's brought this on?'

'Dunno.'

If I said anything about the cheese she'd go next door and make a fuss. I wouldn't be able to stop her.

She sat on the edge of my bed. 'Was it that boy again?'

I rubbed the bridge of my blocked-up nose. It didn't help. She sighed.

'Shall I put some Dettol in that bucket?'

'Uh! No.' Neither of us said anything for a bit, then I asked her: 'Are they really going?'

'Looks like it,' said Nan. She bit her lip. Even though she was angry with Irma for liking Shawn Bull better, she still cared. And if Irma moved away Nan wouldn't be able to keep an eye on her.

'How far?' I asked.

'I think he'll get a transfer.'

I wanted to ask her what she'd told Irma all those years ago. But then she'd know I'd been listening.

'We'll miss her,' said Nan. But she was thinking of the old Irma, the one who'd already gone.

As for me, I'd been wishing hard that Bully would move somewhere so far away he wouldn't be able to come back to our school and then I would never have to see him again. Maybe my wish was going to come true – and there was nothing I could do about it.

I was sick twice that night, woke up sweating, but made it to the toilet, my head thumping as I hung over the bowl, thinking, if only this would stop, life would be so sweet. I won't ask for anything else if I can just feel well. At last I slept again and when I woke in the morning without a headache I breathed a sigh and snuggled down. I just wanted to enjoy the feeling that the poison had gone.

When Nan came in, I opened my eyes with a struggle.

'Are you getting up, Michael?' she said.

I moved my lips as little as possible. 'I don't think I can go to school, Nan.'

'But it's your last day of SATs.'

'I can't. Not today.'

'How's your head now?' she asked.

'Better *if* I lie still.'

'It's going to be a HUGE palaver, you do know that? And I have to go work. There'll be no one here to look after you.'

'Tha's OK. I can stay on my own.'

'You can't stay here on your own.'

I waited for her to work it out. It wasn't as if there was no one she could ask.

Nan sighed. 'I suppose Irma would look after you.'

I was careful not to punch the air, but I smiled to myself, just a little.

Nan went away. I was going to listen but I must have fallen asleep. She woke me up to say, 'All right. I rang the school. You can take the test on Monday but you are not allowed to speak to *anyone* from your class: so no Internet, no texting your friends on my phone, no speaking to that boy next door.'

'Why would I want to speak to *him*?'

'OK.' She started folding up clothes while she was talking. 'The school were not happy about it, but I said, they shouldn't have let someone bully you into eating cheese. It's OK,' she said. '*Irma* told me. I guess she feels responsible. Only the school said they didn't know anything about it. You have to tell your teacher when these things happen.' She came over and put her hand on my forehead. 'Mmm. You're a bit clammy. Well, I've got to go.'

Nan left but it was only quiet for a minute then I heard Irma tripping upstairs.

'Your nan's gone,' she said. There was a funny gleam in her eye. 'I'm in charge. Have you had anything to drink?'

'No,' I said.

She tutted. 'Tea and toast then,' she said. 'And if you're feeling better I'll make you some of my lovely chicken soup for lunch. Do you want Ted?'

Ted was up on a shelf. Nan said I would get teased less if the other boys didn't think I still slept with my bear. And anyway, he was too old to be cuddled: his paws were coming unpicked, his eyes pointed in different directions.

At least she hadn't tried to give him away, like she gave away some of my best toys to our neighbour Mrs Rogers for the charity shop. I had to go round there and get them back. I had to pay!

'But they were under your bed gathering dust!' Nan said. 'You can't have played with them for ages!'

She didn't know they were my shock troops: Action Man and Fireman Sam and all my dinosaurs. I couldn't tell Nan I had put them there to keep me safe from the man with the knife. He lay on his back under my bed waiting for me to go to sleep. He was never there when the light was on or when Nan was in the room – only in the dark when I could feel my own heart beating. Then I heard him sliding about under the bed and the knife whispering out of its sheath, ready to stab upwards through the mattress. I would roll over to escape the sharp blade. With all my allies under the bed I felt safer because they wouldn't give him any room. I'd even sent Squawky, the remote-controlled T. Rex, on patrol in the dark – until she fell over and the batteries ran out. I had almost forgotten about the man. The toys were still under there though, where I'd put them back, including Squawky. She was a present from Irma and she liked me to look after my toys especially the ones she gave me. She was right in a way. I'd never have sent Ted down there.

'It's OK,' I said. 'I don't need him.'

'Well, he's watching over you,' said Irma. I heard her go back downstairs and fill the kettle. Usually she would switch on Radio 4 and make herself at home. Instead I heard the front door open, which was odd because she usually came and went by the kitchen door that was on the side, facing her own house. I sat up slowly so I could see out of the window. There she was scuttling down our front path and back round to her own gate. Shawn Bull's police car was still parked up. I lay down again. After a bit I heard two doors go clunk and an engine starting. Bully getting a lift with his dad. He'd have to eat his own sandwiches today.

Even the walls seemed to breathe more easily once Bully was gone. I wouldn't have to see him now until after the test on Monday.

I got out of bed and walked carefully to the bathroom, had a long pee and washed my hands, looking at myself in the mirror. How do you feel, Michael? Is that really you? When I looked at that boy in the mirror, I couldn't always seem to see myself, the boy inside. I heard the side door open and then Irma busy with kettle and pot in the kitchen. My room smelt like a sickroom when I went back in: no Dettol but Nan had given me a hanky with a smear of vapour rub folded inside to help me breathe through my nose. As always it was the special big cotton hanky with the blue M stitched in one corner. M for Michael. It was my grandad's name too: it was his hanky. I wished I could remember him, but Nan said I was just a baby then. There isn't even a picture of the three of us together, only one that Nan keeps in a drawer of her dressing table of her and Grandad together somewhere by the seaside. Nan has spiky hair and tight black trousers; Grandad is wearing a suit and pointy shoes. They are both very thin and blown into curves by the wind: they probably didn't have much to eat in those days.

Irma came up with a tray. She'd put on her blue smock, the one she wore for cooking and for cleaning the house. Nan always said it made her look like an artist. 'All right, little man?' Irma said. 'I'll have to pop next door now and then. I'll make the soup in there. Save messing up your nan's kitchen. But I won't be far if you need me. Is there anything you want?'

She brought me the phone and Nan's digital radio from downstairs. I said, 'It's nice you're looking after me again.'

'Oh Michael,' she said. 'I'll always look after you!'

She must have forgotten she was moving.

She looked around. 'Shall I tidy up a bit?' she said. 'It could do with it. Look at this carpet. I could hoover? Oh, but no, you don't want a lot of noise with your bad head, do you? What about a steam inhalation?'

'It's all right,' I said, holding up the folded hanky.

When I woke up again the tray had gone. Irma must have been in to check on me, creeping about the room while I was asleep. She'd left me a drink of orange. I couldn't hear anything downstairs. I turned on the radio for the start of *Test Match Special*. From outside came the beeping of a van reversing. The door went and Irma bobbed back up the stairs. 'Shopping delivery for Violet,' she said, meaning Janey's mum. 'She was standing on her doorstep looking at the path like it's made of quicksand. How come the rest of us don't get swallowed up? How does she think *we* manage?'

It seemed like Irma had forgotten all about Janey's dad.

She smiled at me. 'I've got the chicken soup started. I'm glad *you* like my soup. George prefers the tinned stuff, if I'm honest. And he doesn't like *any*thing with bits in it.' She shook her head.

She said would I like to come down after lunch and watch *Poirot* with her and *Murder She Wrote*?

I said I wanted to listen to the cricket.

Her face fell. 'Oh, but you used to love those!'

I was going to tell her it would help Janey if I knew more about cricket. If Janey would only play the game her mum liked then maybe her mum would get dressed and go out and watch her. But there wasn't much point talking to Irma about it because she was moving away. She wouldn't know us any more. She wouldn't know about anything that happened to us. It would be like we were dead.

All morning, Irma flew between her house and ours like she was trying to be in two places at once. Just before twelve she dashed in, quite pink, and said, 'I'll bring your soup in about half an hour, OK? You've got the phone.' And away she ran again before I could ask for another drink. I watched her go. Irma turned in at her own gate and hurried down the path to her house and then I couldn't see her any more.

Five minutes later, Shawn Bull's car was back. I saw him coming up the path, already unbuttoning his jacket. I went downstairs. Standing at the sink to fill my glass, I looked through the window with its wavy lines and saw shapes floating in the window of Irma's kitchen: a face, low down by the sink, like someone was being sick. A scrap of blue and I thought I could make out Irma's hair swinging, her head nodding like a chicken. Above her was a blur of white and another head, like it was on a higher shelf. I stepped well back so they couldn't see me. I hoped Irma was all right.

Back in my bed, I fell asleep again and woke up hungry. In test match time, lunch had come and gone. Strauss and Trott were settled in at the crease and halfway to tea. I lay there listening to the murmur of the crowd, Henry Blofeld repeating: 'And there's no run'. My tummy rumbled. I reached for the phone and dialled Irma's number. Ansaphone. Leave a message? I don't think so.

I pulled on my dressing gown and went downstairs, belt trailing, knowing there was no one around to tell me to tie it up in case I tripped. Through the kitchen window I could see a blue shape moving in Irma's kitchen. I thought about ringing her again but I'd left the phone upstairs. Maybe she had just changed her mind. Anyway, it was a bit warm for soup. I ate a banana and drank a glass of coconut milk. The radio was still going upstairs, but I couldn't be bothered to get that either so I found the digital radio station on the TV and lay on the sofa for a change. Nan says a change is as good as a rest, but I was having a change and a rest. The school day was nearly over, the weekend coming and Monday far away. Nan had a good reason to tell Bully's dad to keep him away from me until after I'd done the Science test. I was starting to feel better.

The radio and the TV weren't in sync so there was a kind of echo. 'And there's no run': *And there's no run.* After a while, I went upstairs to switch the radio off and to make it worth the effort had a little nose around in Nan's room. She goes through my drawers so I think it's only fair to have a look at hers. She says we don't have secrets from each other but then I'm not really interested in her big knickers and her woolly tights. Tucked into one corner of the top right hand drawer is the key to her firebox, the treasure chest where she keeps important papers. The firebox is on the top shelf of her wardrobe and she can reach it by standing on the bed, but I can't. I've tried: I'd need the stepladder. The firebox is the thing she'd grab if she had to run out of the house and yet it's also the only thing that won't get burned up if there's a fire. I think she should keep it somewhere I can get at it in an emergency because what if there was a fire and she wasn't home? She says that will never happen. But it could today. There could be a fire this afternoon. Maybe just a small one.

It sounded like someone was coming in the house so I quickly shut the drawer and skipped back to my room. False alarm. Must have been Irma's door closing. I go down and lie on the sofa again, but still Irma doesn't come.

Trott gets his fifty just before Tea. Janey will be coming home from school. Maybe she will find her mum putting the shopping away, listening to the radio, or half asleep on the sofa. Maybe Janey will come in and fall over the shopping trays and bags in the hall and have to rummage around in there for something to eat. Janey's mum doesn't even check the order these days. The same things come every week whether they need them or not. I don't know why Janey doesn't go online and change the order herself. I would. And I would unpack the shopping. I think I would do that. Janey says I have no idea what it's like when everything hurts like you've been knocked down and trampled by wild horses. I tried to imagine what it would be like if Nan died, but then I decided I had better not think about it, in case I make it happen.

Janey's counsellor told her you can sometimes feel guilty even though you haven't done anything wrong. Even when you're not responsible.

Nan sent me for counselling but I don't know what for. The man asked me about my mum and dad but I don't remember. I learned some things though: some of us are worriers; some of us think too much.

The teams are coming out again after Tea. First ball – too gentle. 'No no no no,' says Sir Viv. The doorknocker bangs and makes me jump. Then the doorbell rings. I look from behind the curtains: it's Bully. Just like him to come round when he knows I'm not allowed to speak to him. For all he knows I'm in bed – ill. But he keeps on knocking and calling and ringing. I'm looking for a piece of paper to write 'GO AWAY'. I'll put it up to the window. I won't let him lure me out of my ground. But he goes on banging and shouting and there's a funny screechy sound in his voice that I've never heard before. I go into the hallway to get a better listen.

Is he – crying? He loses his words and what comes out is a high breaking wail. He's really putting in the effort. The letterbox opens. He sees me standing in the hallway and bangs on the door with both hands.

'Go away!' I shout. 'I'm not allowed to talk to you!'

'Help! Open the door!'

I stay exactly where I am.

'Ambulance!' he shrieks. 'Police! Let me use the phone!'

'What's wrong with *your* phone?' I shout back. 'Call your dad!'

'I *can't*.' His voice breaks.

I say quietly and firmly, like Nan would: 'I'm not allowed to talk to anyone from school.'

'Puh-lease!' It sounds like he really is crying.

I open the door just a crack to have a look at him, ready to shut it if he laughs in my face. It isn't even locked. Irma must have left it like that. Bully could have walked in any time. Tch-tch. Wait till I tell Nan.

Bully's eyes are stretched wide and his hair's on end. 'You've got to come,' he says, grabbing at me. I step back, pulling my dressing gown tight and doing up the belt. I wished I did judo or karate and I was tying on a black belt right now, *then* let him try and pull me about. His arm drops. 'You have to dial 999,' he says. His voice is hoarse, like he's been shouting. His face is boiled red.

'Oh yeh? What's wrong with your phone? Why don't you ask Irma?'

He just stands there shaking his head. 'Hurry,' he says. He doesn't try to push past me or grab the phone. He just waits for me to do something.

'OK.' I pick up the hall phone and hold it out to him. 'You call if you really want to. *You* dial 999.'

He lunges at me, snatches the phone and jabs three times with one finger. A little voice says: 'Which service?'

'Ambulance,' he says. 'Police.'

Right, I think and march out the front door and up the path. I'm going to talk to Irma. I feel a bit silly when I'm out on the pavement in my dressing gown and slippers, but I keep going, through Irma's gate and down her path. As I pass the front of our house I can hear Bully's voice, saying 'No!' and 'I can't!' If he's playing a trick and pretending to be me I want Irma on my side. She'd better – or Nan will never be her friend again. I go to the side door and knock. No answer. I try the handle. The door's locked.

That's funny. Maybe she had to go out and that's why she didn't bring me my soup. But she wouldn't go out just like that when she was meant to be looking after me. I get a tingle down the back of my neck but I shake it off and think, if she's left me hungry and all by myself, all afternoon, for no good reason, Nan will give her a right telling off.

I kneel down and look through the dog flap into the kitchen. Behind the legs of the table, I see Irma's feet. They've fallen outwards, the toes pointing away from each other at what I can't help noticing is an obtuse angle. It's like she's fallen fast asleep on the kitchen floor lying on her back.

I pull away and stand up. I breathe the outside air. I can still hear Bully on the phone. I take off my dressing gown, kneel down again and put both hands through the dog flap, like a diver, reaching for the floor. I keep looking at Irma's feet. I want them to move but if they do I know I will jump.

My shoulders get stuck. I haven't tried climbing through the dog flap for a long time – not since the Bulls moved in. If I stay stuck, Bully will come and kick my bum, while my head will be in the kitchen with Irma. But she needs my help so –

I remember to twist to get my shoulders through and after that it's easy. I walk forwards on my hands: my hips and legs and feet slide through. The dog flap clacks shut behind me.

I stand up inside. It smells of onions in here, of warm carrots and chicken broth. Irma is lying on the far side of the table near the cooker. A strand of grey hair has fallen across her open mouth. Her eyes are open. Suddenly coconut milk and bananas burn at the back of my throat. I call her name three times getting louder: 'Irma! IRMA! **IRMA**!' She doesn't move.

Pictures flick through my mind. I have seen a dead baby frog before, like a tiny plastic toy at the bottom of the dog's water bowl. I have seen a dead cat, stiff and flat, with its mouth open: still yowling soundlessly at the car that hit it. I know what dead looks like. Terrible. But they were all small creatures and I didn't know them so well. This is Irma. How can the house still be standing? It ought to fall down with a thunderclap. And yet everything's so still.

What's on the floor? It's Irma and not Irma. This is what they mean when they say someone has gone. I still want to believe that if I shout loud enough, she will blink and shudder and close her mouth and break this spell of death that's on her and be alive again.

Trembling, I close my eyes and wish very hard. When I open them she has not moved.

I bend down and touch her forehead. It feels like cold stone but I snatch my hand away like it's burning.

I think about those Vinny Jones ads: Press Hard and Fast to 'Staying Alive'. You don't have to kiss her. Her mouth looks kind of sticky. I don't want to touch her again; I don't want to leave her on her own; I don't want anyone to know I didn't try. I push myself out through the dog flap, getting it all wrong and taking some skin off my arms. Then I put on my dressing gown again and I walk back up the path on wobbly legs. When Bully comes out I'm leaning on our gate. His face floats towards me, wet and pale now. 'I'm gonna wait here for the ambulance,' he says. 'So they know which house.'

It seems a long time that we stand there on the pavement saying nothing. I pull my dressing gown tight around me again and re-tie the cord. My arms hurt but I know I mustn't look at them. We hear the siren getting louder and louder. Bully is waving his arms before the ambulance comes up the slope and round The Middle towards us. The paramedics pull in and turn off the siren, leaving the blue lights flashing. They get out: a man and a woman in green overalls. The man has cropped hair going grey, deep lines in his face. The woman is shorter, younger, fatter, with a blonde ponytail. For a second, before I brush the thought away, I wonder what it would be like if she were my mum.

'It's here,' says Bully. 'She's in there.' He points down the path. They are already walking to the house. Bully follows. 'It was me that called you.'

And the man – 'Is it your mother?'

'No.'

'What's the lady's name?'

When they get to the door Bully unlocks it for them. He stands aside to let them in, looks back to where I'm standing and waves me away. I stay where I am until the man comes back. Bully follows.

'Was it her heart?' I say. My own heart is bumping hard in my chest; it's getting tighter and harder to breathe.

Behind the paramedic, Bully clenches his fists.

'Were you there when it happened?' says the man.

I say, 'No. I was next door. She was all right before. She was making me soup.'

'He doesn't know anything,' says Bully. 'He just makes things up.'

36

The paramedic nods. To him I am just a kid. A kid in pyjamas in the afternoon.

I have to go on: 'No, but, was it an electric shock?'

The paramedic gives me a funny look.

'All right, son, all right,' he says. 'Calm down.'

Bully jumps in again. 'He's always telling stupid lies. Ask him about his mum and dad! My dad says...' He shuts his mouth again, as if he's remembered he isn't supposed to tell me what his dad says.

The paramedic shakes his head. He writes down Irma's name and our names and the addresses and what Bully saw and did when he found her. 'I couldn't do anything,' he says. 'She was already...' He bursts into tears and the paramedic pats him on the back.

A few of the neighbours have come out of their houses to look. They see us standing there, just a couple of kids on our own with the ambulance – no one asks if they can help. (Mrs Rogers, who is our nosiest neighbour, must be out. She'd have been straight over.) At last, a police car arrives. Now we'll see. But the policeman who gets out is Shawn Bull. And he's on his own.

'What's going on?' he says, hitching up his trousers. He looks us over, frowning at me in my pyjamas.

'Right,' says the paramedic, walking Bully's dad along the pavement so they can talk. He looks back at me and Bully as if he's talking about us, too.

Shawn Bull doesn't run. He doesn't shout Irma's name. He just nods and walks towards us, but he doesn't stop and he doesn't ask Bully if he's all right or say to the paramedic, 'This is my son.' He doesn't say, 'I live here.' He walks down the path like he's going to the house of a stranger. And Bully watches him go like he's never met him before.

I'm going to say something to the paramedic but then I see Janey coming back from school; she starts to run towards us.

I push past Bully and go to her, my arms spread wide like I'm catching a runaway horse. 'It's all right,' I say. 'It's all right.'

She stops in front of me, searching my face, trying to read the whole story.

'It's not your mum,' I say. 'It's Irma.'

Relief floods into her eyes. She ducks her head. 'Is she OK?'

'No.' Why did I say it was all right? It isn't all right. 'No. She might have had a heart attack.'

'Oh no!' Janey puts her hand to her mouth. 'Is she?'

I lower my voice. 'She's dead.'

'Oh no!'

'But listen,' I say, grabbing her arm. 'Listen, *she was making soup.* What if she had another shock? The dodgy cooker...'

Janey can't seem to take it in. She keeps looking past me as if Irma might be creeping up behind, apologetic, giggling, secretly pleased to find out that we care after all. She'd start singing one of her old songs or call out, 'False alarm!'

'Did you tell Mum?' says Janey.

I shake my head. 'I wanted to stay here.'

'Oh,' she says.

'It's not your fault,' I say.

She tosses her head, like Irma did, right here on the pavement, yesterday. 'Can't they do anything?'

We walk back to the gate together. Bully is shivering now. 'Are you OK?' asks Janey. Shawn Bull comes out of the kitchen door. He stands there on the path, looking at the ground. Like he can't take it all in. Like he can't believe what he's done.

We're still standing there when Nan drives up, parks all slanty and gets out of the car. 'Michael?' she says, hurrying over.

When I tell her, she too puts her hand over her mouth. 'Oh no,' she says from behind her fingers. 'Oh no!'

Another car slows down and pulls up with two wheels on

the grass of The Middle. A man and woman get out. They're wearing suits.

They come towards us. 'Jane?' says the woman. She's thin and her short hair is pale and feathery round her face. The man has dark hair and stands back waiting for her to finish speaking to us. 'Are you all right?' she says.

'Yes,' says Janey. 'Thank you.'

The woman looks at me and Nan and Bully, glances at the neighbours in the distance then goes on down the path to Irma's house. The man in the suit follows her. Shawn Bull comes up the garden path to meet them.

'How do you know her?' I say.

Janey says, 'She's the mum of someone at my school.'

'Who?'

'No one you know.'

'Are you all right, George?' says Nan. His face is the colour of paper and his legs are shaking. She puts out a hand as if she wants to touch his shoulder, then takes it back because Shawn Bull is walking up the path towards us, slowly, as if he's very tired.

'All right, Son?' he says.

'It'll be the shock,' says Nan.

'The shock,' I repeat, nodding.

'What are they doing?' says Bully.

'They'll do everything they have to do,' says his dad.

'I wanna go home,' says Bully.

'Well we can't go back in just now,' says his dad. 'We have to wait until they tell us it's OK.'

'I'd better go and see Mum,' says Janey. And she leaves us.

Nan puts her hand on my shoulder now – to push me down the path to our own house.

'No,' says Bully. 'I want to go *home.* I want Mum.'

'Not now,' I hear his dad say.

In Irma's house the lights flash on and off like a signal. In a minute the police will come out and take Shawn Bull away. They will say, 'We arrest you for the murder of Irma Gordon.' He will go to prison and with a bit of luck Bully will go back to his mum.

I suddenly feel lighter and I can hear Irma saying, 'Every cloud...' That's what she said when Janey's dad died. She and Nan were talking about the things he'd arranged to make sure his family would be all right and the benefits Janey's mum could get because she still had two children to look after. 'It isn't a lot,' Nan had said. 'But enough to keep them going.' And Irma said, 'Every cloud...'

I asked what about clouds? Irma was a bit embarrassed when she had to say about the silver lining. She said of course it would have been better for Janey and her mum and Melissa if there had never been a cloud.

I know better now what she meant: Bully and his dad going away, that would be my silver lining.

So I can't believe it when Nan turns round to them and says, 'Why don't you come in with us while you're waiting? I'll make us all some tea.'

Shawn Bull gives her a what's-in-it-for-you? look. 'All right,' he says. 'I think George needs to sit down.' He asks the paramedic to let the detectives know where we'll be.

There is cheering in our front room and Nan looks round to see where it's coming from. *Test Match Special* is still talking out of the blank black TV screen. Irma is dead and Andrew Strauss has made a century. He'll be taking off his helmet, showing his bald spot and raising his bat to the dressing room. I pick up the remote control and switch off the TV. Silence falls on us with a thud.

Nan drops into one armchair and I sit in the other; the Bulls take the sofa, Shawn Bull sitting forwards, right on the edge, Bully burrowing way back and hugging a cushion.

I rub my arms. They're still sore from being scraped by the dog flap.

'Are you boys cold?' Nan asks.

We both shake our heads.

Shawn Bull's eyes are going round the room. He likes to notice things: he noticed the tax had run out on Janey's mum's car. Irma had to go round and remind her. It wasn't as if Janey's mum ever drove the car, but that didn't matter. She could still get into trouble. The reminder was in her great pile of unopened post. 'Shawn would rather not notice things sometimes,' Irma said. 'But if it's right under his nose...'

And now here he is, the man who murdered our friend, looking round our living room, as if we could have something to hide. Nan hasn't said anything about suspecting him. I decide that as long as Nan is doing such a good job of pretending to be sorry for the Bulls, I'd better go along with it.

She jumps up and says, 'I haven't even put the kettle on. Coffee? Tea?'

'Coffee,' says Shawn Bull.

'I can make a pot of filtered,' says Nan.

'Just a *normal* coffee,' says Shawn Bull. 'Two sugars.' It's very hard not to get up and follow Nan and be safe with her in the kitchen, but I make myself stay in my seat. I keep my mouth still and my eyes on Bully and his dad. The silence gets heavier and heavier and presses against my ears and on my heart. Under my fingers I can feel the rough lines of the flowers stitched into the arms of the chair. Not quite the same feeling each side. My fingers search to try and even them up. Bully's dad sees it. I freeze. Think about something else; this is no time to be taken over by The Twitch.

It used to go like this: if I was walking along, say, to school, and I felt a stone through the sole of my right shoe, then I would have to try and step on another sharp stone with my left foot to even things up. But it would never feel quite the same. So I'd have to find another stone to step on with the left foot and another to step on with the right foot. And then because I'd gone right left left right I'd do it all again, left right right left. And repeat starting from the left. Doubling and doubling and doubling. The thought that it could never end made me feel sick and dizzy but I still used to try. Sometimes I stopped because I had to get to school, or because I'd reached home or – because someone noticed.

Standing in assembly, I'd started feeling the ridges of the woodblock floor through my feet. I'd be jigging away trying to get things to *feel* right – the same on both sides. Anyone else might think my feet were tapping out a code. Left-right right-left. Right-left left-right.

Then The Twitch began to spread to my hands. If my right hand brushed against my leg or if I pressed my fingers together I wanted to get the same feeling on the other side and I thought – now I'm in trouble: I have to find a way to stop; I can't go on my whole life like this, twitching and jiggling. A man passed me on the street one day and shouted, 'Hey, Riverdance!'

I didn't ask for help. I just decided that I had to stop. All by myself. I did it by always thinking of something else whenever the need to start The Twitch came over me, so I didn't let it take hold. It felt good, like loosening something that had been knotted too tight. I let it all go and thought about how good that felt. By the time Bully arrived at our school, I was nearly over it. I'd got myself down to a six-second limit if the urge to do The Twitch was too strong. But Bully took one look at me and he seemed, somehow, to *know*.

Now they are both looking at me. The Bulls.

I let out a slow breath. I keep my fingers still. I tell myself to say nothing, do nothing. You're nearly the youngest. It isn't up to you to start a conversation. Just don't take your eyes off them.

Nan comes back with coffee and tea on a tray and a big plate of biscuits, quite a few different ones, arranged in a circle. I know which ones I can eat, and pick up two of them before Bully and his dad can take any.

Nan doesn't even tell me off.

'How long do we have to wait?' Bully wants to know.

'I told you,' says his dad. 'The police always have to come when there's a Sudden and Unexplained.'

'But you *are* the police,' wails Bully.

'It doesn't make any difference,' says his dad. 'I told you. It has to be somebody else.' He studies his mug of coffee and says to me, 'I didn't know you had a day off school.'

'I ate some cheese.'

'See anything?'

'I was sleeping a lot.'

A nod. He knows I've been downstairs, because of the TV. I think about those faces at the window.

'And where were you?' he asks Nan.

'At work,' she says. 'I've been at work all day.'

'So was Michael here on his own?'

'No no. Irma was looking after him.'

He looks annoyed, and then his face crumples. Sorry for what he's done to Irma? Or only thinking that he will never be able to tell her off again?

Nan offers him some kitchen roll. He shakes his head but takes it anyway, tears off a few squares and holds them.

Next door, the police will be examining the cooker. Even if he's put the socket back together they will see something's wrong, but anyway I don't think he had time to fix that while the paramedics were there.

Nan keeps looking at me and her eyes are all warning.

She turns to Bully. 'Are you all right? It must have been a terrible shock.'

'A shock!' I say and laugh. I can't help myself.

'What?' says Shawn Bull, staring at me.

'Michael!' says Nan, sharply.

We sit there. My tummy rumbles.

'It's taking a long time,' says Nan.

'It'll take as long as it takes,' says Shawn Bull. 'I mean ... sorry, if we're in the way we can go.'

'No, you're all right,' says Nan.

In my head, two words start chasing each other round and round: Sudden and Unexplained. Sudden and Unexplained. Like something off *Sesame Street. CSI Sesame Street. CSI Sesame Street* is brought to you today by the words: Sudden and Unexplained.

'Where would you go anyway?' says Nan.

'Can we go and see Mum?' asks Bully.

'No,' says his dad. 'I told you, she's too far away.'

Nan asks if she can get them something to eat. Some toast maybe? Shawn Bull looks at her as if toast is a dirty word.

'I'm sorry,' I say, 'but I'm hungry. I didn't have my soup.'

Now Bully and his dad both stare at me.

'I'll get you something,' says Nan. 'Do you want to come and help me?'

'I'll stay.'

'Michael,' says Nan and I have to follow her to the kitchen.

She turns on the radio. Fills the kettle and switches it on. Drops slices of bread into the toaster and presses the lever. Then she turns to me and bends to look into my face. She says in a whisper, 'Michael, are you all right? What did you see?'

I want to tell her about the faces at the kitchen window, but instead out tumbles, 'She was on the floor. I couldn't do anything.' I want to cry but the tears don't come. I say, 'What are we going to do?'

'We'll be all right,' says Nan. 'Just you and me.'

But I meant about them. What are we going to do about them?

The front doorbell goes and someone calls, 'Hello?' It's the woman in the suit. She says her name is Detective Inspector Dunbar. We go back into our living room and sit down. Another woman in police uniform stands in the doorway, holding her hat under her arm.

'I'm so sorry, Shawn,' says the inspector. 'I thought I'd come myself.'

'I'm honoured,' says Shawn Bull, looking at the carpet.

'Perhaps we should talk outside?'

'It might help the boys to know what really happened,' says Nan.

'I'm sure you'll understand that I can't give you a definitive answer.'

'But she was never ill,' says Nan.

Shawn Bull clears his throat and says, 'That's not quite true.' He looks at the inspector. 'She'd been to the doctor.' He moves his hand over his chest. 'She'd felt something – something with her heart.'

'And she was being treated?' says the inspector. 'Perhaps we can call her GP?'

Nan gets up. 'I have the number.' She finds it in her address book and writes it down.

The uniform goes to make a call.

Nan says, 'She was here this morning. She was absolutely fine.'

'Yesterday she didn't feel so good,' says Shawn Bull. 'But we were moving. And things have been … difficult here. So we put it down to stress.'

We wait. This is when we should say something about the cooker. But Nan looks at the ceiling and my tongue feels stuck. We wait. The uniform comes back and shakes her head.

The inspector sighs. 'I guess he's not willing to sign off on this one for whatever reason. So we'll see what the coroner has to say. I'm sorry, Shawn.'

He nods. 'Got to follow procedure.'

'Do you know who'd be the next of kin?'

'She didn't have anyone,' says Nan. 'I mean: no family.'

'Shawn?'

'There's only me,' he says.

Nan frowns and pulls in her chin but says nothing.

'Then, you'll want to be in charge of the arrangements?' says the inspector.

He nods.

Nan's face clears. She says, 'I've got a letter. Things she wanted. It was something we did ages ago.'

'Ah,' says Shawn Bull.

'I'll find it,' says Nan. 'I'll bring it round later.'

'See if the medics can do transport,' says the inspector, turning away, 'then come back and just take everyone's names for the record.'

The uniform nods and disappears again.

'What about us?' says Shawn Bull. 'Do we need to find somewhere else to stay?'

'No no!' says the inspector. 'We're not treating this as a crime scene, are we?'

I want to say, 'Why not?' But Nan's eyes are telling me not to speak.

'Thanks,' he says. 'I'll appreciate that.'

'We'll need a formal identification. Tomorrow will be OK. Don't worry about your shift. Perhaps we can have a chat with George tomorrow too? It was you that called 999 wasn't it, George?'

Bully nods, his face all squashed.

'You did well. I'm sure your dad's proud of you.' The inspector gets up to go. 'We'll do everything by the book, of course. But we'll try to make it as painless as possible. I'm really very sorry for your loss.'

We all stand up. I want to say something. What about the

soup? What about the dodgy socket on the cooker? What about the *murder*!

Just as she gets to the door the inspector turns round and says, 'When did you say you last saw her, Shawn?'

'I err ... popped back late morning.'

The inspector's eyes rest on him but all she says is, 'And she was all right then?'

'A bit flustered,' he says. 'It was just a quick ... I wanted to check on her. I had calls in the area all afternoon.' He pats his chest. 'It's all in my notebook,' he says. 'I mean, I had no idea she was ... she was running about. Doing too much.' He looks hard at me. 'She was *fine* when I left.' He wipes a hand over his face. 'I just can't take it in.'

The inspector nods. She has that same look people used for Janey's mum. Lips pressed together, mouth turned down. Sad face.

This is all wrong.

They're ready to take Irma away. Nan and the Bulls go out to say goodbye. Nan doesn't make me go too: she just leaves me behind in the doorway.

As they move towards our gate, the trolley carrying Irma is already on its way up the path next door. You can only see a shape. I push our front door half shut and go back through the kitchen and out the side door. I run down the garden and through the gap in the fence and straight up to Irma's house. The kitchen door should be covered in crime scene tape: there should be a forensic team in white onesies. But instead the door's wide open and there's no one inside. I step into the kitchen. No saucepan on the cooker. No plates in the washing up rack. Everything cleared away. Was it like that before? When Irma was lying here? I don't remember. But it must have been.

I step over the place where Irma was lying. The socket for the cooker looks OK. Not hanging off anyway. And – it's a different cooker. It doesn't even look electric. I turn one of the knobs and gas hisses out.

Oh.

And no soup.

All I can find is a wooden spoon. I only notice it because it's the wrong way up in the pot where Irma keeps her spoons and mashers. She always puts them handle down. The spoon's still damp. I sniff it. I can't say it smells of soup – it's been washed – but forensics would be able to detect a little molecule of chicken – wouldn't they? I have to get it away before Bully and his dad come back. It's obvious the soup is evidence of some kind and they've tried to hide it. The door's been open all this time: so they've even got rid of the smell. I look in the pedal bin, careful not to make it go clang against the wall. Nothing. Maybe it's in the food waste or the wheelie bin. I wrench open the fridge door and the beer bottles rattle. No big pot of soup in there. I could have raced up the path, waving the spoon shouting, 'Stop!' But I think, I have to show Nan. She'll know what to do.

I hurry back and put the spoon into a plastic freezer bag from our kitchen drawer. The freezer! I should have checked that next door. But it's too late. I bump into Nan in the hallway of our house. 'She's gone, Michael,' says Nan. 'She's gone.'

And she hugs me. I let her hold me until it gets hard to breathe and then I struggle free. I show her the wooden spoon and tell her what I found.

'Oh, Michael,' she says. 'You shouldn't have done that!'

'But, Nan. This is evidence!'

'No, Michael,' she says. 'If it ever was evidence then you've spoiled it by bringing it into this house.'

She will not call the police to come back. She rubs her eyes and says, 'Michael, will you please, please shut up about the soup.'

My mouth hangs open. Telling me to shut up! After the day I've had.

Then she says, 'I am so sorry, Michael. But it would be better if you could just accept it.'

It's a long time before I get it: it's bad enough that Irma's dead; Nan doesn't want to think that her best friend has been murdered.

That evening, Nan goes rummaging in the drawers of her desk in the hallway. 'Here it is,' she says, holding up a blue envelope. She taps it and runs her hand along the top, but she doesn't open it. 'I know what's in it,' she says. 'More or less. But I shall have to take it round next door. I'll go tomorrow. And maybe I'll be able to smuggle in that wooden spoon.'

I wish I hadn't shown it to her now.

It's a weird evening. I try to read a book. I don't want to watch TV. Nan says, 'I suppose I should just see the news.' She stares at it until after the weather forecast. After that we play Uno and I let her win, even though she forgets to say Uno when she has only one card left. Nan is usually a bad loser but she doesn't even argue or complain.

'Irma used to forget to say Uno,' I say.

'She used to let you win.'

'No, she never.'

'You mean, "No, she didn't".'

Whatever. Irma never got cross about losing.

Nan sends me to bed before the sun goes down. I pull Ted from his shelf and hug him.

The silence in my room is very loud. I keep seeing Irma lying on the floor with her eyes and mouth open. Looking at me. Looking through me.

And then I hear her voice. 'Aren't you going to help me up, Michael? Aren't you going to help me?' Like she's under my bed now. My heart squeezes and I hold Ted tight against my chest. Where's Nan put that wooden spoon? Imagine Irma having hold of that and jabbing at me with it.

I hear her say, 'Don't worry, Michael. I'll always look after you. The way you looked after me.'

I feel heavy, like I've swallowed a rock. When I turn on my side my heart knocks loudly in my ears. Slowly, slowly, darkness gathers in the corners of my room until it is solid and ready to pounce.

Downstairs, Nan switches the TV on again. I turn on my light and wriggle to the end of my bed, climbing over the chair before I touch the floor, afraid of the hand grabbing at my ankles or the knife slicing off my feet.

Escaping downstairs, I stand outside the living room, like I did when I was little, just waiting there and hoping Nan will know that she needs to open the door and find me. Cold creeps up from the floor into my feet and up my legs. From deep inside the room I hear Nan crying.

Saturday morning. Nan doesn't go to work. She says, 'They were just talking about it on the radio.'

Irma in the news. I missed it. 'They're not treating it as suspicious,' says Nan. 'Though I think they mean "suspect".'

I don't know what to do next. Nan says maybe I should get ready for the Science test I have to take on Monday. Wouldn't that be cheating? She says, no, because when I was ill I missed a whole evening of revision so I could do a few hours now. If I wanted to. If I could concentrate.

I sit on my bed and try. I'm studying bones but I keep looking out the window. I see Janey being picked up in a car. She's going to play in a tournament. End of season stuff. Just like normal. 'The hip bone's connected to the thigh bone,' Irma used to sing when I was trying to remember words like 'pelvis' and 'femur'. Silly old Irma. Soon Bully's dad will have to go and look at her body. When they pull back the sheet, he will see her face and say, 'Yes that is her.' I hope he takes Bully with him. I don't want Nan to offer to look after him again. What will Bully tell the police? He got home, the door was locked; she was lying there, dead on the floor. He isn't going to say, 'And I think my dad killed her!' And what can I say? I don't even know how he did it.

Nan goes next door with the blue envelope. She isn't gone very long. And when she comes back she's on her own. Good. When I go downstairs, Nan is sitting hunched at the table, cheeks squashed by her two fists. In front of her, the blue envelope with Irma's writing. It hasn't been opened.

'No longer required,' says Nan. 'Nothing to do with us.' She puts her hands flat on the table and sighs and shakes her head. 'He did say there'll be a post-mortem in a few days. Don't hold your breath.'

'That's too late,' I say. 'They should come and look for evidence *now*.'

'Oh and I tried to take back the spoon. I thought I might be able to slip it into the pot without them noticing but they did not leave me alone for a second.'

'We should take it to the police.'

'And say what?'

'You know.'

'OK. We could say there was no sign that she was making soup except for a damp spoon. Which you have handled. Which I have had up my sleeve.'

'They've probably eaten it by now.' I think of them sitting at the table spooning up Irma's soup and smacking their lips like they are eating *her*.

'Or taken it away and dumped it in a ditch,' says Nan. 'Soup isn't going to stay evidence for long, is it?'

I should have stayed up all night and watched them. I should have done *more*.

'But *you* believe me, don't you? That she was making soup? For me?'

Nan sighs. 'She was very fond of you, and I know it's hard

but please, Michael, don't go thinking that it's all a big con-
spiracy.'

But she can't just have died.

'We're going to have to accept what's happened,' says Nan.
'There's absolutely nothing else that we can do.'

I think that's why Irma started to talk to me and not to
Nan: she knew Nan had already made up her mind that the
best thing would be to leave the Bulls alone.

We can't stand to be at home. Nan says, 'Let's go and make
sure Janey's lot are OK.' She hasn't bothered that much with
Janey's mum lately. We take the blue envelope with us.

Janey's mum unlocks the front door to let us in.

'Everything all right, Violet?' says Nan.

'As can.' She clutches the dressing gown around her. 'Janey's
not back from football yet.'

'Where's the tournament?' I ask.

Janey's mum looks guilty. 'Umm,' she says, turning back
down the hallway to the kitchen. We follow. Two birds fly away
from the feeders outside the window. Janey's dad used to say,
'That's a siskin, that's a chaffinch. The blue tit has a mask like
a little bandit.' Now Janey is the one who fills the feeders. 'We
must have a fixture list somewhere,' says her mum. 'Have you
been listening to the cricket? Jonny Bairstow went for 16.
Poor lad – and in his first test.' She doesn't say a thing about
Irma. How can she think about anything else?

'We haven't been listening,' says Nan.

Janey's mum frowns at the tatty piece of paper stuck to the
fridge with a magnet shaped like a red-and-black football.
Next to it is Melly's picture of her family: three on the ground
– her mum (big with black curly hair), a small Melly with a
brown line either side of her head, and Janey in the middle
with a squashed-looking ball at her feet. Up in the sky a huge
man is flying.

'That's last season's,' I say, pointing to the fixture list.

'Michael!' says Nan.

'What?'

'Don't be rude.'

'I'm not!'

'It's fine,' says Janey's mum, putting the list back under the fridge magnet. 'I'm a Bad Mother: it's official.'

'No, no,' says Nan, her voice dry as a dead leaf. Her fingers twitch. She wants to get hold of that old list and put it in the recycling. Janey's mum can't throw anything away; she says you just don't know what's valuable and what isn't, what funny little things might mean a lot one day. Because you never know what might happen. So if Janey got knocked down by a lorry, at least her mum would have her 2010-2011 fixture list to cry over.

'I'm sorry, Michael,' says Janey's mum. 'I just keep getting it wrong.'

'It's OK.' But it isn't really. Once, I heard her say to Janey, 'Your dad's not here to see you play any more so I don't know why you bother.'

There's a pain in my stomach, like a bread knife sawing at my guts. Is that what Janey feels − all the time? I miss her dad too − but this is different. No one expected Irma to die. No one except Shawn Bull.

Nan and Janey's mum sit in the kitchen and drink coffee and then they do talk about Irma. 'She always said she'd leave the house to Janey and Michael,' says Janey's mum. 'But I don't suppose that will happen now.'

I go into the living room and sit with Melly, who's having a busy day sucking her thumb and watching cartoons. I don't know whether I should talk to her about Irma. She's maybe too young. After a bit I hear a car door go clunk and then Janey comes in with sweaty hair and mud on her socks. She's carrying her boots. 'How did you get on?' I ask.

'Yeh, got through to the quarter finals,' she says.

'Oh. That's good, isn't it? Are you going to play for them again next year?'

'Dunno. I'm gonna have a trial for the County. But...'

I find myself doing that sad face. Playing for the County would mean a lot more travelling: even their home ground is sixteen miles away. And who knows when Janey's mum will start driving again.

'Anyone else going?' I ask, trying to brighten things up.

'One girl. Don't know if she'll get in.'

'You've got to hope.'

'I've got to have a shower,' she says and goes off upstairs. I sit with Melly a bit longer and then go back into the kitchen.

They're still drinking coffee. I like the smell. I wonder when I will be old enough to like the taste. It made me gag last time I tried it. I say, 'Janey's gone up for a shower.'

'Right,' says her mum. 'Thanks, Michael.'

'They got to the quarter-finals.'

'Oh. Well, never mind.'

'Janey's got a trial for the County, Nan.'

'Well done her,' says Nan. She could help me out a bit by asking Janey's mum how she would manage to get her there but they are just too busy looking at Irma's blue envelope.

They still haven't opened it.

'If I'm right,' says Nan. 'She'll have asked for lilies and roses and a wicker coffin. A woodland burial and for the music she wanted 'Final Taxi' by Wreckless Eric.'

'Really?' says Janey's mum. 'That sounds a bit ... I mean, I thought she might like something more...'

'Traditional?'

'Easy for other people. Not everyone has the same sense of humour.'

'Not even Irma,' says Nan. 'Not at the end. She changed. With that man. Some kind of strange chemistry.'

Janey's mum puts a hand on Nan's arm. It must be nice for her to comfort someone else.

Nan shakes her head. 'I feel like I lost her weeks ago. But I thought she'd just go somewhere else and start again. She'd still *be*. Not this.'

'Are you going to open it?' I say.

'I don't know. It feels a bit like opening someone else's post.'

On the envelope it says, 'To Whom it May Concern'. Isn't that us?

'*He* didn't want it,' says Nan. 'That's for sure.'

'He might just change his mind,' says Janey's mum. 'Grief can take you all ways, can't it?'

Janey comes down with joggers on and wet hair. She looks in the fridge and the old fixture list flaps. 'I'm starving, Mum,' she says. 'What's for lunch?'

Nan says, 'Will you all be coming to the funeral?'

Janey slams the fridge door.

I say, 'I want to go.'

'Umm,' says Janey's mum. 'I'll probably have to stay and look after Melissa.'

Janey looks at the ceiling.

Sometimes it's hard to know what goes on in other people's heads and sometimes it's easy. Right now Janey is thinking: Oh, Mum. Even now. *Any*thing to avoid going out.

We all eat a sandwich while we're there because Janey's mum likes to prove she has food in the house. She might not get to the shops but nobody starves. Then Nan goes home, taking the unopened envelope with her. I say can I stay a bit longer? Janey and I go up to her room. She lies on her bed looking at the ceiling. I go to the window and look out. If the Bulls leave their house I could go round and check the compost heap for onion skins and carrot peelings. I could look in their bins. There might be chicken bones. I could go back through the dog flap and check their freezer.

I sit down on the end of the bed and tell Janey about the wooden spoon. She listens with her eyes shut until I run out of things to say.

'Janey?'

'Mmm?'

'I thought you'd gone to sleep.'

'No,' she says. 'I'm thinking.'

'What?'

'Maybe how stupid you'd look if you told the police you'd stolen a damp spoon.'

'It could be evidence,' I say.

'You know what?' says Janey. 'You should wait and see what happens.'

'For how long?'

She shrugs. 'Anyway, you don't know for sure she was making you soup. And if she was, what does that even mean?'

'She was and if it doesn't mean anything why get rid of it?'

'Maybe she was just saying it.'

'She wouldn't. And I could smell it.'

Janey puts the back of her hand on her forehead like I do when I have a headache. 'Maybe you're starting to make things up again.'

'I'm *not*.'

'Why would anyone try to hide some *soup*?'

'That's what I'm *saying*.'

This is as close as we ever get to an argument.

After a bit she says, 'Maybe George threw it away because he just doesn't like you.'

'How would he even know the soup was for me?'

'Maybe he doesn't like chicken soup.'

'Or, maybe he came home, found Irma dead, knew that *his dad had done it*, panicked, threw the soup away and washed up.' But he'd have to do all that with her lying dead on the floor.

And *then* lock the door and come round to my house. That would be – impressive, weirdly impressive – and cold. He was really upset when he came round. 'Maybe he was scared.'

'Maybe *she* was scared,' says Janey. 'Maybe she was scared of *that man* telling her off for looking after you. Maybe she threw it away herself.'

'And then he killed her.'

'Why?'

There has to be a reason. It can't just be because of the soup. 'I bet he gets the house.'

'Maybe. Do you mind if it isn't us?'

'Dunno. I know she said it would be ours but – she was leaving anyway, wasn't she? So she probably changed all that.'

'Maybe she just … died.' Janey shrugs as if to say, that's what happens.

'But then why get rid of the soup?'

'How do you *know* she was making it?'

I'm starting to feel dizzy. I try a new direction. 'So, you know this Detective Inspector Dunbar?'

'Well, I know her son.'

'Her son?'

'Harry.'

'Oh. Harry.'

'Yeh. He's at school with me. In the year above.'

Ah. 'So … do you ever go round theirs? Maybe you could ask her. Find out what's happening. Say you really want to know what's going on because Irma was your neighbour. No, say she was like family. I need to know they're doing it properly.'

'They're the police, Michael.'

'*He's* the police.'

'I can't tell her how to do her job.'

'But you can tell her you're worried.'

She half sits up. 'Worried about what?'

'Worried about living next door to a murderer!'

'Oh that,' she says, lying back again.

I go home. Nan has found her *Wonderful World of Wreckless Eric* picture disc and is playing 'Final Taxi' loud enough for them to hear the la-la-las next door.

'Everything all right?' she shouts.

I mouth some words and she turns the music down.

'Is Janey all right?' she asks. 'It will be extra hard for her, you know, because she and Irma weren't getting on.'

I think, you're talking about yourself, Nan. And anyway, *I* was getting on all right with Irma and it's quite bad for me, too.

'Have you done your homework?'

'Don't have any.'

'Oh, your Science test!,' says Nan. 'You weren't supposed to talk to that boy.'

'I *know.*' It wasn't like I could help it.

'Just don't mention it at school.'

Now I *am* worried. Did I do something wrong? 'Why? Why can't I say what happened?'

'It's not as if you talked about Science while you were waiting for the ambulance. So there's nothing really to tell. It's best left.'

That night, the worry stops me from sleeping.

'That's your grandmother.' I can just hear Irma saying that. 'If there's a problem, she'd rather not talk about it. You know what she's like.'

It's true. Like she says about my parents: 'Best left'. Because they don't send cards or presents or even letters or emails; no text messages or phone calls. Nothing. I don't even know where they are exactly, in what prison, or what they look like. Somehow – and I know this can't be how it really is – I always imagine them in a cell together. Like they went on being a family, only without me, and *in prison*.

I think Irma knew more about them than I do.

And now – nothing. Her body is lying in a fridge somewhere. Shut away. Dark and cold. *Flick*. I see her on the floor of her kitchen with her eyes and mouth open.

'It's all right,' says Irma. 'I'm not really still there.' She sighs as if she's comfortable under my bed with the fluff and the crumbs. 'I've moved your toys to make room. Squawky says hi by the way.' Irma gave the T. Rex that name when she first heard her roar. 'Everyone says hi. You can have a look if you like.'

Why would I do that? When I leaned down, my head would dangle and my neck would be in just the right place for a sword to go *swoosh*.

'Still,' she says, 'every cloud... Now I'm here, you don't have to worry about the man with the knife any more.'

On Sunday I make myself look at the Science revision website again. This time I'm studying Forces in action; How we see things; Changing circuits.

There is nothing about how you can stop someone's heart – but that's OK. It's easy to look it up on the Internet. I wonder: does the shock have to be an electric shock?

Your heart uses electricity to tell its cells to squeeze to pump blood from the upper chambers to the lower chambers and then from the lower chambers all round your body. The cells all have to squeeze at the same time or the pump won't work: the heart just shivers.

So maybe her heart didn't stop straight away like a heart attack. Did she lie there thinking, *You know what? My heart doesn't seem to be working*. Did it hurt? Like a boulder landing on your chest? Or did it feel like a jelly shaking? Like a million butterflies beating their wings out of time?

Sunday night. I can't sleep with Monday creeping up on me. I have my Science test. I'm going to have to see Bully and I don't know what I'm going to do about that. And Nan wants me to tell a lie. On top of everything, Irma's been murdered and it's maybe going to be up to me to prove it. I'm all alone.

Nan always says you're not the only little boy who feels like this: scared of tomorrow. So how would I feel if I was Bully now? He has to carry round this terrible secret: that his dad's a murderer. I almost feel sorry for him but Irma prods me in the back and says, 'Don't you dare!' I think she wants someone to be angry that she's gone. I don't know why she's picked on me. I'm not the angry type.

Monday morning. School. It's funny walking across the play-ground. Everyone's running, skipping, standing about in circles. Like always. No one seems to notice what's happened to me. I don't see Bully.

I go straight to the headmistress's office. Her secretary has a desk in a sort of corridor. She looks at me as if I'm in the wrong place. She doesn't seem to change her mind about this, even after I explain. She makes me wait and I get so nervous my hands sweat.

The headmistress calls me into her office. 'Hello, Michael,' she says. 'Sit down. Feeling better now?' She squares up some papers, takes up a pen and says, 'Have you had any contact with children in your class?'

Nan's 'say nothing' won't help me here. So I say, 'Yes.'

'Oh?' She puts the pen down. 'Well that wasn't supposed to happen, was it?'

I tell her I couldn't help it. That George Bull came round and banged on my door because he needed an ambulance.

'Oh. Oh. Were you involved in that?'

'It was an emergency.'

'But why did *you* answer the door?' she says. 'Were you on your own?'

'No,' I say. '*She* was looking after me.'

'Who?'

'The one who died.'

The headmistress thinks about it for a minute. 'You might as well take the test now,' she says. 'And I'll speak to George's father about it.'

Why *him*? 'I didn't want to answer the door.'

'I understand that it was an emergency,' she says.

I don't say anything about the murder. She might tell Shawn Bull.

After the test she asks me, 'How do you think you've done?'

'All right,' I say. 'I like Science.'

She nods. I was worried before in case I did badly and now I'm worried because if I do well she'll think I'm a cheat.

She sends me back to my classroom. Bully isn't there. The teacher says everyone has been signing a card for 'Georgie'. They talk about Irma and call her 'Georgie's stepmother'. I want to say 'She wasn't his stepmother' but I don't want to put up my hand. The teacher talks to us about how we will behave when 'Georgie' comes back.

'Just include him as you normally would,' she says. 'The worst thing is to be ignored.'

No one remembers that I might be upset too.

'Michael?' the teacher asks. 'Perhaps you could take the card home?'

I take it. I think about ripping it to pieces but I don't. Instead when I get home I go slowly down the path to Irma's house. I could just put the envelope through the letterbox in the front door but instead I go round the side and very quietly lift the lid of the wheelie bin. Inside there are black bags and carrier bags, all neatly tied up. I close the lid gently and move to the kitchen door and knock. No answer. I think I will push the card through the dog flap, but there's a piece of wood across it. It's been nailed shut. I have to go to the front and knock again. No answer there. Maybe they've gone away. Maybe Shawn Bull's been arrested after all. Or maybe they're just hiding, waiting for me to go. I look through the letterbox, squinting in case something strikes at my eyes. It's all quiet inside. I push the card through and hear it fall.

In the evening paper Nan brings home, there's a report about Irma. It goes:

> A 52-year-old woman was found dead at her home in Buckington on Friday afternoon. A spokesperson for the emergency services confirmed that police and ambulance were called just after 4pm. The deceased was found in the kitchen of her home and could not be revived. She was pronounced dead at the scene. Police are awaiting the outcome of a post-mortem on Tuesday. The incident is not being treated as suspicious.

Tomorrow is Tuesday. Tomorrow there will be some answers.

Nan sends me to bed and I lie there looking at the wallpaper: the donkeys in their field; the geese with their triangular feet. My heart begins to flutter and I put my hand on my chest.

'Don't worry,' says Irma. 'You're too young to die.'

I don't think that can be true. Maybe Janey's right: it can happen to anyone. Any time.

Tuesday. After school I'm waiting for Nan to come home with the paper so I can read what they have to say about Irma. Bully's in the back garden next door kicking a ball against the shed. He wasn't in class again today. I decide I'm going to speak to him.

'Did you get your card?' The teacher asked me and I want to be able to say 'Yes' tomorrow and know that it's true.

He shrugs.

That is just annoying, so I go on. 'They were cutting her open today.'

He looks away.

'Yep. Weighing her brain. Checking her *heart*. They'll find out what really killed her, won't they?'

'Shut up.'

'I mean I think it's good. But maybe you're scared.'

'I'm not. I didn't do anything.' But he still runs away into the house.

I was going to shout after him, 'What about your dad?' but I don't – in case his dad is home.

But there's *nothing* about Irma's post-mortem in the evening paper. I look all the way through it – twice. And I ask Nan.

'I don't know if they report on post-mortems,' she says. 'Or maybe there's nothing to tell. Maybe it just isn't news.'

But Irma was murdered by a police officer. Maybe that's *too* much news.

I want to talk to Janey about it, but she hasn't been coming straight home after school. Her mum says she has extra football practice so I go past the school field and there she is, doing free kicks even though the goal posts have been taken down for the summer and the track is laid out for athletics, brown lines in the grass like giant fingerprints. She's with a boy. He's taller than she is. He has blond hair that he shakes out of his eyes.

I go and sit on the grass and watch them. She puts up her hand to say hi. The boy looks my way and then sweeps his hair across his forehead. Janey sends him the ball; he chests it down and traps it at his feet, steps back a few paces, runs up and kicks. The ball goes up and down and Janey doesn't have to chase far to get it. He's nearly as good as she is. I can see why she wants to practise with him. I get it.

I have to wait for ages. When they give up and come over to me, Janey says, 'Hi,' and that is all. She mumbles something to Golden Boy and then she and I walk off together.

'Is that him?' I say. 'Is his mum the detective?'

She nods.

We walk on.

'Have you asked him?'

'Yeh, but he can't talk to his mum about her job.'

'So you haven't asked him?'

'Yes,' she says. 'Embarrassing.'

'So what did he say?'

'Nothing. He doesn't know anything.'

'Nothing? But he *lives* with her.'

If Nan was a detective I'd have found out all about it by now. I want to know: did they look for scorched fingers and burnt-out nerves?

'Should *I* maybe talk to her?' I say. 'If you go round his house, can I come?'

'No,' says Janey. 'And no.'

'How would you send a message without anyone knowing who you are?' I ask Nan. It's the kind of puzzle she likes.

'Why do you want to know that?'

'It's a project.'

'A school project?'

'Communication studies. I'm interested.'

'Mmm. I suppose in the old days you could ring up from a phone box. You'd have to go to a different town. But I wouldn't know where to find a working phone box these days.'

'You could use a mobile.'

'Traceable. Though there must be ways. You could cut letters or words out and glue them onto paper and put that in the post. Only that always looks like hate mail. But anyway, I don't think modern printers are as individual or traceable as old-fashioned typewriters.'

'So you could just write a letter and post it.'

'Unsigned. And you'd still have to send it from a different town to have less chance of being found out. And *then* you'd have to make sure you could prove you were nowhere near that place when the letter was posted. And not be seen on CCTV. And delete it permanently from your computer. When you come to think about it, crime isn't all that easy. I wonder how anyone ever gets away with it.'

'But it isn't a crime to send a letter.'

'Depends what kind of letter it is. Like I said, if it was hate mail. That isn't good. Or libel. Do you know what that is? It's when you write down a lie about somebody. A lie that could hurt them – or their reputation, which for some people is the same thing.'

So I don't think I can tell her I was going to write a letter to the papers or the police saying, 'Irma Gordon was murdered. That policeman did it.'

Bully comes back to school on Thursday. I'm ready for him. If he starts to have a go at me I'll be *glad*.

Everyone is nice to him. I watch him. He doesn't speak in class. He looks at his hands or at the board or at the screen or out of the window.

At break time he just hangs around at the edges: I want to run and because I'm looking at Bully I knock over some little kids playing Coconut Crack. And then, even though I am helping put them the right way up again, the teacher comes out and says, 'Michael, stop showing off.'

What does *she* know? Nothing.

She knows nothing about how I feel.

Everyone is quiet around Bully. Quiet and careful. The grown-ups look at him as if they're sorry or like dying is something you could catch. He has a tear in his eye and the teacher almost puts her arm around him but then she just sort of holds it there like she's comforting the air. She says is he all right to stay? Does he want to go home? He says there isn't anyone there.

'Oh dear,' says the teacher. 'No, of course there isn't.'

'I wish my mum was here,' says Bully, which is just confusing for the teacher because she's been acting like Irma *was* his mum. But I'm the one who knew her all my life. He just lived in her house for a bit. Her house.

Now *I* follow *him* home, ten steps behind. When he stops and turns and looks at me, I stop too. When he walks, I start walking.

He stops. I stop.

'Stalker!' he calls. 'Weirdo!' But he doesn't come near me.

We walk on, like we're holding a long pane of glass between us.

He has new trainers. They're black and look almost like school shoes, but they're still trainers. When did he get those? Was that what they were doing when he wasn't in class? Shopping? When they were supposed to be so upset.

Nan says it's not up to me to judge.

But who else is going to do it?

The neighbours want to know when Irma's funeral will be. Mrs Rogers has been round. But we don't know. No one dares to go and ask the Bulls.

Friday. At school, I keep thinking: this time last week...

Now England and the West Indies have moved on to play the Second Test. It's funny how the cricket goes on and doesn't know what's happened to us. 'Jonathan Agnew always sounds so cheerful,' says Nan, sadly. But you can't expect Aggers to know how things are here. Aggers didn't even know Irma.

Irma's funeral is next Wednesday. Bully's dad told us, when he came round our house with an envelope. 'I was going through Irma's things and I found *this*,' he said, holding the blue envelope between two fingers like a dirty five-pound note. Nan hoped it was a message from Irma but then she saw her own handwriting. Inside were her own last wishes. She didn't open it. I think she just put it in the firebox with all the other stuff. I suppose I'll have to open it one day.

At school, I see Bully *smiling* and I want to smack him in the mouth. I don't, because I know how *that* would look. I bet he thinks he can get what he likes now, do what he likes, because everyone feels sorry for him. He's probably blackmailing his dad.

After school, I drag myself home, past Janey's house, past Irma's house with the For Sale sign with the word 'Sold' slapped across it.

Nan brings home the weekly paper. There's just a few lines about Irma and it says she died 'of natural causes'.

'What does that mean?' I ask Nan.

'It means it was nobody's fault,' she says. 'Shawn Bull says the post-mortem concluded it was her heart. So – there we are. No inquest.'

'No way.'

'We have to accept it,' says Nan. 'It's just one of those things.'

'No! It isn't.'

'Like *I* have to accept that her funeral's at the Crem, which isn't what she wanted at all. But there's nothing we can do about that either.'

Irma's funeral. Janey's coming with us, which is good because I think she's been avoiding me but bad because her mum won't be there with her. I told her I was thinking of going to Crimestoppers. She said, 'You're on your own there.'

The Crimestoppers website says 'Fight Crime without revealing your identity' and there is a man in a kind of Zorro mask.

I can't decide what to do.

Bully's dad has made all the arrangements for the funeral himself. Nan offered to help but he just grunted. I agree with Nan. If I was a policeman, I wouldn't go around grunting. Nan makes a call to the headmistress so I can get the day off school. There's a bit of an argument but Nan is firm because Irma was like family.

Everyone already knew that Bully was going to have the time off. He made sure of that, still going around looking sad, most of the time, so the teachers would be nice to him.

Nan says, maybe he really is sad.

I say I would be sad if I knew my dad was a murderer.

'You can't go around accusing people.'

'Why not? Was my dad a murderer too?'

She takes in a great big breath and holds it, like Melly does when she wants to get her own way. Then she sighs. 'The only thing you need to know, Michael, is that you're much better off without him.'

'You always say that.'

'Because it's true. And I don't want to discuss it.'

On the drive to the Crem I sit next to Nan in the front and Janey goes in the back. Nan says we will respect Irma's wishes and so we listen to the lonely strumming guitar and Wreckless Eric's sad and jokey croaky voice beginning to sing 'Final Taxi':

'A black cavalcade winds its way through the back streets
'Flowers piled high on a wooden box

'With friends and relations sat in rows in the back seats
'All looking shaky cos it came as a shock.'

I pull down the visor so I can look in the mirror at Janey. She's just staring out the window. Then the chorus crashes through the car and through my head. I shut my eyes and move my lips to the words while Nan sings as loud as she can. When the song is over we drive on in silence. I see other people just walking around like it's a normal day, in and out of shops, stepping into the road, impatient to get past a wheel-chair or a double buggy. I hold tight to the door handle as if the door might fly open. A woman on the kerb waiting to cross stares at me.

We wait outside the chapel for Irma to arrive. Bully and his dad turn up wearing suits. Shawn Bull says we should go in and sit down. Mrs Rogers is there and a few more of our neighbours and people I don't know, maybe from the office where Irma used to work though she was leaving there anyway: a different kind of goodbye. Then the funeral men bring in the coffin with Irma inside it. Nan shakes her head and whispers, 'MDF'. Bully and his dad walk behind and sit at the front. The flowers are chrysanthemums: Nan wrinkles her nose. She and Janey and I each hold an Order of Service for Irma Felicity Gordon (18 March 1960 to 18 May 2012). On the back it says: *Donations to the British Heart Foundation*.

All through the hymns that were not Irma's choice, I wonder what we should have been listening to. I can't join in. Neither can Nan. Janey sings. She has a good voice. I think Nan might jump up and shout, 'This is all wrong' and Janey and I will have to decide whether to try and hold her back or let her get on with it. Bully is crying – too loudly, I think. His dad puts his arm around him. I want to cry too. My throat aches but nothing will come out. Shawn Bull gets up and says something about Irma: that she was the kindest person he had ever met. It should be Nan talking about her: she knew her the best and the longest. Nan's arm feels hard in her jacket, like she's wearing armour.

It's not good to see the curtains close round Irma's coffin. Nan puts her hand over her mouth when the wheels start to squeak. It's all wrong. Irma wanted to be buried in a wicker basket. She wanted to go into the ground among the trees. She wanted a *natural* burial.

Bully and his dad wait outside, and look at the people as they come past. Bully's face is tight and pink. His dad's is kind of misty like it's being rubbed away. Nan manages to shake his hand and say, 'I'm very sorry for your loss.' I put out my hand to Bully and to my surprise he takes it and jerks my hand up and down, up and down.

I still think of them as 'the new people', and here they are saying thank you to Irma's old friends. But they don't invite us not even for a cup of tea afterwards, so we go straight back to Janey's house to tell her mum all about it. Nan says of course she will want to know, even if she couldn't be there in person.

As we leave I turn back one last time. Bully and his dad look at each other as if to say, 'Job done.'

'Where has she gone?' asks Melly.

Gone. So simple it makes my head shake.

'Nothing was the way that Irma wanted it,' says Nan. Her eyes are wet now. 'Nothing.'

It seems wrong that we left while Irma was still being burned to ashes. What will he do with them? Scatter them or leave them on a shelf? He isn't our friend so we won't know where she is in the world. She will become atoms. She could be anywhere. And because of that I think she could be everywhere.

'It means we won't see her any more,' says Janey. 'Like Daddy.'

'Oh,' says Melly. 'You mean because she's dead.'

Janey's mum doesn't ever say, 'He passed away' or anything like that. She says 'He died' and 'She's dead.'

But when Nan talks about Irma, she always says that she is lost.

II

FRIENDS OF THE DEAD

Half term. Some houses round The Middle put up bunting and hang Union flags from their windows. It's the Queen's Diamond Jubilee or, as Nan says, 'A lot of hoo-hah.' Mrs Rogers wants us to decorate our house too.

Nan says, 'No. I don't approve of the Union flag – it doesn't include Wales.'

Mrs Rogers: 'I didn't know you were Welsh.'

Nan: 'I'm not but what's that got to do with it? I used to live there and it makes you think about these things.'

Mrs Rogers: 'I don't have to think about that because for sure I am never going to live in Wales.'

Nan: 'In any case, I'm a Republican.'

Mrs Rogers: 'There is no such political party in this country.'

Nan: 'That is not the point and those are not the values I am talking about.'

There's going to be a party out in The Middle. Nan has the Bank Holiday free and a few days of half -term. She said maybe we would go away or something. Then she decides that we should go to the party after all, because Irma would have liked it. 'Funny how she turned into a Royalist when there was a do.'

Janey's going and Melly. Everyone is taking food. Nan is making Irma's special trifle. Janey's mum – she isn't going but she says she will make a quiche or something. In the end, Janey hands over a bag with some crisps and a couple of pots of dip. Mrs Rogers looks inside the bag and says, 'Thank you so much.'

The woman next to her mutters something and Mrs Rogers says in a loud whisper, 'Ssh. She can't help it.'

At the party, Janey, Nan, Melly and me all sit together at one end of the long table. A man in a paper crown sits at the other end and acts like he's in charge. No one wants to be near us. The Bulls don't come out. If they did everyone else would probably shuffle up and make them sit with us – we are Death Corner.

So we eat and drink as much as we can: we make people pass us food from the far end of the table. Nan keeps asking Mrs Rogers to check if I can eat it and then we hold on to all those things down at our end. If they won't be nice to us they can feed us instead.

We have brought some elderflower champagne. 'Is this alcoholic?' says Mrs Rogers.

'Oh no,' says Nan. 'It's only a week old. It'll be like lemonade.' She doesn't let Melly have more than a sip of it though.

I am drinking it. And Janey and Nan. It's like drinking summer even though the day is cold and drizzly. In London, the Queen and Prince Philip are standing on a boat for hours getting damp. Nan says it's almost as if someone has arranged it on purpose to kill them off.

The bubbles rush through my blood like a train. Whoosh, they gather in my head and make it light as a balloon.

We picked the elderflower on that one sunny day from the tree that hangs over the fence from Irma's garden: flat white clusters of tiny perfumed flowers as big as dinner plates. The best blooms were on the other side, facing south, but we made do.

Last winter, Shawn Bull wanted to cut the tree down but Irma wouldn't let him because it is unlucky and anyway, what about the elderflower champagne? He said you can't call it champagne.

Nan says the new thing is to call it prosecco. I think she would have liked to talk to Irma about it. I'm not much good at taking her place.

While we were picking, I saw Janey's mum opening an upstairs window in their house. She held on to the handle and the blue sleeve slipped down her bare arm. I waved but she didn't see me.

I used to wonder if my mum had dark hair.

The elderflower fizzes out into the glasses.

When the trifle is served up, Nan gives me my special one with the non-dairy custard and cream.

'How did your trial go, Jane?' asks Nan.

Janey swallows trifle and says, 'Good.'

'Did they offer you a place?'

'Mmmhmm.'

'Janey might have trouble getting there,' I say. 'I told you.'

Mrs Rogers and her friend are trying hard to look like they're not listening. They know Janey's mum is stuck. She's stuck like her feet are in toffee. Stuck like a sheep with its head through the fence. Where Nan used to live there were sheep and they would cry and cry because they couldn't get free. They'd stay there all day, and die if you left them, if the farmer didn't come. So, Nan said, you'd climb over the gate and walk through someone else's field and only then, when they knew you were coming near, would the sheep start to tug and struggle, wrestling their heads out from the square of wire. They'd be free and running off before you got within ten yards. But if you did nothing they would just stay where they were and die.

I eat my trifle – and think of Bully. I think of throwing trifle at his face. I'm glad he isn't here because people would think I was the nasty one.

'Is it all right?' Nan asks.

'It's lovely, Nan. Thank you.'

Nan looks at everyone else tucking into the trifle and she raises her voice to let everyone know: 'This is Irma's trifle.' Some of the people near us hold their spoons in mid-air and look at the trifle and look at each other.

I want to explain, 'Irma didn't make it. Nan did.' But I'm not brave enough to speak.

Bully and his dad come out of their gate and there is a woman with them. She has fluffy blonde hair in a wide cut that stops between ears and chin; she wears a stripy dress and a thin cardigan; she has nice pale shoes. 'Ooh. Is that his wife?' says the woman next to Mrs Rogers. 'You've got to wonder. She looks like something out of my catalogue.'

'One thing's for sure,' says Mrs Rogers. 'He didn't waste any time.'

Bully's dad puts a bag into the boot of the car and then he rests his hand on Bully's shoulder and guides him to the passenger side. He even puts a hand on his head so he doesn't bump it getting in.

'Once a policeman...' says Nan.

The woman doesn't kiss Bully's dad good-bye; she just gets into the driver's seat. Bully's dad watches them go then he turns back to the house. It's like we, the long table, the bouncy castle, the bunting, all the people – are not there. Ghosts we are to him or less than ghosts.

Nan stands up at our end of the table and shouts, 'Everyone! Everyone!' until they stop talking and look at her. She raises her glass and says, 'A toast.' I see that her hand is shaking. Janey and Melly and me, we pick up our glasses. Everyone else does the same. The man at the far end wearing a paper crown is the last.

'To Irma!' says Nan. She drinks, and the glass rattles against her teeth.

We join in with the echo, 'To Irma', and drink.

'She's dead,' says Melly to Mrs Rogers. 'Like my daddy.'

'It's all right, Melly,' says Janey. 'You don't have to explain.'

There is a long silence while we finish the trifle: soft, slithery, sweet. Makes it easier to swallow.

Afterwards there are some games for the little ones and we

watch Melly running about. We want her to have a good time. We want her to be happy. Her hair flies up as she jumps on the bouncy castle. She is only five. She is allowed to laugh.

At home I talk to Nan again about Janey playing for the County. 'It's the School of Excellence. There's training twice a week, matches at the weekend. Even for the home matches you have to drive miles to get there. And then there's the away matches.'

'Don't they have a bus?'

'People go with their mums and dads.'

'Michael, I can't help it if her mum isn't bothered.'

'I wish I could drive. Or if I had enough money for a taxi.'

'Oh, Michael. We can't do everything.'

'But it's important.'

'I can't just take time off work.'

'What if *I* wanted to play?'

'Err … it's a girls' team, Michael.'

'But...'

'And yes, think about it, what if you do decide there's something *you* want to do on a Saturday and I've committed myself to helping Janey.'

'I'm not going to.'

'You don't know that.'

'I do.'

'We don't even know if she's going to get in.'

'She will.'

'Well, let's see if she does.'

'If she gets in will you help her?'

'Let's see.'

I wish she would just say yes so I could tell Janey. I really want to. 'Her dad would have taken her,' I say.

'I know, Michael,' says Nan.

Shawn Bull goes back to work and everything carries on like it's all normal again. Like when you throw a stone in the river. Plop. Splash. Ripple. Gone. But I always think of the fishes underneath and maybe one of them getting a bump on the head.

Bully is away all half term, staying at his mum's. I don't even have a photo of mine. If I did it would be like one of those head shots with starey eyes they put in the newspaper, photoshopped over the scene of the crime.

'It's better not to have photos, isn't it?' I say. 'Janey's mum doesn't know what to do with all hers.'

'At least we won't be cluttered up with the stuff that Irma's left us,' says Nan. Because Irma has left us Nothing.

I sometimes think she will come tripping down the path like before when she and Nan were best friends. Nan says, don't feel too sorry for her. I think she enjoyed herself quite a bit this last year.

Now Janey and I will never live together in her house.

Maybe it's for the best. We might have been too sad. We might always have been stepping over the spot where Irma fell and when we were having breakfast I'd think about her lying on the floor. Or maybe we would have got used to it. Maybe we would have started to laugh about things – and then we would remember. Janey would know what to do, because of her dad. Only he didn't die at home – and it doesn't matter now anyway because it isn't going to happen. We are never going to live in that house.

Nan says she doesn't mind that we got nothing because she only cares about losing Irma.

Yeh, Nan. 'So why did you google "Right to see a will UK"?'

'How do you know that?'

'Nan, it's easy.' She doesn't know about stuff like deleting her browsing history and I'm not going to tell her.

She's found a way to get a copy of someone's will. 'I just need to know,' she says.

None of the offices you can go to are anywhere near us so she writes a letter and sends some money. 'Worth £5,' she says. She thinks it could take a long time but one day there it is in the post.

'I guess she had all her affairs neatly tied up because of the move,' says Nan.

Bully's dad gets everything.

'Doesn't that make you suspicious?' I say.

'You mean, does it make me suspect something?' says Nan. 'No: I'm learning to mind my own business.'

The For Sale sign is still up. It still says 'Sold' at an angle across it – but they don't seem to be getting ready to leave. Nan says they can do what they like once the house is legally theirs. She says it would be nice to get a neighbour she likes but it will be 'the end of an era' when all traces of Irma are gone.

So the summer goes on without Irma. The West Indies draw the Third Test and go home. No more Sir Viv on the radio. Nan shops and drives to work and comes home. She cooks tea and tidies up. She makes it look easy. I go to school. I wonder if I'm making it look easy too.

Bully gets over feeling shy with me and tries to play Coconut Crack on my head. No one else stops him so I push him hard and look him in the eye. I wag my finger at him and I say, 'Irma won't like it. She'll come and find you.'

His face goes red and swells up like it's going to burst. I nearly feel sorry for him.

I think of Irma shaking her head at me. She was never nasty to anyone. She didn't like arguments.

Nan used to say, 'Irma, you can't sit on the fence all your life.'

I thought, no it isn't comfortable.

But when Irma got off the fence she ended up on the wrong side. And now I am the one trying to make things right for her. So she shouldn't be shaking her head at me: unless she's telling me to be careful. I don't feel like being careful. Irma was careful – and she died anyway.

At school, I say to Bully, 'Officially, I was the last person to see Irma alive.' It sounds good. I almost wish that people would point at me and say 'You see that boy? He was the last person to see her alive.'

Bully doesn't say anything.

'What's it like?' I say to Bully. 'Now your dad's a murderer.'

I'm ready. If he jumps on me I will throw him. He doesn't. He runs away.

I run after him. 'Your dad. What did he do to her?!'

He's a good runner, Bully. He runs to the teacher and stays with her. I think he's going to tell her what I've said. But nothing happens.

All afternoon I watch him. Nothing happens.

At home I think, he'll tell his dad. I think his dad will come round here soon and knock on the door. He will shout at Nan. Or maybe Bully will call his mum and tell her what I said.

Nothing happens.

Janey says I shouldn't be so mean.

'Mean? Me?' I can't believe that. Bully knows his dad killed Irma. He's helping him cover it up. And I'm *mean*?

'How did he do it then?' says Janey. 'Where's the evidence? The police haven't found anything.'

'So, did you ask – Harry?' I nearly said 'Golden Boy'.

'She died of a heart attack.'

'Oh and you think that someone can't make you have a heart attack?'

'You don't know anything.'

I try to be patient. 'Even a small electric shock could have stopped her heart. Have they even thought of that?'

'Say she did have a shock,' says Janey. 'It could still have been an accident.'

'So why hide the soup? Hiding what happened is bad too, isn't it?'

'Maybe you think it's your fault. Maybe you want someone else to blame.'

'How can it be my fault?'

'I'm not being funny,' she says, 'but I've already got Mum to worry about.'

'You don't care about Irma any more. But I do. And she was murdered.'

She looks me in the eye. 'Everyone's got their problems.'

Someone comes and takes down the For Sale/Sold sign. That's it: run away while you can. There's a little flame of hope – maybe I won't have to do anything. Only, Shawn Bull's still a murderer, even if he doesn't live next door.

Nan says, no, they're not leaving. They're going to stay right where they are.

Oh-oh. Well, that's clever. But I'm watching them. I've already written down everything I can remember about the day Irma died, because it might be needed in court. If I see anything now I will write it down.

Weirdly, for a while, still nothing happens. Except I get taller. My feet are longer. I'm growing and the things that are me are still alive.

In my nightmares sometimes my body dissolves at the edges. Or my feet get stuck. I'm like Janey's mum. I wave my arms and struggle and I can't move forwards.

When I'm awake, I worry about cars mowing me down when I cross the road. I see myself falling out of trees and smashing my skull.

Life is very dangerous – but being dead is nothing. Nothing at all.

Bully's mum comes to fetch him away now at weekends. I like it better when he's not around. I can breathe.

Then one day Mrs Bull is in Irma's back garden, hanging out washing. That isn't right. She can go down the garden now and pick Irma's peas. Eat her strawberries. Reach up into that apple tree.

Why is she even here?

Nan says someone has to look after George. I think she feels sorry for the Bulls. I see Bully's dad coming and going in his uniform, like they've always lived next door and Irma was never there.

Why am I the only one who cares?

I want to talk to Janey but she just keeps moving, kicking balls at me, throwing balls at me, hitting balls at me.

To please her mum we play French cricket out in The Middle. You don't need stumps. Just the bat and ball that Janey's dad gave her.

'You could be the next Charlotte Edwards,' her mum says, waving us off.

Janey doesn't answer.

Melly plays too, patiently rounding up the ball and bringing it back. She agrees to do this as long as we agree that she's a sheepdog called Lily. It works out for everyone.

'I'm being Jonny Bairstow,' I say, patting my chest before Janey bowls at me, though I shouldn't be giving her any hints about where to aim. 'Who are you going to be?'

'Paul Collingwood.'

'Ah, Tough Guy! But he doesn't play international cricket now.'

'Neither do we.'

Tough Guy. That's what Janey's mum used to call Janey's dad too – when he was ill and being brave. Janey doesn't like me saying it. I don't mean to upset her so I try looking sad but it just makes her more cross, and while she's staring at me and standing there like a teapot, Melly is running around howling and barking and setting off the dogs in houses and gardens all over the hillside. So we just get on with the game. 'Come on,' says Janey, when it's her turn to bat. 'I'm gonna smash a six.'

A six is anywhere over the rooftops. Hitting a house or a fence or a car is a four, but mostly we don't try to score boundaries as it makes people shout at us. We just try not to get out. 'Look,' says Janey. I turn round.

She's looking at Irma's house, at the upstairs window. A face keeps bobbing up and falling back. Bully, running at the windowsill and pushing himself up. Playing.

'We could ask him to come out,' says Janey. Bully's face bobs up again, like a balloon on a stick.

'No,' I say. 'I can't.'

'Come *on*,' barks Melly.

'OK,' says Janey. 'But he's seen us.'

I shrug. I don't care about Bully. I feel a little stab of pain because Janey does.

It's a lonely kind of feeling.

Maybe that's why Irma talks to me again. You should try being dead,' she says. That's really lonely. And no one cares.'

'I'm sorry. I'm sorry. Nan says, nobody could help it. You just died.'

'"Nan says." Do you always believe what your nan says? You *know* the truth, Michael. What are you going to do about it?'

'I'm sorry. I'm sorry. But there's nothing I can do.'

'Now, Michael. You know that's just not good enough.'

One thing: I don't let Bully push me around any more. When he tries to get me in a headlock I elbow him in the guts. He tries to hit me and I thump him in the eye. This time he does go crying to the teacher and the teacher tells his dad.

He tells Nan to keep me away from his boy. His boy has a black eye.

Nan says, 'Oh, Michael. What is happening to you?'

Bully's mum is there all the time now. She comes round and says, 'I have a bone to pick with you about your grandson.'

Nan says, 'I'm sorry? I'd like you to know that your son has been a menace since the day he got here.'

I want her to say, 'And who are you anyway, living in my friend's house?'

Nan sends me up to my room while they talk. Their voices sound like angry bees.

Wimbledon. Janey goes all Andy Murray on me and we remember we might be interested in tennis. She borrows her dad's racket and I borrow her mum's. We play out in The Middle after school – when it isn't raining – and use all the tennis balls in the tube so we don't have to keep fetching them. Janey puts out two chairs and a table. We carry them from the shed in her back garden and wipe them clean, but her mum doesn't come out to watch us play. Melly sits in one of the chairs with her sunglasses on, even when there is no sun, and she calls the score and giggles every time she says, 'Love.' Janey wants to let 'George' play with us and I say no.

When it rains, Janey leaves the chairs and table out. She thinks her mum might go and get them. The next day they're still there. Janey says her mum looked at them through the rain and said they were only chairs – just 'stuff' and 'stuff' doesn't matter.

'So why does she find it so hard to get rid of it all?' says Janey.

'Maybe we should put it all out in the rain.'

It rains so much that on days when it doesn't rain we stay out as long as we can – until the swallows turn into bats.

I see Nan from my bedroom window walking down the garden and puffing out smoke. When she kisses me good night she smells of ashes and peppermint.

'Why are you doing that?' I ask her. 'You don't smoke.'

'I used to,' she says. 'I just felt like it.'

'It's bad for you.' If she dies, I'll have no one. Except maybe Janey. I wish I could live at her house.

'OK. I'll make a deal. You stop bothering that boy next door and I'll give up smoking – again.'

'I don't bother him. He bothers me.'

'All right but keep away from him. Otherwise it will be us who'll have to move.'

'Yes, cuz it's kind of dangerous, living next door to a murderer.'

She sighs. 'You certainly weren't like this before they moved in.'

Before Irma was killed, she means, but she can't say she thinks the policeman did it, because then she would have to do something. And maybe we wouldn't be safe here. And we'd have to leave. I don't want to go. If I'm not here, who will I be? Who will I become? It makes me feel all tangled up inside. 'They're the ones who should go. Not us.'

'I really need you to drop it now,' says Nan. Don't go after that boy and his dad any more, Michael. I mean it. Let it drop.'

Let it drop. Let it drop. Let it drop. The words keep sounding in my head even when I'm trying not to think about them.

Nan says, 'Giving up is part of letting go.'

Sounds easy.

'Is someone telling you do this, Michael?'

No. Irma isn't saying anything. But I know she's still here.

Saturday afternoon. I go round to Janey's. Melly lets me in.

Janey's out and her mum's sleeping. The radio is talking in an upstairs room. Applause. Grunt. Pock. Pock. Grunt. Pock. Applause. We are halfway through Wimbledon.

In the living room there are felt-tip pens all over the floor. As I get to the sofa I tread on one and hear it crack. I sit down with my left foot covering the pen. If I had The Twitch now I'd have to break another and another and Melly would have no pens left. She climbs into her dad's chair and puts a hand on each of the arms, like it's her throne. There's a long pink streak of felt tip right across her cheek. I wonder if she's done that on purpose to make it look like a scar. She stares at me.

'Sorry,' I say, moving my foot. I pick up the broken felt tip and put it on the table.

'Don't worry about it,' she says, waving her hand. It was a thing her dad used to say. It sounds funny – and how does she remember? She was so little when he died. I think what it would be like if her dad was still here. There wouldn't be pens all over the floor for me to tread on. He would be in that armchair watching Wimbledon.

I look up at the shelf where our chessboard should be. But it's gone.

Things don't stay the same. I used to watch the cricket round their house. And the football. They had Sky Sports then. Janey wasn't happy when her mum cancelled. 'See,' Janey said. 'She can sort some things out when she wants to.'

That last summer, Janey's dad spent most of his time sitting here watching TV. He would watch any kind of sport. Sometimes I'd sit with him, even if it was indoor bowls. He didn't mind. If the news came on and there was something about a bombing or a murder he turned over. He said, 'I don't want any more bad news.'

'Where's the chessboard?' I ask.

'Mum moved it,' says Melly.

'Where?'

'In Daddy's room.'

I think she means the study. 'Can I put on the tennis?' I say.

I remember when we were watching cricket and Janey's mum would run in and stand behind his chair. He'd say, 'What?' and she'd say, 'Wait.' And then the next ball would be a wicket or a six or a dropped catch or – something. For a long time I thought it was a kind of magic, like Janey's mum could see into the future. And then I found out that if you listen to the cricket on the radio it's always a few seconds ahead of Sky Sports on TV. So Janey's mum might have been sorting out something to eat with the door shut because of the smell, or getting ready his next lot of medicines and she knew when to come running in.

Melly is still looking at me.

'Are you doing a sponsored stare?'

'No.'

'Shall I go and come back later?'

She shrugs. 'How do I know?'

'What are you doing anyway?'

'Nothing,' she says, warily.

'Not colouring?'

She shakes her head.

'So you were just sitting here, not doing anything at all?'

She nods.

'That's boring,' I say.

'I know.' She rolls her eyes.

'So why don't we put on the tennis?' I say.

She gives a big sigh. 'OK.'

Serena Williams is having a battle on Centre Court. Bobby Charlton is in the Royal Box and Geoffrey Boycott, Andrew Strauss, Alastair Cook, Dame Kelly Holmes. Lots of sporty people. I think, it must be nice to be so important that people invite you to watch a match at Wimbledon. You'd have to be really good at something first though. That might happen to Janey one day. Maybe.

I don't feel like going home. I just sit there, feeling thirsty and a bit sad.

We hear the bed creak upstairs and then Janey's mum comes down. Her eyes are red and puffy. She's wearing Janey's dad's big dressing gown over her own, like she does sometimes when it's cold. I stand up when she comes in.

'Oh, Michael,' she says, looking round for Janey.

'I was waiting.'

'Where is she?' says Janey's mum.

Melly makes the noise that sounds like, 'I don't know.'

'Didn't she say where she was going?'

'She said she was going out with the boy next door and I thought she meant this one.' Melly points at me.

'Maybe it's that boy she knows from school,' I say.

'What boy?' asks her mum.

My chest goes tight but I can't suck the words back in. 'Oh, you know, the one whose mum is a detective?'

'Oh, him,' says Janey's mum.

I breathe out. At least I didn't give away a secret. Still, I wish Janey wasn't talking to her mum about Golden Boy.

'Do you want a drink or something, Michael?'

'OK,' I say. 'Yes please.'

'Come into the kitchen then and tell me what you'd like.'

I sit down at the kitchen table and she doesn't ask, she just gives me a glass of blackcurrant. She's forgotten I only like orange. She makes tea for herself. She puts the teapot on the table and sits down. 'So, Michael. What boy is this?'

'Oh, umm.' Now I'm trapped.

'Michael?'

I'm still hunting for the right thing to say when I'm saved

– the side door opens and in comes Janey, followed by Bully. In their hands they both hold tennis rackets.

I can't believe it.

'Oh is *that* who you were with?' says her mum.

'Hello, Michael,' says Janey. 'What are you doing here?'

Bully's eye is yellow. He doesn't say anything. He skulks next to Janey, just inside the doorway.

Janey says, 'We gave up cos the balls were getting wet.'

Melly wanders in, climbs up into her mum's lap and snuggles against the big soft dressing gown that used to be her dad's. She puts her thumb in her mouth and holds onto her mum's lapel with the other hand and strokes it.

What if Janey says, 'Come on,' to Bully and takes him upstairs. Or just into the other room to watch telly. Leaving me there with her mum and little sister.

I'm not leaving; I'm sitting here. I've got all this glass of squash to drink.

For the first time in that house I feel like I don't belong.

'I've got to go,' says Bully.

Yes! Retreat! As soon as he's gone I raise my glass and take a long celebratory drink. Ugh!

Janey looks at me and raises her eyebrows. Her mum says to her, 'You and I need to have a chat.'

I push the glass away and say, 'Anyway. Thanks.'

Janey comes outside with me. She doesn't ask me why I've come round.

'Nice game of tennis?'

She shrugs.

'He's just making you feel sorry for him.'

Janey wrinkles up her nose. 'Well, look who's talking.' As soon as she's said it, she turns away and goes back indoors.

I spit into a bush – just to get the taste of blackcurrant out of my mouth – then check round. Melly's at the window. Her mouth is an O.

I'm trying to do something about the murder. I really am. I try Crimestoppers. There is a long form to fill in.

Nan doesn't know I'm online. She's mowing the lawn. The mower stops now and then but she's only emptying the cuttings. She says she doesn't like to make so much noise on a Sunday. Not that she's religious. She's a Republican and an atheist she says. It's just a shame to make a racket when other people are trying to enjoy their gardens. I don't know why she worries about our neighbours. Bully's mother is here so much now I think she's moved in. So make lots of noise, Nan.

The form says try to say as much as you can about the crime. Shall I give the names of the people who did it?

Mmm.

I can say when it happened and where. I can say that I think she had a shock. Only I can't say it came from the cooker. There are other kinds of shocks. Maybe not something that would burn her fingers or fry her cells. I can say that I'm afraid to say anything to anyone because the people who did it might find out.

They tell you how to delete your browsing history here too. Nan will be safe. No one will know it was me.

It's been three days since I sent a message to Crimestoppers. I'm keeping an eye on things in case the police come. A car pulls up but it's Bully's dad, as usual. He hesitates before opening their gate. Looks down the path as if it's very long. Then he puts his shoulders back and starts walking.

If they've told him, asked him questions and if he thinks it's me, he will look at our house. He'll look up at me, looking down at him from my bedroom. I should move, but if I do he might see me, the way you sometimes only see the blackbird when it flies out of the bush. I make myself stand still and watch.

He doesn't look up. My heart is beating so hard I think it will stop. It swells up inside my chest and I can't breathe. I drop onto my bed. I'm sweating. My heart is going bumpety-bump like a bike racing down a stony hill.

Maybe I was wrong. Maybe this is what happened to Irma. She got scared – of something. Her heart went faster and faster until it started skipping and tumbling. Maybe it was that kind of shock.

I lie on my side, curled up, put my hands over my face, close my eyes and breathe slowly. I don't want to die.

Think of something happy. Waves on the beach. A boy was killed there, playing chicken with the waves. A giant one scooped him up and took him out to sea. No, then, an island in a river – rowing out in a boat, little ducklings bobbing past with their mum. Don't think about crocodiles.

It's easier to breathe now. I go on lying there and thinking, what could have scared Irma?

The same thing that scares me: Shawn Bull.

'I don't get it,' says Janey. 'Why do you want to be friends with him now?' Downstairs, her mum is playing a song called 'It's Raining Again'. Very loud. It hasn't stopped raining since yesterday. The news said, a month's worth of rain in twenty-four hours.

I don't really want to be friends with Bully. But I don't want anyone to think it was me who called Crimestoppers.

Another weekend, another week of school gone by. We've had Sports Day. My last ever Sports Day with egg and spoon races (or spoon and small potato: Irma always said it's not quite the same).

I didn't have a partner for the three-legged race and neither did Bully. Our teacher said, 'You two are about the same height. You'll make a perfect pair.' I never thought we were the same in any way. I said, 'No.' The teacher said, 'Come on.

93

Wouldn't it be good if you could help each other out?' She said which one of us was going to be 'generous'.

'We might as well,' said Bully. 'I don't mind.'

Maybe it was only because the teacher was there, but it was the nicest thing he'd ever said to me.

We had to put our arms around each other because if you don't, you can't run. The teacher tied our legs together and she said, 'Now, if you can't get on, you'll both fall over.' She got up and dusted off her hands.

'Begin with the middle leg,' said Bully. It was annoying but he was right. We tried a few steps. 'We can beat them all,' said Bully.

'Try running now,' I said.

We both called out, 'One-two one-two one-two.' I thought we were going to fall over, that one of us would stumble and bring the other down, but we didn't. In the race, I could even tell when he wanted to speed up a bit. I felt it through my side. We were brilliant. We won.

The teacher said, 'Congratulations! I knew you could do it.'

She left us to untie our own legs.

'OK?' I said.

'Yeh,' he said. 'You?'

'Yeh.'

Then we both looked around. We were getting on so well and no one was there to see it.

'Did your nan go to Sports Day?' asks Janey.

'She had to work.'

'Oh.'

Irma was always a good stand-in for the mums' race. Nan used to sometimes run too because they don't have one for grannies. Nan says that's because they don't think grannies can run. Last time she ran she came somewhere in the middle.

She did OK but she wouldn't have been any good at it this year because of the smoking. She hasn't stopped yet. She says she's cutting down.

I remember when Janey's mum ran and she was always so far ahead of the others it was like the rest of them were in a different race. I was glad for Janey. It was good she had a mum who liked running. Janey was proud that her mum could run fast and laugh about it afterwards, waiting for the others, not being at all out of breath.

When her dad ran he always won easily too. Everyone remembered it. Janey's mum and dad were best, like the Queen and King of races. Two years before Janey moved to Big School, her dad still won but he had to sit down afterwards. He didn't run again.

Janey's mum didn't go to any Sports Days this year. Janey said she could've done if she'd been trying.

'Let's go out,' she says. 'When she starts playing that music, you know she'll just be looking at Dad's stuff and crying.'

'Maybe we could help?' It was like it would make up for not helping Irma.

'She doesn't want help. If she had help she might get better. She just gets things out of boxes, looks at them, cries and puts them back again. Or not even. There's stuff everywhere.'

'At least it's all in one room now.' Janey's mum has been steadily moving everything that reminds them of Janey's dad into his study. She's trying to work out what to keep and what to let go. 'Maybe we should take her mind off it,' I say.

'Or we could go out,' says Janey. 'It's stopped raining. We could go and see Georgie.'

Georgie. 'Aren't you meeting your boyfriend?'

'What?'

'What's-his-name. Harry.'

She hit my arm. 'He's not my boyfriend. You're as bad as Mum.'

'Maybe it's not such a good idea. It's too wet to do anything. Except swim or fish. Or swim like a fish.'

'I'll just go and ask Georgie then. See if he's got any good ideas.'

She slides off the bed and goes downstairs and I have to follow. We slip out without Janey's mum knowing and go next door. Knock and stand back. Fat drips of water fall on us from the porch roof. We step in closer just as Bully's mum opens the door.

She looks at us, crowding right under her nose.

Janey says very politely, 'Oh hello, Mrs Bull. Can George come out with us?'

'Oh,' she says. She gives me a stern look. 'I'll see,' she says. 'You'd better come in.' Janey and I find our way to the kitchen of doom and stand there looking around while Mrs Bull goes upstairs.

There's a different cloth on the table. The washing–up rack is silver instead of white. I'm glad I took that wooden spoon. Bully's mum would probably have thrown it away. I remember Irma telling Nan that Shawn Bull complained about his wife. She was 'hard to please'.

Bully comes slowly downstairs. His mum says, 'Are you sure you want to go out? I don't want you getting soaked.'

He stands there without saying anything. Then the phone rings and we all jump. Mrs Bull answers it while we three wait. I'm trying hard to think what to say or do next. Mrs Bull puts the phone down. 'That was your father,' she says. 'There's a flood warning. He wanted to know if we were all right.'

'We never flood here,' I say.

Bully's mum says we have to be careful and not go too far. 'Just out to the green perhaps,' she says.

I want to tell her it's called The Middle. But what's the point? She doesn't belong here and if she stays she'll just go on calling it the green anyway. She might get everyone else to do the same. She'll probably start a petition.

We go out. The Middle is so wet that when we run across it we spatter each other with brown water. The cars are passing slowly on the road below the hedge. We run down the little slope to have a look.

The road is like a river, but shallow in the middle with cars going in one line. I've never seen it like that. When a car comes through, it has to go slowly, like a boat, pushing water out of the way. The people inside look straight ahead.

'It's like Noah!' says another voice. Melly. She's come out in her slippers. 'We need a Nark!' she cries.

'Oh, Melly,' says Janey, taking her by the hand. 'Does Mum know where you are?'

She pulls her little sister back up the slope to their house. Bully and I follow, trying not to walk as if our middle legs are still tied together.

News of The Flood has sent Janey's mum into a panic. There's a big pile of things at the bottom of the stairs and more at the top. 'Bring up those golf clubs,' she shouts. 'We have to get all your father's stuff up into the attic.'

The hatch is already open: a dark space above her head. She's trying to hook the folded-up ladder with a pole but can't reach. She comes to the top of the stairs. Looking down at us makes her face fall away from the bones. 'Can you get me the stepladder?'

We don't move. Janey says, 'Mum. We're not going to get flooded.'

'Or a chair. One of you can go up the ladder, can't you?'

Not me. Climb a ladder up into that dark space and step off at the top onto those creaky boards? No. It would be stuffy up there, hard to breathe. If you slipped and your leg came through the ceiling … I feel sick already.

'I'll help,' says Bully, quietly, to Janey. 'If you want.'

Her mum has ears like a bat.

'Oh, George, that's so kind of you.' She sounds relieved.

I can't stop a babyish voice in my head going, 'Oh, George, that's so kind of you!'

Janey slumps and shakes her head and then heaves her dad's golf clubs over her shoulder and up the stairs. She won't let us help, so we each pick up a box and follow. A fat envelope slides about on the top of mine. It's marked 'CHRISTMAS CARDS 2010'. Janey's dad's writing. I'd know his capital letters anywhere. Janey drops the heavy bag and it falls over at her mum's feet, the golf clubs rattling.

'Jane! Be careful!'

'Why?' says Janey. 'It's just stuff, isn't it?'

'If it was "just stuff" I wouldn't be worried about it.'

'But you always…'

'Muum!' Melly calls from downstairs. 'I want a drink!'

'We can help carry things,' I say. 'But I can't go in the attic.'

'I don't mind going up the ladder,' says Bully.

'*No,*' says Janey.

'I just want to know that it's all safe,' says her mum. 'So I don't have to worry about it.'

'Mum. It's not even up to your knees at the bottom of the hill.'

'But the news said…'

'If the water comes up this far, the whole town will be drowned. We'll have to leave in a boat. There'll be dead cows floating past the windows!'

Her mum looks up into the darkness above her, then at us. 'Don't say that.' She goes soft in the middle, like she's losing air. 'If you won't help me put it up in the attic, can you help me carry everything back down again?'

'No! says Janey. 'You had this mad idea. You do it.'

Her mum says her words carefully – like throwing stones

at a target: 'Your father would be very disappointed in you, Janey.'

Janey doesn't speak. She just turns and goes down the stairs. Bully and I give her mum wimpish smiles and then we stampede after Janey and out the front door, leaving it open.

'Where are you going?' calls Janey's mum.

She doesn't answer. The last thing I see are Melly's big eyes looking at us and her mum's bare legs coming down the stairs.

We follow Janey down the path. She walks fast, cutting across the puddled Middle, feet slapping like a duck. My plan is to give her some space but Bully catches up with her. 'We've got all kinds of things in our attic,' he says.

Yeh: I bet you have.

I don't know why Janey thinks she has to explain to him, but she says, 'I don't want it up there. She'll never get it down again. It'll just sit there for the rest of our lives.'

'My dad's sorting things out,' Bully goes on. 'It takes a while. Your mum'll get round to it.'

'She's had ages. There's papers and stuff about money. And things dad collected. All mixed up. Lost. And broken. She doesn't even know what she wants to keep.'

'Maybe you could help,' says Bully.

She stops and glares at him. 'You know what? She won't move that stuff. She won't do *anything*. She'll just lie down on the sofa and wait for me to come home.'

They go down the slope and along the road. A passing car makes brown water wash over their feet and Janey yells, 'Thank you! Thank you so much.' Further on, the road is dry again and the cars speed up, passing the two of them talking and walking ahead of me. Like I'm not there.

If I just stop?

How long before they notice?

I catch them up again.

'Well, I *am* upset,' Janey's saying. 'She doesn't care about me.

She thinks she's the only one who's allowed to be sad.' She takes a deep breath and I think she might cry but instead she starts to run. Bully and I look at each other. We don't know where we're going but we run too.

I hope Janey will run right out of town and keep going like Forrest Gump and we will run with her, out into the big wide world, but we only get as far as the roundabout. It's partly under water, the cars passing one at a time. Traffic is backing up the hills in both directions.

I hope Nan will be able to get home – but the inland road is probably OK.

'Let's try up there,' I say, pointing to where the road rises up the hill into town, but Janey splashes straight across. She doesn't wait for us on the other side. She marches on down to the meadows where people walk their dogs by the river. She goes through the kissing gate. We catch up and find a new lake. You can't see the river. Fences and gates stick up out of the water, with seagulls perched on them as if this is the new harbour. In the next field, a boy is running through knee-deep water and throwing himself onto a body board. Further off, two girls are wading with their arms up.

'I don't want to get that wet,' I say. 'And there'll be dog poo.'

Janey doesn't seem to hear me: she goes down the path, which is on a raised spine, and her feet splash water. If she stays on the path it won't be too deep.

'You coming?' says Bully.

I shake my head.

Instead of going straight ahead, where Janey's walked, he goes off to the right. It's only a little deeper – at first.

I wait and see. Then I'm about to call out, 'Bully!' and I think: I can't call him that. And I can't bring myself to just call him George.

He's trying to get ahead of her. Circle round and meet her. She's not even looking, just walking on, head down, slop slop. It's only up to her ankles.

'Janey!' I shout. Bully looks over but she doesn't stop. I wave to him, 'Come back!' But he just turns round and keeps going.

'Janey!' I shout again. I start to run after her, kicking up water and calling. When she does look back, I see she's crying. Then she wipes her eyes because she's spotted Bully way over to the right. He takes another step, calls out and goes under with a big splash.

'Oh my god,' says Janey. 'He's in the river.'

Bully bobs up again and pretends he meant to do it, lying on his back and letting the river take him. He's laughing!

'Swim!' shouts Janey.

He turns on his front and starts to swim. It's not a wide river.

'Why did you let him do that?' says Janey.

'I didn't tell him to go there.'

'You didn't stop him.'

'I was calling.'

'Help!' Bully's still swimming but he isn't getting anywhere. The river is pushing him the way it wants him to go. All he had to do is steer a bit one way or the other and he would've found the bank. He's fighting now, his strokes getting shorter, faster. If he panics...Yeh. He's panicking.

'The weir,' I say and we both start to run, lifting our knees high to splash across the field. The water slows us down. We cut across to get downstream of him, heading for where the fence posts slope down to where the riverbank should be. If we can get there. If there are no potholes.

'Swim this way!' shouts Janey. 'Kick!' Bully's got his back to us, flapping his arms. He's forgotten what to do. The current turns him. His eyes are very big and his mouth opens and closes. His hands beat the water, like he's trying to grab on to something.

'This way!' I shout.

He sees us and starts to scrabble. Far away, a tiny man is running towards us across the new lake.

If Bully goes through the metal gates of the weir he'll be chopped up like an egg.

I go as far down the fence as I can to where the riverbank should be. I'm in among some reeds now, climbing over them, crouching low, grabbing at a clump with one hand and reaching out with the other. My feet slip but I have to go in deeper. I turn my back on the river, take hold of some reeds with each hand, twist a loop round each wrist, grabbing hold again near the roots. I lower myself down into the water; the reeds tighten as the river takes my legs, trying to tug me away.

'This way,' I hear Janey shout above the roar. There's nothing I can do but hang on. When Bully grabs my ankles I gasp and swallow water and spit it out again. Hold on. Just hold on. Don't think about the reeds slicing into your hands, the shitty brown water soaking through your shirt, floating up the legs of your trousers. Don't think about what will happen if you let go.

If he starts to drag me away to the weir, will I kick him in the face to get free? No one could blame me if I saved myself. Could they?

Splashing. 'Let go!' shouts a voice. Bully's grip tightens. 'I've got you, son. Now let go.'

Bully lets go and the man drags him past me. I start pulling myself up, trying to find my feet, but my legs won't go down. 'Hang on, son,' says the man. He reaches down and grabs the back of my top and pulls.

We hold on to the fence, gulping and shivering. My legs are wobbly. Bully's face, pale as porridge, runs with water.

'I thought you were going to *die*,' says Janey.

'What the bloody hell did you think you were doing?' says the man.

A police car pulls up on the bridge over the weir. Bully's dad gets out. I can see his baldy head. He's putting on his hat. I see a girl holding up a mobile phone like she's filming. Bully's dad stops at the edge of the water like he doesn't want to get his feet wet. He can see us – some silly fools who are probably all right. He shakes his head. Then he looks harder and starts to stride towards us, forcing the water out of his way. 'What's happened?' he shouts as he gets near. 'Are you all right?'

Bully nods. 'I think so.'

'Did someone push you in?' He glares at me and Janey. 'Was it these two?'

Bully shakes his head.

The man who helped us says, 'That's a bit strong. Lucky I saw them though. They might have both gone down the river. Only, this lad...' he drops a kindly hand on to my shoulder, 'is a real little hero. He put himself in danger, helping your son.' Shawn Bull stares at me with his tiny eyes. He doesn't believe it. He doesn't want to believe it. 'Thank you,' he says to the man. 'George, what do you say?'

'Thank you.' He says it to the man. And then he looks at me. He doesn't say anything. I think he's going to cry and I feel tears stinging my eyes too.

Janey is crying hard now. 'I thought you were going to die,' she says again. I feel warm because at least some of her tears are for me.

Silently, I show the wounds in my hands. I stand there like Jesus.

Shawn Bull tells us all to get into his car. He's grumbling about getting the seats wet. He has two silver survival blankets and he makes me and Bully sit on one of them in the back and tells us to put the other round our shoulders. We crouch under it like it's a tent, as if it's raining in the car. If Bully were my friend we might giggle about it – but we sit quietly, careful not to touch each other. Janey's in the front. 'You're the only one who had the sense to stay dry,' says Shawn Bull, even though her feet and legs are soaked through and her face is wet from crying. He talks to us all the way home about 'the stupidity' of what we've done. 'I'll have to have a word with your mother,' he says to Bully. 'And yours,' he says to Janey. He looks at me in the mirror and I pull the foil blanket closer. 'Your nan's got a thing or two to answer for.'

He's driving a bit too fast. What can you do about a police-man who drives too fast *and* kills people? I feel scared and a bit sick: I only swallowed a few drops of water. Bully must have swallowed more. He probably has a whole lot of dog poo inside him. I feel even more sick thinking about that but I don't want to throw up in the back of Shawn Bull's police car.

He sends Janey home. Nan isn't back yet, so he takes me into Irma's house. Bully's mum is all, 'What's happened?' Shawn Bull says he can't stop: he's still on duty. More impor-tant things to do. 'Keep an eye on them,' he says. 'A bath and clean clothes and something warm to drink. Not too much in case they're sick. Get those cuts washed. I'd rather they didn't go to A&E. Makes it all so official, doesn't it, Michael? Remind your nan of that when she comes home.'

He goes. Bully's mum leaves me downstairs dripping onto a sheet of newspaper while she takes him up for a bath, clucking over him, and asking him if he's all right. She doesn't ask me.

I call up the stairs, 'Nan's back! I'm going home. Thanks!'

I don't wait for an answer. By the time Nan does get home I've already showered and changed. My wet clothes and my trainers are in the washing machine. I set it to 'rinse'. I bet Bully doesn't even know how to do this.

'Ooh, it's like the Apocalypse out there,' says Nan when she comes in. When she sees the things in the machine she just says, 'Well done. Did you get very wet?'

I say yes. It isn't a lie.

'My god,' she says, 'What have you done to yourself?'

Nan puts bandages on my hands the first night so I don't get blood on the sheets. It's hard to sleep. Another June day, windy, grey and cold. The cuts are burning sore and I can't bend my fingers. I keep expecting Shawn Bull to come round and talk to Nan. I see Bully walking across that field again and it's like I'm pushing him into the river with my long invisible arm.

Nan and I watch the Wimbledon Men's Final. They stop the game to close the roof on Centre Court and Andy Murray loses in four sets. When he has to make a speech, he can't help himself: he cries on camera.

I feel my eyes getting damp too. It's been a very wet weekend.

Summer isn't summer. It just goes on raining. The way east is blocked by water. There are even floods for Nan on the road north.

I don't know how it happens, but I'm a sort of hero for about a week. There's a YouTube video of the rescue and it gets on the local evening news. Some journalists want to come and talk to me and take my picture. Nan says no photos: she doesn't want it all going to my head. At first I'm all: 'It was nothing really.' But then, I think, I'm missing my chance and the next reporter who rings I start to tell him about Irma and the policeman who murdered her – only Nan snatches the phone out of my wounded hands.

One evening there's a ring at the door. 'I'll go,' I say, thinking it might be another parent with a little kid, wanting to meet me and get my autograph. Like Andy Murray, I sign them all.

It's Detective Inspector Dunbar: Golden Boy's mum.

'Oh,' says Nan, appearing behind me as if by magic. 'It's you.'

We all go back into the living room. Nan forgets to ask the inspector if she would like a drink. The inspector settles herself, Nan sits on the arm of a chair and I perch on the edge of my seat. I know what this is: she's been sent here by Crimestoppers. I just want to hear her say it: 'You were right, Michael, your good friend Irma Gordon was murdered. We're re-opening the case.'

But she says, 'I'm not here on official business.' She smiles at me. 'Did you go to see the Olympic torch relay? Harry got absolutely soaked. It's a wonder they were able to keep it alight. Let's hope it's brighter for the Games, eh?'

She goes on smiling. 'Michael, your grandmother and I thought it might be a good idea if you and I had a chat.'

Nan looks down at me. She looks sad.

'I'm just wondering,' says the inspector, raising her eyebrows, 'if you're the sort of boy who likes to make up stories?'

'Excuse me?' says Nan, sitting up like a meerkat.

'You sometimes tell people that your parents are in prison, don't you? That they're, haha, International Jewel Thieves? Now, that's not true, is it?'

'Now just you hold on,' says Nan. 'This isn't what we talked about.'

The inspector puts her head on one side. 'I'm just saying that sometimes, for whatever reason, we all try to make sense of things. Sometimes even perhaps by making things up? I expect you miss your friend Irma very much. You feel that it shouldn't have happened. But things do happen, Michael. Look at your friend Janey. I'm sure you're a good friend to her – and she needs you. Perhaps that's something you could think about a bit more.'

I don't get it. Why do I have to choose?

Nan says, 'You're too young to be worrying about all this, Michael. Irma would understand. It isn't your responsibility.'

'But you don't care!'

'Of course I do,' says Nan. 'Only, you're not helping anyone by going around saying that our neighbour, a *police officer*, has murdered my best friend.'

Why can't they see it? The Bulls have got Irma's house and everything that belonged to her. They've taken over her life.

'I know it probably doesn't seem fair that you've lost someone, Michael,' says the inspector. 'But what you have to remember is that Shawn Bull and his little boy, they lost someone they cared about too.'

Not Bully. He doesn't care. Not now he's got his real mum back.

'What if she had a heart attack and he just left her there?' I say. 'What if he made her heart go like a jelly? And he took away the soup.'

'Oh, Michael!' Nan shakes her head.

The detective inspector takes a deep breath. 'I believe we reviewed the case thoroughly at the time, Michael. We can't go second-guessing ourselves. But I was going to suggest that, if you need to talk to someone, your grandmother could see your doctor about sorting that out for you?'

'I don't need the doctor.'

But I see the inspector mouthing the word 'counselling' to Nan.

Nan sees her out, comes back and hugs me for no reason. 'You've heard it from the police now, Michael,' she says. 'You have to leave it alone. You've done your best.'

My wounds heal and the reporters stop calling. I know I'm not really a hero. I can't save everyone. Every day there are new stories of people who die in accidents or because they're ill.

'It's different for me!' says Irma, poking me in the back. 'This isn't natural. Don't. Forget. About. Me.'

For the first time I shout, 'Leave me alone!'

'Michael?' Nan opens my door. 'Are you all right?'

'Nothing,' I say. 'It's nothing.'

Nan comes and sits on the bed. Of course, Irma keeps quiet while Nan's there. Nan says, 'I don't like to think of you worrying about these things. It's too bad.'

'Not as bad as being dead.'

'Michael!' Nan sounds shocked. 'Is this how Janey talks?'

'I don't know.'

'Perhaps the inspector was right. You could concentrate on trying to help Janey, if you feel you must help someone. I know Irma would be happy with that.'

'I'll ask her,' I say.

'You'll ask Janey?'

'Yeh, that's what I meant.'

The summer term hasn't even ended yet and the Back to School ads are already on TV. 'We'll wait to get your clothes,' says Nan. 'Who knows how much you'll grow in the next few weeks.'

Nan is trying to be a bit more friendly again with Janey's mum so she asks her advice about preparing me for 'Big School'.

'First rule of Big School,' says Janey's mum. 'Never call it Big School.' Although it does make our primary school look tiny.

We have our orientation days. Bully seems smaller in among the tall people and the big buildings. I know I look small too but I don't mind: I'm going to try and grow faster than he does.

My last few days at my little school. We have the open day where rellies can come and look around the classroom. Nan likes the mural on the big window best. We were each given a space to fill in for ourselves. In mine, Nan sees a woman holding hands with a boy and she's pleased because she thinks it's her, but it's not, it's Irma. I stand in the way of the other bit so Nan can't see the headstone and the RIP.

Then Bully's dad comes in. The teacher gives him the sympathy smile. I step away from the window so he can see the whole of the picture.

Our last school barbecue. I want to go on the bouncy castle. Nan says, 'Aren't you a bit old for that? Oh go on then.'

It's damp and slippery but in here it doesn't matter if you fall over. I remember when I was little I could feel happy just bouncing. I'd like to feel like that again. After this I will be too old – until some time when I'm grown up enough to get drunk and pretend I'm a kid again.

Near the end, some of us climb the hill and look down on the football pitch and the circle of stalls and attractions, the hoop-la, the tombola. Little figures in bright colours move around, the smoke from the barbecue blows across the field, the playground is covered with toy cars, and the classrooms fit together like matchboxes.

We run down the hill for the last time. Next term we will all be wearing long trousers: no more blue knees in winter, except for games.

Goodbye, Little School.

'School's out' thunders from the radio. 'Alice Cooper,' says Nan. 'This came out the year *I* left primary school.'

Summer holidays: always hopeful at the beginning, with a long slow sinking into boredom and the fear of things to come. This year we have the Olympics to look forward to and the worry in case it all goes wrong. The weather is still cold, windy and wet.

Probably there will be no real summer and in no time I'll be on the other side. Feels like I should do something important first. Something that matters. Because nothing stays: everything changes.

Bully and his mum and dad go away – somewhere. I hope they won't come back. Irma's house is all closed up – curtains drawn – like it has its eyes shut. Irma goes quiet as soon as they leave. Or maybe she doesn't feel like telling me things any more.

A week into the holidays and Nan lets me take my bike up the lane and over the hill. I ride past our old school. They have already scrubbed the windows clean.

The strangest times I have that summer are at Janey's house. I'm trying to help her, like Nan and the inspector want me to, but I think I just get on her nerves. I have to be there most days when Nan's at work and I never used to think that Janey didn't want me around but now she sometimes goes out and leaves me with her mum and Melly. Like I'm just a kid her mum is babysitting.

So she doesn't want my help.

I bet she's getting help from Golden Boy.

Janey makes it into the county football team. She thinks her mum will be pleased, but no.

'I couldn't do that long a drive, not the first time,' says her mum. She hasn't driven the car in months. Not even sat in it.

'You've got two weeks to practise,' says Janey.

'It's the holidays, Janey. You should be having fun.'

'It would be fun. I would be so happy. Ha ha ha.'

'Just play. Play with Michael. Play with that lad you like from school. Or you could find some other girls to play with.'

'Mum, I'm not nine.'

'I don't know why you couldn't stick with your old team.'

'I want to play with people who are good, Mum.'

'Nobody likes a boaster, Janey.'

'As good as me – or better.'

'Why don't you do some normal things? Have your friends round. You never have any friends round.'

Err. Excuse me?

'I can't have friends round because you're too weird,' says Janey. 'They don't want to come.'

But I'm here.

'I am as I am,' says her mum.

'Dad would have taken me.'

Her mum sticks out her chin. 'But he's not here, is he?'

'It's not very Judy Murray of you, is it, Mum?'

'I don't want to see my girl crying because she lost.'

Janey walks out. I think she might be crying already.

I try to tell Janey's mum. 'She's really good.'

'You mean "for a girl"?' She says it teasingly.

'No. I mean she's *really* good. Better than anyone I know. I think she could play for England.'

'Oh,' says Janey's mum, 'that would be *terrible*. I want her to have some kind of career, not play her heart out for no money.'

'But she likes doing it. And she could get paid.'

'And then what will she do for recreation? Because football won't be just for fun, any more, will it, Michael? It won't be "just a game". She's already finding that out.'

Nan says what a shame for Janey. 'She just wants her mum to be proud of her. Poor girl. She might as well take drugs and get pregnant for all the notice her mum's going to take.'

'Can't we help her?'

'We can't do everything, Michael. And we shouldn't rob her mum of reasons for trying. Really, she ought to see a doctor.'

So we do nothing. And all the time Janey is getting more and more grumpy.

I'm at Janey's again but she's out – again.

Melly says, 'Do you want to play a game?'

'I know,' says her mum. 'We'll play the Memory Game.'

'I suppose,' says Melly.

Her mum goes away and brings back a wooden tray. On it are an old penny, a golf tee, an RSPB badge, a gold ring, a pair of Ray-bans, a torn-off ticket from a trip to the cinema to see *Lord of the Rings: The Return of the King* in December 2003 and a ... but that's all I have time to notice before her mum drops a cloth over the tray. Not any old cloth, but her husband's faded blue Hard Rock Café T-shirt, with the little holes around the neck like it's been eaten by insects. She says, 'Now you write down how many things you remember, Michael.' She pushes a piece of paper towards me.

Melly starts to speak but her mum says, 'Wait for Michael to finish.'

'Hurry,' says Melly, 'or I'm going to forget.'

'Usually we play this just the two of us,' says her mum apologetically. Then she stops talking because she knows she's putting me off.

Melly has her eyes shut and her lips are moving.

As soon as I put down my pen Melly begins: 'Daddy's golf tee; the special penny from the year Daddy was born; Daddy's last trip to the pictures; Daddy's wedding ring...' She gets everything.

'You win,' I say. 'You're really good at this.'

'It's how I help her to remember,' says her mum.

'I do remember,' says Melly, nodding. 'I miss my daddy.'

'I know you do,' says her mum and her voice is thick with tears.

'Do you miss him?' Melly asks me, narrowing her eyes.

'I do,' I say, nodding. 'I do. He was teaching me chess.' Maybe it sounds like that's the only reason I miss him but that isn't what I meant.

Janey's mum asks if I want to see the board.

'Oh no. That's OK.' Though I would have liked to, very much.

'Then shall we play this game again?' she asks Melly. 'I can change the things on the tray.'

'No,' says Melly. 'Not today.'

Her mum looks disappointed but Melly is firm: now she wants to play at being a teenager. She tells me: 'I'm your son and you're my dad. You're telling me off because I'm coming home late from the school prom.' She staggers about. 'I'm drunk,' she says.

'I don't know where she gets it from,' says her mum, shaking her head. She looks at the things on the tray. She picks up the wedding ring and slides it on her thumb, turns it round and round, takes it off again and closes her hand around it. 'I'll just put these things away. Maybe I'll try to do a little sorting out while you're here. Is that all right, Michael? I'll only be in the study.'

Melly waits for her to leave then comes up to me and whispers, 'She's going to have a cry.'

So we let her do that and get on with playing the game. I have to put on a deep voice and tell her: 'What time do you call this? It's not good enough.'

'Now I'm going to be your mum,' says Melly, 'and you can be my son who's coming home drunk.'

'Why don't you stand on a chair?' I say. 'Then you can feel what it's like to be a grown-up.'

She likes this idea.

'Not the armchair,' I say. 'I'll get you a chair from the kitchen.' I go down the hallway and stop outside the door of the study and listen. I don't hear anything. No weeping. No papers being shredded.

Her mum opens the door. She takes a breath and holds it. 'Michael?'

'I just wondered...' I was going to ask, are you all right? But instead I say, 'Could I look at the chessboard, after all?'

She lets the breath go and gives me a big watery smile. 'Of course you can,' she says.

Inside the study are all of Janey's dad's things that have disappeared from round the house. It's like they have gathered here because they wanted to be together. Now there is so much of Janey's dad here – it's like he might walk in and say, 'Hello!' Next thing he'd say would be: 'What a mess!'

He liked to have things neat. He used to say, 'A place for everything and everything in its place.' Now there are boxes piled up, clothes spilling out of ripped bin bags and dangling on hangers from the bookshelves, golf clubs and sports bags, racquets and shoes, and piles and piles of paper. There were always two desks: one for Janey's mum and one for Janey's dad. Her desk is all clutter, books and envelopes. His desk is the only tidy space in the whole room. It's like an altar. Janey's mum beckons me closer. There's a smell of polish. Everything has been carefully placed: in the centre is the chessboard, dusted; to one side is the photograph of Janey's dad, guarded by a small plastic knight with a sword; in the other corner, a photo of Janey's dad on the beach and the little plastic trophy her mum gave him one Christmas as a joke with the label 'Most Improved'; there's a heart-shaped stone and a tiny pile of shingle, like peas, coloured orange, grey, purple, white, brown and black, some shells and a scrap of pink-and-white – a piece of someone's false teeth washed clean and rubbed smooth by the sea. What Janey's mum calls 'treasures'.

'This is as far as I've got with sorting things out,' she says.

'It's lovely.' Then I look at the chessboard and say, 'Oh! One of the pieces has moved.'

'Really?' She peers at it. 'I thought I put everything back exactly as it was.'

'It's only a pawn,' I say. My fingers hover over it but I look at her to see if it's OK.

'If you can put it back in the right place,' she says.

I only have to move it one space back but before I can do that, she says, 'Hang on. Whose turn was it? Last time you played, how did you leave it?'

'I made the last move,' I say.

'So, how do you know he didn't make another move after you'd gone?'

He always waited till I came back. He said it would be more fair if he didn't look at the board – so we'd both have to remember and figure out what to do next.

I still haven't touched the pawn. We both stare at it – as if Janey's dad only just now moved it into place.

'Let's leave it,' she says. 'I can't decide.'

She looks at all the other stuff and says, 'There are probably all kinds of things in there that are precious but you know what, sometimes I think the gypsies have the right idea.'

I don't know what she means.

'Oh you know, burning everything.'

'Please don't burn the chessboard.'

'Oh, no. I won't do that. Everyone's allowed to keep one thing.'

As we leave the study, the big waterproof coat that belonged to Janey's dad moves on the back of the door. It gives me a funny feeling to see it; I wonder what it would be like to put that coat on.

The front door goes bang and Janey comes in, out of breath, her face lit up. 'Can we go and see the Women's Team GB play football? The school's getting all these free tickets.'

Her mum doesn't look at her. 'Maybe you can go – if you like. To London?'

'Cardiff,' says Janey. 'It's the very first thing for the Olympics. Before the opening ceremony!'

'So you can go with the school. Yes?'

'No. You have to take me. Michael can come too.'

'And who's going to look after your little sister?'

'You'd like to go and see football wouldn't you, Melly?'

Melly shakes her head.

'Sorry,' says her mum.

Janey looks at the ceiling. 'Mu-um!'

'I'm sorry but I'm just not that interested in football. Now, if it was the cricket then maybe...'

'I suppose I could ask Nan,' I offer.

Janey's mum jumps right on that. 'Tell her I'll help with the fuel costs. That is so good of you, Michael.' She sounds really grateful. But Janey's scowling again.

Nan says no to the football trip: it's too short notice; she can't get the time off work.

I haven't said which day it is yet. And it's only in Cardiff. At the Millennium Stadium. I'd like to go there. Even if I do keep saying Minnellium. 'We could get there in two-and-a-half hours. I looked it up on your phone.'

'I know how far it is!' she snaps. 'And I've told you before not to touch my phone.' I wait for her to calm down a bit. She says, 'It isn't my fault you're going to have to let Janey down. You shouldn't make promises you can't keep.'

'I didn't promise. I said I'd ask.'

'Well that's all right then.'

But we know it isn't.

The Bulls are still away. Maybe gone for good. We take two weeks off from worrying to watch the Olympics, though Nan gets really anxious about the Opening Ceremony. 'Please,' she says, 'let us not give the world a bit of meaningless ribbon twirling.' She has this whole catastrophe fantasy about the ribbons getting tangled. Then she has a glass of wine and starts to relax.

At the end we agree it was Amaaaziiing. Nan says, 'What a relief. Well done, Danny Boyle.'

I am a bit jealous now of all the boys and girls who were in it. Why didn't I volunteer? I must have been too busy to think about it at the time. And we do live a long way from London. But now it seems a bit sad that I didn't make the effort. I think, I must try harder to make things happen.

Our favourites are boxer Nicola Adams and Taekwondo girl Jade Jones, who both win gold. We get kind of used to winning shiny gold medals nearly every day. A day without a gold medal feels a bit flat. And it seems now that we have more to lose. So all through the day there's tension: something you just have to watch. Janey's mum is half-excited, half-sad. She keeps saying, 'Your dad would have loved this!'

I don't know why she can't see that Janey wants to try hard too. All the time they talk about 'investment' and 'sacrifice' and 'inspire a generation'. You have to try your very best in every way and have people to help you.

It feels like things could be different; you hear about people being nice to each other on the Tube in London and things like that. Even the weather is better for those two weeks. When it's all over, Janey's mum says, 'Back to the real world. What a drag.'

'Maybe we could go to the Olympic Park,' says Janey. 'It won't be so busy now, will it? Or maybe we could get tickets for the Paralympics?'

'The cricket will be on again,' says her mum. She says she will make a definite effort to get on with sorting through all the things she's been putting off. 'I'll do it when we start playing the Third Test against South Africa. I'll do better then because I'll listen to *TMS* on the radio. That will make it easier: I'll do it in test match time.'

In the end it's Nan who takes Janey to her first training session on the beach.

She went round to have a chat with Janey's mum, who was very polite, and said, 'Thank you very much for taking such an interest in my daughter.' Then she reminded Nan that any time I needed 'minding', she was 'as ever' always 'happy to help'.

I let Janey sit in the front so she and Nan can talk. Nan doesn't ask a lot of questions and Janey's quiet on the way up. A bit tired maybe. She had another big row with her mum. Her mum acted like she was the calm and reasonable one, while Janey was stomping about getting more and more cross. 'You're entitled to a holiday,' her mum said. 'You don't have to go.'

'Come on then,' said Janey. 'Take us on holiday.'

Her mum said they were having a staycation.

'A staycation isn't just staying in the house.'

'We're having a summer of sport,' her mum said, sweetly. 'Olympics. Paralympics. Test match cricket. You can camp in the back garden.'

'It's raining.'

'It often does when you're camping. Just think how much easier it is to come in and get some clean dry clothes.'

'Clean!' said Janey. 'I suppose you know that dressing gown smells!'

'OK, I'll let that go because I can see that you're upset...'

'Oh, am I? Thanks for noticing.'

'Janey, I wish...'

'I wish, Mother...' Janey leaned over her mum and shouted in her face, 'I wish I wish I wish that you would JUST GET DRESSED!'

'But, Janey,' her mum said very quietly, 'you know, I Just Don't Want To.'

'You are so, so selfish.'

Her mum's eyes went sort of hazy. She said, 'Selfish am I? I'm here, aren't I?'

'You might as well not be.'

They didn't see Melly standing in the doorway, looking scared.

When Janey's mum spoke again her lips were very tight. 'Do you know what I'd do if I really wanted to be selfish? Do you have ANY IDEA?'

'Stop shouting,' I said. 'Please.' Janey and her mum both turned to me then. I thought, that's done it. I'll have to go now. Maybe I'll never be able to come back. It's all right for them. They can argue all they like: they live here.

'Yes,' said Melly. 'Stop shouting.'

We all stayed still. Janey and her mum went down like novelty inflatables losing air, both ashamed, and both still searching for a way to be right. Janey said, 'You don't care about anything.'

'I do.' Her mum softened then. 'Sweetheart. I do.'

I thought Janey was going to cry and her mum would get up and give her a hug. Instead, Janey glared at the ceiling. Her mum picked at the arm of the chair and said, 'Anyway, it's summer. You should be playing cricket.'

We arrive at the faraway beach. It's one of the few sunny evenings. The cry of seagulls, the shush of sand, the swash of the sea: this is what it could be like to go on holiday. There's a car park full of girls and their parents. Janey says we don't have to stay and watch.

'If you're sure?' says Nan.

'No. They like it better if parents stay out of the way.'

Not quite as out of the way as her mum, we think but do not say.

So Nan and I wander away along the beach, looking back now and then to see the girls scampering about on the sand, pony tails flying. It's one lovely evening, with the sun still warm. We find a place where we can eat and start studying the menu for things I can have: no pizza, no ice cream.

'I suppose I'm going to have to carry on doing this, now I've started,' says Nan. She means the driving.

'It would be good,' I say. 'Unless you could maybe get Janey's mum out of the house and driving again.'

'I don't like meddling, Michael. It's other people's lives.' But she looks thoughtful.

On the way home Nan says Irma used to play football when she was a girl.

'I didn't know that,' says Janey.

'Well, football was your thing. She didn't want to take it away from you. Anyway, she told me she had to stop when she was about seven. Banned by the school. Not suitable for a girl to be running round with the boys. Something like that.'

Janey looks out the window. Is she supposed to be thinking how lucky she is? I don't think Janey has thought that once since her dad died.

'It made her very sad,' says Nan. 'And years later her mum told her that she had been good at football too and was banned from playing for the same reason. "So why didn't you stick up for me?" Irma said. And her mum said, "But I didn't know!" I don't think it had crossed Irma's mind until then that something so big in her own life wasn't all that noticeable to other people, not even her own mother.'

Janey says nothing.

Nan goes on. 'Sometimes you have to make things clear or you can't expect people to know how you feel.'

'OK,' says Janey, half-turning her head towards Nan. '*I* feel like everyone talks about Irma and nobody cares about my dad any more.'

She looks out the window again.

'We all care about your dad,' says Nan. 'We really do.'

I nod but Janey can't see, so I have to speak up. 'I think about him every day. And I don't think everyone talks about Irma. Even though she was murdered!'

'Do you think that's worse than cancer?' says Janey.

'Ah,' says Nan. 'The league tables of grief. But it's not a competition, Janey. Nobody wins.'

On Day One of the test match, Janey's mum shuts herself up in the study. You can hear the commentary and the crowd and the bowler running in and the thwack of the bat through the door like it's all happening in there in that room, sometimes interrupted by the sound of shredding.

When Janey's home she turns on the radio in the kitchen loud enough for her mum to hear that she's listening too.

On Days One, Two and Three, Janey's mum listens to the radio like she's under an enchantment – we even hear her laughing, like when Alice Cooper came in to the commentary box at Tea and Geoffrey Boycott shook hands with the wife because he didn't understand there could be a man called Alice. Janey's mum hasn't done much sorting out – the shredder keeps overheating – but she's glad that Janey's talking to her about the match. Janey has gone to find her in her world of cricket and now there's this opening and maybe she can help her mum find her way out. On the fourth day, Janey says, 'Please will you take us to Lord's?' They're saying that the fifth and final day could be a thriller.

Standing behind Janey's mum I shut my eyes and cross my fingers. She says, 'Too expensive.'

But they keep telling us on *TMS*: tickets for the last day are so cheap and under-sixteens get in free.

'Free, Mum,' says Janey. 'I really want to go. And I want you to take us.'

'What? All the way to Lord's? That would be a bus, a train, the Underground.'

'St John's Wood,' says Janey, pushing a piece of paper under her mum's nose. 'Michael's done a timetable. 'Go on,' she says. 'Please. It'll be fun. And you're always saying, if it was the cricket...'

OK, so Janey's mum can't even get off her own front doorstep. What makes us think she'll go all that way and queue for tickets, rattle along on the Underground, and maybe get crushed by all those crowds, lost in all the colours and the noise? When I think about it I feel like something's leaning on my chest and my fingers tingle. I'm scared – but I still want to go. I too want the miracle to happen, that Janey's mum will take us, that she will get dressed and brush her hair and be like in the old days, when she was brave. Like she was when Janey's dad was ill.

Nan says, most ordinary people can be amazing in a crisis, but there are no medals for just getting on with your life.

So we're giving Janey's mum a challenge and we hope it's big enough. Suddenly there is a gleam in her eye, like doing something impossible is just what she needs.

Then Janey has to go and say, 'Do it for Dad.'

Her mum doesn't cry. She doesn't crumble. She stays still and silent for so long it gets scary. Then she says, 'What about me?'

Janey nods and she's the one with the wobbly chin.

Her mum relaxes. 'I know. I'm sorry.'

Janey nods again and makes a funny kind of squeak that isn't even a word.

'All right,' says her mum. 'I won't think about it. Let's just do it. Oh, but what about Melly?'

Janey swallows and says, 'She wants to go too.'

'She'll be bored.'

But we have worked on Melly; she likes the people in the crowd in fancy dress. We haven't said there will definitely be knights and warrior princesses but somehow she's got the idea that Lord's is a kind of Disneyland. We haven't told her that's only on Saturdays.

'And how will we get to the station?' Janey's mum looks at my timetable. 'The bus takes nearly an hour!'

'Nan said she'll drop us at the station on her way to work. Those times are – here.' I point to the bottom of the page.

Janey smiles at her mum. She doesn't give her a hug or anything but she looks hopeful.

'Ah, you're nice to me when you want something,' her mum says. But she does look pleased. 'All right,' she says. 'All right. I suppose I'd better find something to wear.' She pulls her dressing gown a bit tighter around her and frowns and says, 'Shall we take sandwiches?'

When she sees us so excited, jumping about, she even laughs.

Day Five. Monday morning. My eyes are gritty and the early morning air outside feels sweet and cool. The houses round The Middle are still dreaming of the day to come but I'm up – I'm in it. I shoulder my small rucksack. Sunhat: check. Sun cream: check. Bottle of water; train fare; hoody for later; spending money: check.

Nan's nearly ready to leave. She can't be late for work.

At Janey's house the upstairs curtains are still drawn.

I knock on the door loudly because they are all supposed to be wide awake too. No answer. I look through the letterbox. Janey's sitting at the bottom of the stairs. She's dressed. Good. But her head's down, cheeks squished by her two fists. Bad.

'Janes!'

She heaves herself up and opens the door. I'm still hanging on to my hopes but she says straight away, 'It's not happening.'

'Wha…?' I can't finish the word with my mouth hanging open. I hear myself wail. 'Nooooo!'

'Yup, well. What can I do?'

'Why?'

Her mother shuffles through the hallway in her dressing gown, pressing a wet flannel to her head, a glass of water in her other hand. Her voice is like blowing through a cobweb.

'I'm sorry, you guys. I really am. If only I didn't feel so bad.' She is already heading for the stairs.

I'm trying to think what to say to make her change her mind. 'You'll feel better in the fresh air.'

'If only,' says Janey. 'I mean, it's not like she can *help* it or anything.'

Her mum says, 'Anyway, to go all that way. It will probably be all over by lunchtime. Geoffrey Boycott says we don't have a cat in hell's chance.'

'He's been wrong before,' I say.

'Well,' she says, and she's already halfway up the stairs, 'it will probably be a really dull day.'

Janey pushes me outside.

'Let's you and me go anyway,' I say.

'I don't have the train fare.'

Her mother calls feebly, 'Can you look after your little sister for me, love?'

'She's not even up!' shouts Janey.

'Please, love. My head.'

'Sorry,' says Janey to me. 'Sorry about my rubbish mother.' She goes back in and shuts the door.

I'm left standing there. Across the road, Mrs Rogers opens her curtains and looks out. I'm still half-expecting things to change. How can our day have ended already? It should be just beginning.

I walk back past Irma's house. The petals are falling from her roses. And I have seen the peas she sowed in her back garden in the springtime are withering, unpicked. Nan would have picked them for her, if Irma was just away. I go and lie down in The Middle on the grass; the damp creeps into my clothes and I don't care. I can't get up. I look at the sky and feel the weight of the earth underneath me: gravity pulling me into the ground. I hear Nan calling, 'Michael? Michael?'

I might never move again.

Someone comes to lie down beside me.

Nan's voice is still far away. She's talking to Janey. Hasn't seen me lying here. Must have gone to their house.

The person lying next to me sighs.

I don't have to look to know it's Irma.

'Don't worry about the peas,' she says. 'Don't make your nan worry about you. Deal?'

'Do you see your dog now?' I've been meaning to ask her this. I want to know if he's old, with bad breath and back legs so stiff they move as one or if he's young again, like he was when he loved running. He always had bright eyes anyway until the very end when he died but his body changed until he was a furry sack of knobbliness and nothing.

She doesn't answer.

I turn my head.

Nan's legs are coming. 'Michael,' she hisses. 'Get up from there!'

I don't move. She stands over me. 'What's the matter with you?'

She's standing just where Irma must have been lying. I want to tell Nan this. What's she so cross about?

She grabs my arm and tries to pull me to my feet but the earth is still holding on to me.

'Oww!' I say.

She looks around and lets go. 'Get up. I know you're disappointed.'

'You're standing on Irma.'

Nan looks at her feet and moves them. Then she gets even more cross. 'Just stop it,' she says. 'Get up and don't make such a fuss.'

That's what she's worried about: people looking.

'I can't,' I say. 'I'm stuck.'

It feels like no force on earth could move me. But I forgot

about the power of Nan. She kneels down beside me and puts her arm under my shoulders and sits me up. I'm like a half-closed penknife. 'Do I have to carry you like a baby?' she says. She puts her other arm under my knees and pretends she's going to lift me. She thinks I'll find I can move again and scramble up. But I can't.

While she's carrying me across the grass, over the road and through our gate, down the path to the kitchen door, while I keep slipping out of her arms and she's puffing and swearing, I think: Tough! I didn't ask for help.

Nan calls work and tells them I'm ill and she'll have to take the day off. I can move again but I don't seem to be able to speak. She tells them it's an emergency and she's very worried about me. When she puts the phone down she says, do I realise she could lose her job? She tries talking to me. Then she gets cross again and says, 'Please stop sulking.'

I leave my shoes and go up the stairs like I'm climbing a ladder. I get into bed with my clothes on and huddle up until I fall asleep.

When I wake, I see Nan has brought my bag and the radio. The cricket commentary has started: they keep talking about all the kids in the crowd. That should have been us. At lunchtime there are scratch games of cricket on the outfield. I eat my sandwiches and stare at the wallpaper. I always feel sorry for the donkeys and I think they feel sorry for me too, although one of them is showing his arse and that is repeated across the walls.

I haven't exactly got a pain or anything. I turn over and grip the pillow, put my arm across my face. I can smell my own armpit. Nan has been telling me to wash more. Just this morning she said, 'Gone are the days when you can make do with a lick and a promise.' I was too busy feeling excited about our day out to care. Imagine if I had gone to the cricket smelling bad. Aggers would be saying, 'There are a few empty seats; rather funny, they all seem to be around that one boy; maybe he forgot to wash or something.' I never used to stink. I give the armpit a proper sniff. It's like ... mmm ... baked beans.

I have to get out of bed to go to the bathroom. Nan calls up from downstairs. 'Since I've got to take time off, we could go and get your school uniform.'

Oh happy happy day.

Janey's mum does all their shopping online. But it's no use telling Nan that.

She comes up the stairs. 'Did you hear me?'

I shut the door and run the taps for bathwater.

'Why are you taking it out on me?' says Nan through the door.

I open it. 'I'm not.' I'm not even thinking about Nan. Why can't I just care about my own feelings for once? I go and get the radio.

'Careful,' says Irma.

'It's only batteries,' I say.

'I know,' says Nan.

'You're not coming in, are you?' I say.

'Of course not,' says Irma.

'Of course not,' says Nan.

Lying in the bath I waft the water around with my hands. It's funny lying there all bare. My body is strange: I wash my doofer like Nan showed me years ago. It used to be my tinkler then. She calls it 'doofer' now, if she has to say anything at all. It still looks very small. I think it ought to be bigger. I have seen it grow. And shrink. It's a magical thing. Sometimes I can make it happen. Sometimes it happens all by itself. It's nice to stroke the water round it, gently, gently.

Only, what if someone climbs up outside and puts their face against the window? What if there are tiny cameras in the window locks? Ah but I can hide: that's what bubble bath is for. I turn on the tap and pour some of Nan's blue bubble bath through it and make foam.

'Are you washing?' shouts Nan through the door.

'Don't come in!' I shout back.

Soap makes the foam dissolve again. I have a few strands of hair, waving like weed in a fish tank.

I need to tell someone.

I have no idea who.

Nan says we have to go shopping so we take the digital radio with us in the car. The game could still go either way.

'You must be angry with Janey's mum,' Nan says.

'No.' I don't think I am. I think I just feel sad because I wanted to believe, to make the good thing happen.

We go to a different town, not the one where Nan works. 'I don't think my colleagues would believe me if I said we had to go out for some retail therapy.' We take the radio with us in Nan's shopping bag. It's talking all the time Nan buys me one pair of trousers, three shirts and a new pair of shoes.

England have lost too many wickets for not enough runs.

I feel like lying down on the floor of the shoe shop and letting people walk over me.

Back in the car and on the way home. The atmosphere at Lord's changes again; there's a last wicket stand and a miracle might happen.

Guess what? It doesn't. Geoffrey Boycott and Janey's mum were right. But it would have been exciting to be there and ride the ups and downs.

When we get home, Janey and Melly are out in The Middle.

'Gosh,' says Nan. '*She's* taking it well.'

I open the door and set off.

'Where are you going?' Nan calls.

'Can I?' I want to see if Janey's OK.

'Feeling better? All right then. *I'll* unload.'

I walk over to The Middle. Janey and Melly are frozen like in a cartoon. Janey should have a storm cloud over her head because the air snaps with electricity.

What she has is a white cardboard box at her feet. Now she bends down, as if she's only been waiting for me to arrive. She flips open the lid, palms a ball and straightens up.

'Melly,' she says. 'You'd better get behind me.'

Melly trots round. There are furrows in her forehead.

'No, go further back,' says Janey. 'Further.'

'How's your mum?' I ask.

'Her headache's gone,' says Janey.

'Oh.'

'Yeh. No, it's not like she was pretending. She can make herself ill.'

I didn't know that grown-ups did that too.

'Imagine that,' says Janey. 'Making yourself ill.'

'Mmm. Do you want me to bowl?'

'It would be better if you just got out of the way.'

The ball in her hand is small and white and dimpled. She looks behind her to make sure Melly's not going to be clobbered by her backswing, then tosses the ball up and hits it a mighty wallop, right into the hedge of my front garden. A blackbird flies out with a clatter. Luckily, Nan has already gone inside.

'Oops,' says Janey. 'Hard to get the accuracy.'

'Let me bowl,' I say.

She pushes the box towards me with her foot. 'Go on then.'

Golf balls.

'I'm going to hit them all,' she says, shaking out her elbows.

'O-K.' I bowl underarm, a slow full toss.

Crack. Right over the top of Irma's house.

'Err, Janey...'

'Next!' she shouts. And I bowl again.

This one bounces off the chimney pot of her own house, smacks down on the roof and rolls.

'Wow!' says Melly.

Janey's mum opens an upstairs window just as the next ball hits the front of the house two feet from her face.

'Oh, look,' says Janey. 'There she is. That's as far as she's stuck her nose out in months.'

'Janey!' her mum shouts. 'Come back here at once.'

'Make me!' Janey screams. 'Oh no, you can't, can you?' She's ready for the next. Eight balls left in the box. 'Can I have a go?' I ask. There's all this energy whirling around Janey: I go up to her like a storm chaser getting close to a tornado. I've seen on TV how a twister can tear up a farm like it's a giant jigsaw puzzle pulled into pieces and carried off into the sky.

She looks at me suspiciously, then holds out the bat. 'Take it,' she says. 'I'll bowl.'

What were you thinking? Nan will ask me. I'm thinking about taking the bat away from Janey. And then, Janey throws me the ball and I have to hit it. I'm so scared I feel sick but I just have to.

I can see Janey's mum at the upstairs window.

Crash! The sound of breaking glass.

Right through the bedroom window of Irma's house.

'Oh,' says Janey. 'You missed.'

But with the next ball I hit Irma's house again.

'Michael!' says Janey. Now she gets it. She smiles. So do I. Because even though I'm scared, even though what we're doing is wrong, Janey and I are on the same team.

Oh. Nan's coming for us, shouting. I get jelly-legs. Janey bowls me another.

Nan ducks as it zings over her head.

'Good shot,' says Irma. See, Irma doesn't mind. At least I'm doing *something*.

Nan's running. We wrestle for the bat and she wins. 'Oh, Michael. *Now* what have you done?'

'How many was that?' says Janey looking into the box.

'No more!' says Nan. 'Janey, this is not what I meant. I wanted you to *talk* to your mum.'

'Oh, but I tried that,' says Janey, 'and now we've got to finish the game!'

'I'm sorry, Janey, but this has to stop. I know you're angry.'

'Doesn't matter.' Janey shrugs. 'I just wanted to see if she'd come out.' She looks at Melly, whose face is wobbling, then kicks the box and walks away.

'Where are you going?' says Nan.

Melly wails, 'Muum!'

Her mum waves to her to come on back.

I want to go after Janey but Nan keeps a tight hold on my arm. 'Let's take Melissa home,' she says.

Janey's mum opens the door to us. She seems very calm.

'We need to have a talk,' says Nan.

Melly clings on to her mum, who asks, 'Didn't Janey say where she was going?'

'No.'

'Oh.' Janey's mum looks at Nan as if it's somehow all her fault.

'Someone could have been hurt,' says Nan.

'Michael's just as responsible.'

Nan splutters. 'Janey started it.'

'Janey has every right to be angry,' says her mum. 'I know that. What's Michael's excuse?'

'He broke the window,' says Melly.

'He just...' Nan looks at me and remembers how cross she is. 'What *do* you think you were doing, Michael?'

They go on looking at me, as if they have telepathically decided that if they wait long enough I might have an answer.

'I dunno,' is all I manage.

'Don't know was made to know,' says Nan, automatically.

'Irma doesn't mind,' I say. 'And it's her house.'

Their faces freeze as if time has stopped. I don't seem to be breathing either, though I can hear my heart knocking. Then Melly says, 'Where's Janey?' and that sets things running again.

Nan and Janey's mum look at each other and don't ask me anything else.

'She'll come home when she's hungry,' says Nan.

I want to go after Janey but Nan says, 'For once you're going to stay where I can see you.'

She marches me back to our house.

When we're hungry we eat toast, crunching across a long silence. Twilight gathers at the windows. We don't even turn on the telly or the lights. The phone rings. It's Janey's mum.

I already know what she's going to say: Janey hasn't come home.

The lights aren't on yet in Janey's house either. Her mum is at the upstairs window. She sees us coming and runs down to open the door but her eyes look past us. Nothing. She runs upstairs again. Her cup of tea is cold on the kitchen table next to Janey's phone; we hear Janey's mum come down the stairs, open the front door and close it again softly. She joins us in the kitchen. She says she's called everyone she can think of, including 'Harry'. Nothing. Soon it will be dark.

When Janey's phone rings, her mum jumps like she's been tasered. She grabs it and puts it on speakerphone.

'This is Harry's mother,' says the voice. 'Any news?'

So Inspector Dunbar comes round. 'I'll drive,' she says to Janey's mum. 'She can't be far.' She looks at that dressing gown. 'Do you want to get a coat?'

'But what about my other little girl? I've put her to bed but I can't leave her.'

'We can stay,' says Nan.

'All right,' says Janey's mum. I see her throat move as she swallows. She goes to the study and almost closes the door on us then opens it again carrying that coat Janey's dad used to wear. She puts it on and changes her slippers for her gardening shoes. Her hands are shaking and she puts them in her pockets.

Inspector Dunbar sets off down the path and Janey's mum half shuts her eyes and plunges off the doorstep. Then her legs go and she's flat on her back gasping for air and flicking like a fish. She puts a hand to her chest.

'Oh no,' she's saying, in between shuddering lungfuls. 'Oh no.'

Inspector Dunbar whips out her phone. 'I'll call an ambulance.'

'It's a panic attack,' says Nan. 'She's hyperventilating. Michael, go and find me a paper bag.'

I run into the house. I know where they keep the plastic carrier bags. I just hope there'll be a paper bag in the same drawer. There is.

I run back to Nan. She says, 'You hold the bag, Vi. Just breathe normally. Come on now. Trust me: you can do it.'

By the time the ambulance arrives, Janey's mum is sitting up, gripping Nan's arm like she's holding on to the side of a boat. Blue lights flashing. Here we go again. We get Janey's mum back inside.

The paramedics have gone by the time Janey walks in.

'Where have you been?' wails her mum.

'I just went for a walk,' says Janey. 'Why are you wearing dad's coat?'

Inspector Dunbar looks at her watch. 'Where did you go?'

Janey stares at her for a second then says, 'I walked to the Bay and back through town. No big deal.'

133

'Your mother tried to come and find you,' says Nan. 'And she had a bad turn.'

'Mum?'

Her mum looks kind of blank, bleached out. 'I thought I could do it if I wanted to,' she says. 'Oh but ... I couldn't!'

'You should see the doctor,' says Inspector Dunbar. 'Well, everyone's all right for now, that's the main thing.'

'This isn't – official – is it?' says Janey's mum.

'I'm not on duty,' says Inspector Dunbar. 'Perhaps we should go. Leave you to it.'

Nan and I follow her out and we are by her car when the inspector says, 'I couldn't help noticing there's a great big hole in the upstairs window of the house next door. And I know the family's away. Anything you want to tell me?'

'I did it,' I say, because it's true and because I don't want Janey to be in any more trouble.

Inspector Dunbar listens to my confession – about a game that got out of hand.

'Pretty stupid to play cricket with golf balls,' she says. 'Someone could have been seriously hurt.'

'Michael knows that, don't you?' says Nan. 'And we'll pay for the window to be fixed.'

'That might help, but I am going to have to pass this information on.'

'I thought you weren't on duty.'

'I'm not. But I'll have to speak to Shawn about it.'

'I thought maybe they'd gone,' says Nan.

'Extended leave. Compassionate. You know.'

'He'll think it was deliberate.'

'I can't help that,' says the inspector.

For the first time in months, Janey's mum gets dressed. It's weird seeing her in ordinary clothes. Nan agrees to drive her to the doctor's but when it comes to it, Janey's mum hangs on to the doorframe by her fingernails.

Nan rings the surgery and is quite sharp with the receptionist. 'Yes the doctor *will* have to make a house call.'

We're still waiting for the doctor when a van comes and men climb a ladder to board up the broken window next door. Nan says I'd better think about how I'm going to pay the bill, but Janey's mum says, 'No. It's my responsibility.'

Janey and I go out and lean on Irma's gate to watch the men working.

The Bulls have not come back. Sorry, Irma, but I hope they never will. I even say it out loud and Janey says she feels the same.

I give her a look.

'What?' she says. 'If they don't come back maybe you'll start being normal again.'

'What's normal? Anyway, I thought you and Georgie were friends.'

'Oh,' she says. 'I don't know. Sometimes he was OK. I guess I just wanted to make up my own mind. Like, I know how horrible he was to you. But you were being so weird going on about Irma all the time.'

'Someone had to. And he was horrible to me before that.'

'Yeh, funny in a way,' she says. 'He hasn't been so bad lately. But they never said thank you, after the flood.'

'So you see, don't you? It's not right.'

She shakes her head.

'Do you think I'm making it up?'

'It's not that,' she says, looking away. 'It's … I had mum to think about. And I used to think if only it was someone else who'd died and not my dad. It was hard seeing Irma all happy, dancing and singing, like nothing had happened. But then she died too.'

'*You* didn't make that happen. And she didn't just die, Janes.'

Now she gives me such a look. Like I should know her dad didn't 'just die' either.

I would like to put my arms round her but I just lift my hand feebly and say, 'Sorry. You know I don't mean it like that.'

She nods.

We watch the men climb down the ladder, leaving Irma's house with one eye shut like it's been battered. Unless it's winking at us.

The doctor comes and Janey's mum tells her she doesn't want pills. The doctor says why not give them a try and writes out the prescription anyway. 'I suppose someone could take this for you?' she says, looking at Nan.

The doctor also suggests some kind of special counselling for people who have suffered a bereavement. She says it always helps to talk to someone and she googles something on her phone. But I don't think Janey's mum will go on a cruise. She can't even leave the house! The doctor writes a number down and leaves Janey's mum holding the piece of paper.

She should have kept her dressing gown on. Not combed her hair. Made more of a fuss.

Irma doesn't let us off easy. She sends the Bulls back to us. Nan has to apologise to them, which she hates, and she makes Janey and me say sorry too. Shawn Bull doesn't even bother to look at us. Nan offers to come and clear up the glass that's still on the bedroom floor, but Mrs Bull says no, she'd rather take care of things herself. She tells Nan what a lovely holiday they've all had together. So lovely that now they're going to be together all the time. 'Georgie's already made *so* many friends here it seems easier for me to move.'

So that's it. The Bulls are all back together and living next door. Janey and I look at each other: Happy Families!

We hear them laughing. And other noises.

One evening, Nan is washing up and I'm clearing the table. At the kitchen window in Irma's house there are two faces. One above the other. 'Oh my goodness,' says Nan. 'It's like a farmyard. We'll have to get a blind.' She slaps with the dish-cloth, very cross. 'And with the boy in the house!'

'What are they doing?' I ask. 'It was the same with Irma, the day she died.'

Nan takes a deep breath and says, nodding, 'Oh. Oh yes, I remember he said he came home late morning. Well. Let's hope she died happy.'

We'll have to go back to school while the Paralympics are still on, which is no good because I like watching wheelchair rugby. They call it Murderball.

Nan likes the blade runners and sings, 'Send him victorious, Oscar Pistorius,' and can't stop humming the tune to the National Anthem, though she goes off him a bit when he complains someone else only won because they were wearing longer blades. And she likes the GB wheelchair athletes. 'Half-human, half-chair,' she says, before she realises that some of them are *kneeling*. Nan can get things so wrong sometimes.

I'm amazed by the blade runner with no knees – the way he throws his legs out to the sides. His start is slow and then he gets faster and faster until it looks like he's rocket-propelled. I don't tell anyone this but sometimes when the athletes line up I check them out to see what bit is missing. Sometimes there's nothing to see. Sometimes there's a lot of added metal and it makes them look like cyborgs. Superhuman.

Watching the Paralympics is like being somewhere else. It helps put off the horrible doom that comes when the end of the summer holidays looms up – and I still haven't done any-thing about Irma. I try hard to be *a warrior not a worrier* but the night before term starts I lose it: I cry and cry and can't think how I will get through tomorrow. Ted comes down from his shelf. Nan says I can have him for one night only.

I didn't ask for him. It isn't like I'm a little kid any more. But I put an arm around him anyway, to show him I remember the old times.

'You'll see,' says Nan. 'It will all work out for the best.'

It rained nearly all summer and then we go back to school and the sun comes out: it's sooo hot. Even early in the morning you can tell how the day will be. Everything sparkles under the wide blue sky. It makes me think of diving into a swimming pool. My first schoolday in long trousers and I wish I could be wearing shorts again and no socks.

In my class there's a boy who gets around in a wheelchair. He's called Felix and everyone wants to know what sport he plays. He says he doesn't. I say I would play Murderball if I could get a wheelchair. He says you can't play at being disabled but I don't mean that. I just mean I'd like to play that game. He sits near the front because that's where they make a space for him. I sit on one side about halfway back. It isn't so bad now I'm here. Everyone is getting used to it at the same time; it feels like it might be OK. I only know one or two in my class and they weren't friends of mine at primary school – I mean the friends I had before Bully came along – so it feels like everything can start again.

I feel so much older than yesterday.

Somehow the long hot day goes by and, for a special treat, Janey's mum takes us to the beach. She's nervous about driving the car for the first time. So are we. Janey says, 'Did you take your pills?' So she must have decided she needed them, after all.

The car park at the Bay is full of trucks and caravans but anyway we get a spot outside by the wall where you can park for nothing. This is a good start. Janey's mum says, 'Your dad would be pleased.' He never liked to pay for parking.

We trudge over the pebbles past the metal fence posts that sing when it's windy and over the ridge until we look down on the shimmering blue sea. There's a long flickering line of crime-scene tape running from the edge of the cliff straight down nearly to the shore-line and there's a white forensics tent. Janey's mum hesitates. Not long ago there was a cliff fall about a mile down the coast and a holidaymaker was crushed. There are cameras here and two police officers, a man and a woman. Janey says, 'It's OK, Mum. They're just filming for a TV series.' We don't know if the police are actors waiting to be filmed or real police keeping people away. David Tennant is supposed to be in this – we know him from *Dr Who* – but we don't see him. Maybe he's back in the car park in one of the trucks.

Melly is already running down to the water. It's a bit annoying that we can't cut across but once you reach the end of the tape you can walk along by the edge of the sea as far as you want to go. This is the first time I've been in swimming this year. It might be the one and only time. School's over and I'm making the most of the only hot day we've had. Everything shimmers and sparkles. I'd forgotten what that's like. The air is soft and warm. Even the waves are more gentle today. We undress and put our feet in the water and there's no shock of cold. Janey and I look at each other, surprised. Instead of standing in it up to our knees for ten minutes we go straight in. We're swimming. We don't even have to say, 'Brrr, it's all right when you get used to it' because it's lovely.

When you're in the sea everything is peaceful. Water splashes and plocks around you and heaves you up and down like you're on the chest of a sleeping giant. The waves pat the shore and scrabble at the pebbles trying to hold on, dragging shingle back into the sea. Gulls silently spread their brilliant white wings against the blue or stand in dark pockets in the golden cliffs, squeaking or calling. There the face of the cliff is smooth and new after a recent fall and there it's old and craggy with green grass slipping down. The clifftops make a zigzag line of gold against the blue sky. The water is so warm I don't have to keep swimming. I can just float and relax. Every time I decide it's time to get out I change my mind because I just don't get cold and I might not have a chance to do this again for another whole year. Maybe never. Because you never know. Sometimes people come on holiday and have the time of their lives. Sometimes they never go home.

We let the waves push us up the beach, and we hold on to the shore while they try to drag us back out with them. Sometimes they're stronger, and win, and then another surges in and pushes us up the beach again. Janey's mum watches us all the time: even when she's paddling with Melly at the water's edge she keeps looking up. Then Janey takes her sister in deeper and lets her kick her legs going up and down, parallel to the shore. Take just a few steps and you're out of your depth and you can feel how endless the sea is, how weakly your arms and legs move. When we finally decide to leave the water there's still time to bake dry in the sun. It's so hot. We could maybe even go in again. I keep thinking: Luxury. The luxury of being alive.

'Have you seen all those people lying under the cliffs?' says Janey's mum. 'Do you think we should tell them to move?' They don't take any notice of the big ugly signs saying danger and watch out for falls.

Janey's mum tells us a story and we listen with our eyes shut. We've heard it before but we don't say because we're trying to give her a boost. It's the story of one day when she was fishing here with Janey's dad – way back before Janey was born – knee deep in the sea at the end of a hot afternoon. An old man was walking slowly along higher up the beach, followed by his little dog. The dog stopped to sniff something and the man got ahead, when suddenly the cliff slid and crumpled and massive chunks of rock thudded onto the beach; the man turned half-unseen through the dust and stood quite still until at last the dog trotted out of the yellow cloud as if nothing was the matter.

This time when she tells the story I think: maybe they're both dead by now anyway, but I can still see that man and his dog walking out of that dust cloud on a perfect summer beach.

We get nice and dry in the sun before we get dressed: even our swimming things dry out and that almost never happens. Then we tramp back over the shingle, past the flapping white tent again – if there was any filming going on, we've missed it – and back to the car to dump our things. Then we walk to the harbour and Janey's mum buys us our dinner from our favourite kiosk by the river. I have sausage and chips. We go home tired and salty with stiff hair. I want to sleep with the sea still on me.

'Have a bath,' says Nan. 'I've washed all your bedding. It's been out on the line all day.'

My bed is a puffy cloud. I lie back, pull the covers over my face and breathe. How can sunshine and fresh air get right into the sheets?

'Isn't this a better day?' says Nan.

Yes. Nobody died and it wasn't all about school.

Friday is hot too and everything sparkles, but on Saturday the rain lashes down again. It's much harder to be cheerful when the world is grey and damp. Sunday night is as bad as it ever was. I need to make new friends this week. At least I don't see Bully in every lesson now. I'm ready to say it if anyone asks: 'We're in the same year but not in the same class (ha ha).' His friends are not going to be my friends.

I think I'm doing well keeping out of his way, even in the playground, but we must have been looking at each other, because someone says, 'Are you two in love?' We both swing round away from each other and pretend we haven't heard.

Bully has dark smudges under his eyes. Maybe I would have trouble sleeping if I knew my dad was a murderer. And if he left me to find the body, I would be angry; but maybe I wouldn't want to give him away.

It's not that I've started feeling sorry for Bully but it's hard being the only one who cares about what happened to Irma. I'm glad I've got Janey again. I count up: four months now since Irma died. The Bulls must think they got away with it. I can't tell if Bully's dad feels guilty, because I hardly ever see him. It's like he's hiding from me. I know Nan said I should leave it all to the police but what good is that if no one's been arrested? I think of Janey playing cricket with those golf balls. Maybe the best thing would be to make a lot more trouble. I don't know what to do and the worry is eating my brain.

We have an assembly on resilience and I remember how hard everyone in the Olympics must have worked to reach their goals. And I try to focus on the good stuff, like looking forward to my birthday and Hallowe'en and Bonfire Night. Things are going better than I expected at school: I like my teacher and I like learning things. It stops me from having to think. I'm making new friends. Enough to feel I belong.

Things are better for Janey too. The school houses are competing to be the best in the Christmas Show. Janey wants to be in it. Her mum has promised to come. First she'd promised Melly to go to her nativity play and Janey said good, you can come and watch me and Michael too.

Janey's mum wears ordinary clothes every day now, like (as Janey says), 'Any Normal Person'. I hardly see the dressing gown. She even drives us to school sometimes – if it's raining – and takes Janey to matches on a Saturday. She drives like Mrs Mole, looking over the steering wheel, but Janey is happier – like she's not so on her own. Sometimes Nan helps out by taking Janey and this other girl to football practice because now Janey's mum is trying Nan doesn't mind helping to keep their show on the road. This is the thing about Nan: she doesn't like to say she'll do things for other people in case she lets them down. But if she does take something on, she'll always try to do a good job and be cheerful about it. And that is why she *doesn't* like to commit herself to things. But she's also coming to the Christmas Show.

The theme is Old Time Music Hall. That's why I said I'd do it because I know just the song. Janey agrees. She says, 'We'll do it for Irma. And for mum.' I think about Janey's dad then too and I'm sure Janey does. I don't say anything – should I say something every time? But I hope Janey knows that she isn't on her own.

The show's still weeks away but we're already nervous. Apart from anything else, Melly thinks it's going to be like *Glee* so we have a lot to live up to. There are so many things that can go wrong. Golden Boy is one of the sound techies looking down from a kind of balcony above the hall. He sometimes forgets to press the right button. Or worse, he plays the music but forgets to turn up the sound until it's halfway through the verse. I suppose it's good we can practise what to do when things go wrong. Keep calm and start again. There are other things that worry me a lot more.

Janey's mum says we should sing 'The Boy I Love is Up in the Gallery' but we're not doing that.

Bully wants to be MC and introduce all the acts but when it comes to the audition he crumbles and can't speak. So now he's the MC's runner. They're going to dress him like an urchin or a barrow boy or something. The MC is a big girl from the sixth form. She has a bossy loud voice: doesn't even need a microphone.

With Bully in the show we know his dad will be there. And his mum. Of course they will want to watch their wonderful marvellous son.

One day at school, I get a big surprise. Our teacher tells us, beaming, that someone in our class has been nominated as a Child of Courage in the Pride of Britain Awards. We are all looking at each other and then she says, 'Stand up, Michael.'

My face is burning. I don't want everyone to look at me. At break time, a boy I never talk to says, 'Did you really do that?'

I say, 'It was in the paper.' I thought everyone knew.

The one or two people in my class who were with me at my old school, but not really my friends, come over like they know me and say, isn't it funny that I saved the one person who was so mean to me at Little School? No one can understand why Bully isn't my biggest friend now. Why isn't he more grateful?

Nan says it's not like taking a thorn out of a lion's paw. Bully isn't going to be my friend whatever I do.

Everyone at school is disappointed when Nan says I'm not allowed to be nominated and she gives the teacher a rocket for saying anything without her permission. Nan says I'm not there for the glory of the school and we don't want any fuss. That's not Our Way.

Maybe I would really like a fuss, but now everyone thinks I'm being modest and that I am the Quiet Hero type so I can't really scream and cry about it. Even then, Bully's friends look at me like I'm a bighead. Bully doesn't look at me at all.

Irma says, from under the bed, 'You couldn't have done it without me, anyway, so it's probably just as well.'

'What? You weren't there.'

'Don't be silly,' she says. 'Of course I was. You couldn't have held on by yourself. I had hold of you.'

I remember the feeling of the reeds twisted tight around my wrists and how sharp they were, cutting my hands, and the man grabbing hold of me. What bit was Irma holding on to?

Friday, October 12. A very special day. It's my birthday!

My party is tomorrow. Nan made me invite Bully and to promise to 'try and get on'. Why? But I'll do it. I'll be like a double agent.

Grown-ups. They just want children to be perfect: otherwise they can't cope. One day it will be up to me and I will never do anything I don't want to do on my birthday. It's my birthday.

Saturday. My party's in the afternoon. Everyone is supposed to get dropped off but some of the mums and dads don't leave straight away: they want to hang out in the kitchen and talk about all the terrible things that are in the news. Janey's mum looks a bit pale and shaky because she has to get used to being around people again. No one says 'Well done' to her because they don't know that it's a Big Deal. She has Melly with her. Nan's buzzing round fast as a fly: she wishes they would all just go.

I don't know what they're talking about but I hear the mums and dads say how shocking it is and it just goes to show you don't know who to trust. One dad says that it was a terrible thing that no one listened to the children when they complained and that it took years to find out the truth. I say, 'That's right!'

They all look at me.

Nan says, 'Can we please talk about something else?'

Janey's mum says yes or she'll have to take Melissa home again.

Nan gets us all out into The Middle. She organises us first into running races and then for a game of cricket. Janey helps with the Ready Steady Go and the umpiring. Felix bowls from his wheelchair. Today I am the same age as Janey. My friends are a bit shy with her – like she's my big sister.

Nan has set up a table outside. Bringing out the food keeps her and Janey's mum busy. When it's time to eat we have to hold on to our paper plates so they don't blow away. The best thing is to weigh them down with sausage rolls and sandwiches. Bully is a bit out of place with my friends and he sits near Melissa, being nice to her. I am very nice to him. No one can say I am not super polite. I say, 'Would you like some more crisps, Georgie? Would you like some juice, Georgie? Oh why don't you take this seat, Georgie? Thank you for my present, Georgie.'

The present he gives me is a voucher. It's homemade and says his dad will give me lessons in self-defence. I don't think so. He could break my neck and say it was an accident.

Bully says something and I laugh wildly and agree: 'You are right, Georgie. Oh, Georgie, you are so right.' And for some reason, when I am being so polite, Nan's smile fades and she starts throwing me eye-knives.

We go indoors for the birthday cake so I can blow out the candles and make a wish but when I have my eyes shut Bully blows half of them out and laughs. Nan won't let me light them again. She cuts the cake and I scrape the icing off the slice she gives me. 'I thought you liked icing,' Nan says. 'It took me ages to do that.'

I do like icing but I think Bully probably got some spit on it.

Nan gives me a card with a dragon on the front, because this is the Year of the Dragon. It was the Year of the Dragon when I was born and now twelve years have gone by. The next time it comes around I will be 24.

So, what is it going to be next year? 'The Year of the Snake,' says Nan.

I look at Bully and say, 'Oh. That'll be your year, Georgie. *You're* a Snake.'

'I'm George,' he says. 'And you're the dragon.' He goes to stab me with an imaginary sword.

'The old word for dragon is Worm,' says Nan. 'And a snake

is kind of like a worm too, isn't it? You two are more alike than you know.'

Thanks, Nan. Whose side are you on?

Later, there is a bit of a fuss because I set fire to my eyebrows.

After everyone else has gone home, I think, I'm going to have a second go at making a proper birthday wish. I stick all the candles into the last bit of cake and light them with the long match and shut my eyes and just bend too close. There's a phht! And a horrible smell of singed hair. It doesn't hurt but my eyebrows and my fringe are all crispy and curly at the ends. My eyelashes are fried. I show Janey. She says it is Not a Good Look so I cut my fringe with nail scissors.

We get a talk at school about 'telling someone' if anything is wrong. You mustn't keep it to yourself. Go to an adult you can trust. I put up my hand and say, 'What if you do that and still no one listens?'

Then, they say, there is always Childline.

But I've decided. I'm not letting myself be bothered by anyone.

One day I see Bully bending down to tie his shoelace. He's on his own so I knock him off balance and pin him down. I put my knees on his arms so he can't move and I give him the elephants. Janey and I used to do it when we were little, when her chest was hard and flat like mine (I couldn't do it now!). It used to make us laugh, like tickling. With Bully, I wasn't gentle. I dug in with my knuckles. I was laughing like it was all a joke but he was nearly crying. I must have got stronger over the summer or something because he struggled and couldn't get free. A teacher shouted at us and I said, 'We're practising self-defence, right?'

And Bully said, 'Right.'

I don't tell Nan. She seems a bit scared of Bully's dad. I

never thought she'd be scared of anyone. So now it's all up to me and Janey.

Monday morning. Half term. I fall out of a dream and snuggle down again, relief all through my blood because I don't have to get up and go to school. Nan is staying home today and I don't have to go anywhere.

Irma pokes me in the back.

'You're burning daylight, son.'

I turn over and pull the covers over my head.

'Child of Courage tomorrow,' she says. 'Pride of Britain Awards. Pity you won't be there.'

'Oh shut up!' I tell her. And she does.

Has she gone? I don't want to look under the bed.

There's Ted up on his shelf. I hope he isn't cold. I hope he isn't dusty. I hope he doesn't mind I've left him on his own again. I close my eyes.

All my fear and anger and sadness shrink inside me into something small and hard that sticks under my ribs like a seed that will never grow.

I want it out.

Hallowe'en. I've got the same costume as last year – cloak and fangs. The fangs have been in a plastic takeaway box in a drawer with the robin and the snowman for the Christmas cake.

'Bloody teeth,' I say, giving them a rinse.

'Pardon?' says Nan.

'Bloody teeth,' I say, holding them up. 'Teeth with blood on.' I put them in and practise my evil laugh.

Even though I don't much feel like dressing up I do it because Janey and some of her friends from school are taking their little brothers and sisters out trick-or-treating. Nan says this is a horrible American invention but it's up to me and my teeth to decide. She pretends they didn't used to do anything in her day but I know that's not true – they did magical things. She and Irma used to talk about it.

We go from door to lighted door and fill the darkness between with noise but somehow we all go quiet at exactly the same time, and hear the bushes rustle, just as we come back to Irma's house. The lights are off.

A zombie says, 'I bet they're only pretending. I bet they're home,' and wants to throw an egg. I say no, we'd better not, because we knew the lady who lived there, and she died.

When we've been all round, the ones with little brothers and sisters take them home. Seven of us end up at Janey's: three witches, a ghoul, a zombie, a vampire, and Melly, the Good Fairy.

Janey's mum comes in and says, 'Bedtime, Melissa.' Melly waves her magic wand and bargains for another ten minutes while she finishes the sweets in her bowl. Her mum puts the rest away in a cupboard. She leaves us on our own in the living room. I count my sweets. I only ever take the ones that are wrapped. (Mrs Rogers' face when I said 'No thank you' to her naked pick 'n' mix.) Janey's friends are looking at their phones and exercising their thumbs on Facebook and Snapchat, uploading pictures of each other and their hoards of goodies.

'Why don't we play Levitation?' I say to Janey. 'You remember?'

She shrugs.

'You need both hands,' I say. The scariest part for Janey's friends could be having to put their phones down. 'Come on,' I say. 'It's Hallowe'en!'

Melly doesn't want to take her wings off to lie on the floor. 'They'll get crushed,' Janey says. After a bit of thought we put them on her front. The rest of us kneel around her: me at her head, Janey at her feet and two on each side. We look down on her like cannibals about to feast. Melly isn't scared. She can fly away if she doesn't like it and she has her wand to make everything right.

I begin to gently rub circles on Melly's cheeks, saying softly, 'You are feeling tired.' And the last word goes round, repeated until everyone has spoken.

'Tired.'

'Tired.'

'Tired.'

'Tired.'

'Tired.'

And again:

'You are feeling tired.'

'Tired.'

'Tired.'

'Tired.'

'Tired.'

'Tired.'

Three times in all before my voice changes, more serious now.

'You are feeling ill.'

'Ill.'

'Ill.'

'Ill.'

'Ill.'

'Ill.' One of the girls sniggers and looks round to see if anyone else finds this funny. When no one else laughs she begins to look scared.

I say it again: the word 'ill' strikes over and over like an old clock.

And at last my voice, deeper than I've ever known it, says, 'And now you are dead.'

'Dead.'

'Dead.'

'Dead.'

'Dead.'

'Dead.'

Three times we all tell her she is dead and then I give the command 'Rise' and we all lift her, just with two fingers of each hand, as if she has no weight. The girls look shocked: they didn't expect to be able to do it.

We lower Melly down to the carpet. She lies there with her eyes closed.

'Maybe we could just lift her with our fingers anyway,' says the ghoul.

'Try it,' I say. We can't do it. We nearly sprain our fingers trying.

'Anyway,' says a witch with black lips, 'I'm pretty sure there's a scientific explanation.'

Melly is lying very still.

'Is she all right?' says the ghoul.

'Melly?' says Janey.

'She's got too much magic for anything bad to happen,' I say. 'But maybe we should reverse the spell.'

'I don't think I like this,' says Janey.

Just then their mum comes in to take Melly off to bed. 'Is she already asleep?' She gathers Melly up in her arms. 'Oh you used to go stiff like this when you were a toddler. I'll give you older ones another half an hour.'

Melly's voice, muffled against her mum's cardigan says, 'I'm not dead. I've got too much magic.'

'Woh,' says one of Janey's friends. 'What just happened?'

'She will be all right, won't she, Michael?'

Of course. It's only a game.

'So what's next?' says a witch. Like me, she has blood on her teeth and she looks hungry for more.

Then the zombie says, 'How about a ouija board?'

'Oooh.' And they are all looking it up on their phones.

Janey is slow to get the Scrabble tiles and the glass but she doesn't say no. I look at her dad's armchair and it's like he's here listening and looking and not able to tell us what to do, or what he feels or what he thinks about anything. I feel a cold prickle at the back of my neck even with the collar of my cloak so high. We lay the letters of the alphabet in a circle on the coffee table. By the light of a pumpkin lantern in the window we all sit round and each put a finger on the upturned glass. Two or three take photos, which flash in the dark. And then we begin. 'Is there anybody there?'

Nothing happens. Again: 'Is there anybody there?'

The glass starts to move. Y. E. S.

'That was obvious,' says Janey.

'Who are you?' says a witch.

Nothing happens and then with a scraping sound the glass rushes to the letter I.

My heart freezes. I tell myself this is only a game. The glass waits and waits and then speeds to the next letter, and the next and the next.

R.

Sjoeff. M.

Skrits. A.

'No,' says Janey, looking hard at me. 'Michael, that isn't funny.'

'It isn't me.' I say. 'It isn't me doing it.'

'I don't like it,' says Janey.

'It's just getting good,' says Black Lips.

'How did she die?' says the ghoul.

'Michael, don't!' says Janey.

But we've got to ask. It's the only chance. 'Irma. Please tell us. How did you die?' The glass waits again then shoots across to – the letter M.

'Michael,' says Janey.

'Ssh.'

The glass is moving.

U

R

D

E

R

Some of the girls take their fingers away as if they've been burnt.

The glass falls over.

They all look at me.

'We *should* ask who did it,' I say, setting the glass up again. 'You can all be witnesses. We can't stop now.'

We hear footsteps coming down the stairs. Quickly, Janey grabs the glass and pulls all the letters out of the circle and starts turning them over. Her friends are too stunned to join in. Janey's mum opens the door. 'My goodness. Scrabble? Who'd like some popcorn?' She goes off to the kitchen.

'We should have asked who did it,' I say. 'Even though we know.'

'Too late,' says Janey. 'Mum would go mad.'

The other girls are on their phones again. They don't even notice Janey jerk her head towards the door or when I stand up and leave. I wonder what they're going to say about me when I'm gone.

Janey pushes me outside and closes the door. It's stopped raining. The path home is shiny and dark. I run past Irma's house.

'How was it?' says Nan. 'Get a good haul?' She pauses *Strictly* and the dancers freeze. They have a Hallowe'en theme going too.

'OK. It was a bit scary though. Some of Janey's friends were playing a game.'

She lets me cuddle into her. She puts her arm around me and it's nice and warm. I show her the sweets. 'Do you want one?'

She takes a liquorice lolly. 'I haven't had one of these in ages.' It makes her lips and tongue go black too. 'Better put the rest of these away in my secret cupboard,' she says.

She gets up and I feel her warmth flying; the cold creeps back to my skin.

When it's time to go to sleep, I turn on the big light and leap onto the bed. I don't dare to look under it. If I see Irma looking back at me I'll scream.

Janey's friends were spooked and now it's all over Facebook. A frenzy of Snapchat. I still wonder what they're saying about me. Maybe it's better not to know.

Janey says she asked her friends after I'd gone and they all swore they had not done anything to move the glass. 'So it must have been you.'

'It wasn't.' Why would she believe them more than me?

She says she doesn't even know if she'll do that song and dance number with me now.

'But we have to,' I beg her. 'It's for Irma. And for your mum.'

'Melly had nightmares,' she says. 'She woke mum up and told her she didn't want to be dead. She thinks you have to magic her better.'

'It was only a game.'

When I go round to their house, Melly looks at me very serious. 'She's hardly speaking,' says Janey. 'It's quiet but it isn't normal.'

I say, 'We're going to play the game backwards this time. Just to be sure everything's OK.' I ask Janey to kneel at Melly's feet.

With just the two of us, we have to throw the key word 'alive' between us like a ball.

I even trace the circles on Melly's cheeks the other way, not anti-clockwise this time (what Nan calls widdershins), but clockwise, going forwards again.

When we have reversed the spell, Melly opens her eyes.

'And you must never tell your mum.'

Melly jumps up, slaps me on the head and says, 'All right but don't do it again!' She goes off, probably straight to her mum to let her know she's Alive and Well and Awake.

'Do you want me to go now?' I ask Janey.

'You can stay and help me sort out some stuff. I want to help Mum.'

'Are you still going to be in the Show?' I'm already so scared about it. If Janey won't help me, I don't know if I can do it on my own.

'Help me help Mum,' she says. 'And I'll think about it.'

Janey's mum is still turning out the study. She's been going through it a bit at a time; the pile of things to sort out is getting smaller; the pile of things she doesn't know what to do with grows. In the middle of the room is the shredder, with a stack of papers that still need to be put through it, but it overheats and stops and then she has to wait for it to cool down. She tips the shredded paper into sacks and has a meltdown when it hits her how many times she's destroyed his name: his signature. Janey says, 'Just keep one and put it with your special things.' Her mum sniffs and says that's very wise.

She says if we really want to help we can make a list of everything that's in the shed.

The garden's a bit tidier. Nan's cut back the brambles and the long thorny coils are drying out on the grass, along with the hedge trimmings, ready to go on the big pile we will make for The Burning out in The Middle. Everyone joins in with November 5 – all the neighbours. We have our own fireworks party and make a Guy. It's going to be on Monday, even though we'll be back at school then, because we always do it on the actual day – and will do as long as it's Nan buying the fireworks with her staff discount.

So we go looking for things to burn. Janey's dad always liked to keep his shed tidy but now it's one big mess. Tools lying in dried-up puddles of rust, sagging towers of cardboard boxes, mostly filled with books that have gone mouldy. They should have gone to new homes ages ago. The windows are grimy and thick with cobwebs so old that even the spiders are dead.

'Why are we doing this?' I ask.

'To help Mum,' says Janey, firmly. She has the paper and the pencil. She gives me a pair of gloves.

'Mum says start on the left and work your way round.'

Some of it is just rubbish: some of it could be fixed. There are saws, files, hammers, drills, screwdrivers. We take a few things in to show Janey's mum. 'They just need someone to take the rust off and oil them,' she says.

Who? That's the question we don't want to ask. 'Just make a decision,' says her mum. 'I've already got a big pile of stuff for the charity shop.'

We drift out again. 'Is your mum even going to use any of this stuff?'

'Dunno. Maybe the lawnmower?'

It feels hopeless. Every drawer you open has millions of big and little things in it. Bits of wire, wooden curtain rings covered in blue mould, old tent pegs, tins of nails and screws and hooks.

It's making me feel ill. I keep saying, 'What are these?'

Janey says, 'I don't *know*.' And she doesn't want to keep bothering her mum.

At lunchtime, Nan comes to find me. We've tidied up one end of the shed, wiped some of the tools with an oily rag and filled a bin bag with manky old paper sacks and shrivelled seed potatoes like tiny shrunken heads with tangled beards, a plastic container half-full of wet blue crystals, some empty tins of paint and some plain old oily dirt we've swept up off the floor.

We're filthy and have cobwebs in our hair but I don't mind because Janey says, 'Thanks for helping.' I think we're OK again.

'What are these?' I ask Nan.

We all wonder why Janey's dad needed *three* spirit levels.

Everyone makes a pile in their front gardens of the things they want to burn. We never build the bonfire heap until the day so there's no worry about hibernating hedgehogs getting roasted. People like to have a look at what everyone else is throwing away, so not everything makes it out to The Middle. Sometimes we put out things that aren't really good for burning: stuff that other people can take if they like. You can go and look at someone else's heap, reach over the fence or even nip in through the gate. The rule is that once something's out in The Middle it can't be touched. Whatever's left is taken to the tip.

On Friday, we do our best to finish clearing the shed. By lunchtime we've piled up, in Janey's front garden: a broken wooden chair her dad never got round to mending, some rotten planks and a pallet; in another pile there's a box with old tools, a swivel chair that doesn't go up and down any more, one of the spirit levels, all the mouldy books, some mugs that need a good wash, and a couple of candle holders. Mrs Rogers will like those. She always says that whatever she picks up will go to the charity shop but we all know she sells some of it at the car boot sale down the Bay.

Nan's going to take the clothes to a charity shop near where she works so Janey's mum won't have to see them again or meet someone else wearing them. There's an old shirt and a pair of trousers Janey's dad wore for doing the garden – too many holes and stains to sell – and we ask if we can have them to make the Guy. If we work on it today, we can take him to town tomorrow and collect pennies. Melly doesn't want us to

157

use her dad's old clothes. 'But they are very old,' says Janey. 'And Dad would give them to us, wouldn't he?'

Janey and I tie string around the legs at the bottom and start filling the trousers with shredded paper. When we make the papier-mâché head Melly joins in and we have to clean her up after, before the bits of paper stuck all over her face and clothes set like tiny lumps of concrete.

When the head's dry she gets to choose the colours. The face is very pink. 'Make him pink all over,' I say. 'He can be bald.'

Janey gives me a look.

'What?'

'You just want to make him look like Shawn Bull.'

'Why not? See what he does about it.'

'Oh no,' says Melly. 'We don't want *him*.' She decides the Guy must have hair – very black. We do brown eyes and eye-brows, long eyelashes and red spots on the cheeks. He has a wonky smile – like he knows what's going to happen and is OK about it.

When I go home, Nan grumbles about me being filthy again and all the bits of paper falling out of my clothes but she says yes OK you can go to town with the Guy tomorrow.

'Did you see the neighbours are back?' she calls to me when I'm in the bath.

I didn't know. But I call out, 'So what?'

'Michael!' She doesn't like me saying that.

I stir the water and kick my feet. Maybe I should just drown myself. Maybe I would too – but not in this dirty water.

I think about it until I feel calm again.

'You're right,' says Irma. 'It's always better not to be dead.'

When she was alive, she would never have come in like that without knocking. I try to remember it's only a voice in my head but I feel like I should cover myself with the towel.

On Saturday, we put the Guy into a wheelbarrow. First we show him off to all the other houses around The Middle.

Melly's coming with us. She might be too shy to ask other people but she puts out her hand to Nan.

'Here's two bob.' Nan gives her a ten-pence piece.

Melly looks at the coin in her hand then up at Nan. 'Big deal.'

'I hope you don't say that to everyone who gives you money,' says Nan.

'I hope I won't have to,' says Melly.

'That's *24* pennies in old money,' says Nan.

Maybe we should say a pound for the guy, but Nan says no, that just sounds cheeky.

Then we have to go next door. I don't know why we have to but we do. Maybe because if we leave out the Bulls it will seem like we're scared of them. So we knock – and put Melly at the front. And wait. My heart is thumping. No one comes. Kind of a letdown *and* a relief. They haven't left anything out in their front garden either. I was dreading that too – seeing Irma's stuff out there – but I also wanted to know what things of hers they would get rid of.

We go on round The Middle. Some people are nice about our Guy and some people are all, 'Call that a Guy? We used to put in a bit more effort in our day.'

Mrs Rogers says, 'I hope you're collecting for charity?'

'Yes,' says Janey. 'Cancer Research.'

Mrs Rogers opens and closes her mouth like a fish.

We usually take the Guy into town once we've done all the houses round The Middle. On Saturday it's always busy with the market. Janey isn't sure she wants to go but this is the first year we're allowed to do it without a grown-up *and* take Melly with us, so we just have to. We wheelbarrow the Guy, taking it in turns to push. First we stand by the Town Hall and then when the clock strikes twelve we go and sit on the steps of the Post Office after it closes. Janey keeps drifting off to look at the stalls leaving me and Melly in charge.

We're both too shy to call out but we've written 'Pennies for the Guy' on a piece of card.

We stay in town for one-and-a-half hours. On the way home we let Melly sit in the wheelbarrow on the Guy's lap. We bring the Guy into the house and put him in Janey's dad's armchair. This feels a bit weird but it's not up to me to say so.

We make piles of the coins and count the money – over £15. Janey's mum takes it and says she'll donate online.

Before I go home, I ask Janey, 'Do you want to get a lift with me and Nan to the fireworks?' Another good thing about having our Burning on Monday is that we can also go to the big town fireworks display, which is always on a Saturday night. It means we have to record *X Factor* and *Strictly* again but that's OK. Ex-England cricket captain Michael Vaughan is still dancing. We think he's best when he has to keep his elbow up and his head still. Years of batting practice pay off there big time.

'No, you're all right,' says Janey.

I would say, 'I know I'm all right but do you want a lift?' only I'm thinking of not getting a bruised arm: Janey has a punch like Nicola Adams.

As I go home I take a quick look over the fence into Irma's front garden. Now there's a full box and a small pile of wood. I want to look in the box only somehow I can't go through the gate. And anyway, here comes Mrs Rogers.

Nan drives us down and we park the car on the road and walk to the fireworks field. I see Janey there with Golden Boy. Melly's there too, getting a good look at people's bottoms. Janey is holding onto her little sister's hood. I see some friends from school but I'm shy because I'm there with my nan. Bully's there: his mum and dad flanking him like bodyguards.

When the fireworks begin, Golden Boy sits Melly on his

shoulders. I hope she'll hold on to his ears – but she's patting and smoothing his head, pretending he's a pony. She jumps when the big mortar bangs go off and puts her hands over her own ears. I'm afraid she's going to fall if she doesn't hold on and it takes some of the fun out of watching rockets bursting in the sky. The explosions echo in my chest and I wonder if they could stop my heart beating.

On Sunday, Janey's mum stays indoors. That's OK. For once, Janey and I don't nag her to come outside.

We take out some of the stuff she doesn't know what to do with and stand with it in the front garden. Mrs Rogers is straight over.

'Golf clubs?' she says. 'Are you sure?'

She also gets the shoe rack, the small bedside table, the tennis racquet and the dartboard.

'And it's OK with your mum?' says Mrs Rogers.

'Oh yes,' says Janey. After all, she told us to make the decisions.

Bonfire Night. The Burning. I feel excited. It's not just the fireworks and the flames, the crackle of gunpowder in the cold air, the smell of fried onions: we're helping Janey's mum too. All the things we've hidden in the bonfire – like those boxes of papers that won't go through the shredder – will be burned tonight and she will never have to see them or worry about them again.

I thought about putting Irma's wooden spoon into the heap. It would flame and be gone. I couldn't do it: but what is the point of keeping things you can't use? That night I have another idea. It can be in our song for the Christmas Show.

Bully comes out of his house with his mum and his dad. They are all covered up in coats and scarves, hats and gloves like it's mid-winter. I don't even have a coat on. Nan asks me if I'm cold and I say, 'No. I'm *boiling*.'

Bully wasn't at school today so why's he allowed out? First day back after half term: who would want to miss that? I'm joking, hahaha. But least I got it over with. He still has to face it tomorrow.

Mrs Rogers comes over and introduces herself to Mrs Bull, a bit eager, like Irma was, but she'll never be Irma. She almost bobs a curtsey as if Mrs Bull is royalty.

I'm glad Janey hasn't invited Golden Boy to The Burning. This is just for us: the people who live here. Janey's mum has one arm around each of her daughters. Our poor Guy is right on top of the heap; it won't be lit until after the fireworks. Melly doesn't want to see him burn. 'I painted his fey-hey-hace,' she wails.

'Oh, you poor thing,' says her mum. 'Shall we get you a sausage?'

Janey and I go with her, while Melly stays with Nan.

Mrs Bull comes towards us with three hot dogs piled up in her hands.

'Hello, neighbour,' says Janey's mum. 'We haven't met.'

'No,' says Mrs Bull. 'I haven't seen you out and about.'

Janey's mum takes a deep breath. 'That's right,' she says. 'I haven't much felt like going out since my husband died.'

'Oh!' says Mrs Bull. 'I'm so sorry.'

'I suppose your George has found it hard too. I mean, I know he hadn't known Irma all that long, but still, it's a shock, isn't it?'

'A shock?' says Mrs Bull, blinking as if Janey's mum has thrown cold water in her face. 'I wouldn't know about that.'

'He doesn't ever talk about her?' says Janey's mum.

'We've tried to focus on the positive,' says Mrs Bull. 'He's been terribly bullied you know.' She looks at me and Janey.

'Really?' says Janey's mum. 'Really?' She sounds so surprised, Mrs Bull can't tell if she's being sarcastic.

Black figures with torches go out into no man's land to light the fuses. Stand well back and whoosh! There they go. Pow! Bursts of pink and green and gold stars. These rockets are smaller than the ones on Saturday night but they scream and bang pretty loud. They feel close. They still make the air inside my chest tremble.

'Cyberbullying too,' says Mrs Bull. 'It's the worst kind.'

'Really?'

'Oh, I can't repeat it. It's horrible the way children gang up on one person though, isn't it? Antisocial media, I call it.'

'Umm, I don't know that...'

But having made her announcement Mrs Bull is walking off.

'Who does she think she is?' says Janey's mum. 'The bloody town crier?' And our eyebrows go up and our eyes bulge because Janey's mum swore.

Mrs Bull walks straight past Nan to where Bully and his dad are standing on their own on the other side of the dark heap of the unlit bonfire.

We get our hot dogs and go back. 'Don't drop it, Melly,' I say. Before Janey's dad died and then the dog and then Irma, it was one of my worst memories, the day Nan bought me a hot dog down the Bay and I bit into it at one end and the sausage shot out at the other. It fell to the ground and all I had left was a bread roll and some onions and red sauce. Now I always squeeze the bread roll tight so the sausage can't escape. Yes, worse things have happened to me since then and the loss of a hot dog isn't all the world, as Irma would say, but Melly doesn't know that yet.

When they light the bonfire it smoulders and flickers with tongues of flame, rising higher to lick the Guy's feet. The centre of the pile glows orange, and the wind pulls the fire into tatters flying through the dark. The heat grows fierce like it would eat us up if it could. Ashes blow up into the air and float down and pieces of paper fluttering white.

Janey and I give each other a look. We'll have to check the grass tomorrow.

'What are you two up to?' says Janey's mum.

I almost wish that we could tell her but we don't – just in case she loses it and tries to pull something out of the fire.

'There he goes,' says Janey's mum, as the Guy in her husband's clothes starts to burn.

November 14. We have something important to do so Janey and I finish half an hour early and wait at the roundabout by our school. 'You OK?' I ask.

'Yeh.'

It's just the two of us. We don't need to talk. And it's the only sunny day we've had for ages. It feels special.

Her mum picks us up: Nan and Melly are already in the car so we can go straight to the beach.

'Is that it?' says Janey, looking at the bag Nan is holding on her lap.

'That's your dad,' says her mum.

They went to get his ashes today. Nan took time off work to help so Janey's mum didn't have to go to the funeral director's on her own.

'Was it all OK?' says Janey.

'It was strange,' says her mum. 'Walking back in there again.' She sounds OK but her hands squeeze the steering wheel.

They haven't finished sorting out every last thing at their house but it's much better than it was. Janey's dad's coat still hangs on the back of the study door as if it will always be there. That's OK. But for some reason the chess set has gone. That makes me feel sad. We'll never finish the game.

The tide is out, the beach flat and wide and almost orange in this blue light.

The water shines, turns over into white-frilled waves that run in and dissolve in hissing foam.

We've walked along to the spot where they used to go fishing. The wet grit near the shore is fine today, packed down like sand. There's hardly anyone else around. Nan takes a photograph. We turn our backs to the sea to face her. In front of us is the green cardboard box. Inside the box is a plastic bag. In the plastic bag are Janey's dad's ashes, white and grey and black, with tiny pieces of bone like slivers of fine shell.

It isn't windy. We don't speak. Janey's mum, jeans rolled up to her knees, bare-legged, stands in the water and quickly pours away her husband. The pebbles eat him up. The water drinks him down. He is there. He is gone. He is there! Flying in little puffs. If something of him sticks to her legs and there is dust on her hands, she washes with seawater and he floats away. In time to come he will be atoms in the waters of the Bay and go out into the Channel and maybe round the planet. Some of him will settle or swirl around here forever.

Some of him will go back to Janey's house and sit on the mantelpiece – because at the last minute Janey's mum can't quite tip all of him away. She keeps some: just in a corner of the thick plastic bag.

Later she will have a brainwave and buy a replica of the famous Ashes urn, from the shop at Lord's. It's tiny – about twice as big as an eggcup. And it's £50. But you can't put a price on keeping that last bit of him safe. I have a funny thought about swopping Janey's dad's urn for the real replica one that Australia and England will battle for next year. In cricket it isn't the size of the trophy that matters. This one's only a bit bigger than the plastic one Janey's mum has kept, the one she gave Janey's dad labelled 'Most Improved'. She could have used that, but it doesn't have a lid. And maybe 'Most Improved' is not what you want to say about your husband turned to ashes.

We throw red flowers on the water and wait for the sun to sink. The waves bring the flowers back, swollen and bruised to the beach. I don't want them trampled by strangers' feet so I pick them up and throw them in again but they don't go far. They float back in and are left, wet and battered on the shore. But it's all right because Melly has laid out stones and shells to make a heart. We tuck the flowers into the pebbles in the middle of the heart and leave them there for the tide. The colours seem to glow brighter as the sun goes down. When we get back to the car it's the last one left, all alone by the wall. 'I'm glad we could park here for free,' says Janey's mum. 'It just feels right.'

We drive back into town and go to the pub they liked to stop at on their way home after fishing on those long summer evenings. Now it's dark and cold outside but in the pub it's bright and warm. We order our dinner. We raise our glasses and say 'Cheers!' and 'Chink!' and 'Happy Birthday!'

'Yes,' says Janey's mum. 'He would have been 45 today.'

I go to the beach with Janey and her mum and Melly again in December, early on a Sunday morning, cold and sunny. People are walking along under the cliffs, with and without dogs. I think Melly will get upset that her stones are gone and the flowers but she doesn't seem to mind. She finds a few shells to take home and pebbles she likes. Treasures of her own. No false teeth.

After we leave the beach and Janey's dad behind, we walk up to the car boot sale.

'Are you looking for anything, Michael?' says Janey's mum.

'I thought I might find a Christmas present for Nan.'

'Oh!'

From the way she says that, I'm guessing you're not supposed to buy Christmas presents at a car boot sale, but I'm twelve and I don't have a job. I'm doing my best.

We trundle round together. There's Mrs Rogers fiddling with the ornaments on her table and pretending she hasn't noticed us. Janey and I walk on but Melly and her mum stop anyway.

'How lovely to see you,' Mrs Rogers says, trying to keep Janey's mum talking at her end of the table.

At the other end is a spirit level, some Haynes manuals and a set of golf clubs. Janey's mum looks at them and at Mrs Rogers, who is going red. When a man comes over to check out the golf clubs, Janey's mum says, 'I'm sure those are a bargain.'

He smiles at her and says, 'I'll have a think about it.'

'Don't think too long,' says Janey's mum. She turns to Mrs Rogers and says, sounding quite friendly, 'I suppose you thought you'd get more for them here than in the shop. But it would be a good idea to let people know you're selling them for charity. And the other things too.'

'Oh,' says Mrs Rogers. 'Oh yes! I was just about to do that. Put up a sign.'

Melly is hunting through a box under the table. 'Look,' she says, pulling out something shiny and red. 'It's a wand.'

'Oh that's a hand blender,' says Mrs Rogers. 'Careful, the blade's sharp.'

I take it from Melly and think: that would be good for Nan. It doesn't have a plug though.

'How much?'

'To you?' she says. 'Two pounds.'

I stare at it a bit more.

'Or £1.50,' she says.

'Mmmm.' I feel in my pocket and show her a pound.

'Oh, all right,' she says, 'but I'm not taking it back if it doesn't work.'

'It's OK,' I say. 'My nan knows what to do.'

The man who was interested in the golf clubs comes back.

He decides to buy them. 'If you want,' says Janey's mum, 'you can give me the money and I'll make the donation.'

'I can just put the money through the shop,' says Mrs Rogers.

'That's all right,' says Janey's mum. 'It's no trouble. I'll put it through my husband's JustGiving page. They were my husband's,' she explains to the man. 'My late husband's.'

He gives her the cash and an extra £10 because he says they really are still a bargain.

'Thanks!' says Janey's mum. 'It's nice to know they'll be used.'

She nods to Mrs Rogers and we move on. 'We'll come back in half an hour and see what other "donations" she's trying to sell off.'

'Mum?' says Janey.

'Yes, Janey?'

'We were only trying to help.'

'You did help, darling. Not so sure about all those bits of bank statement flying out of the bonfire but – I know you meant well.'

'You're not cross?'

Her mum stops and puts her hands on Janey's shoulders. They look into each other's eyes: almost level. 'My darling girl,' says Janey's mum. 'I'm not cross.'

Christmas is coming like a red-and-white train. Two weeks to go until we have to do our song and dance. Janey and I are so scared. I think I might be ill.

Melly will be Mary in her Nativity play.

'Are you nervous?' I ask her.

She looks puzzled. 'What for?'

So I don't say anything about the tiger tearing at my guts.

After a bit she says, 'Well. I think the play would be better with a real donkey.'

At home she goes round with a big baby doll stuffed up her jumper and complains about her back. Sometimes she carries the baby in her arms and won't let anyone else hold him. 'I'm his mother,' she says. 'I know what's best.'

'Don't worry,' says Janey. 'Mum won't let her breastfeed at the table.'

Whose idea was this anyway? Oh yes. Mine. But why did they *have* to choose Old Time Music Hall? When we get nervous, we practise. We go to my house when Nan's out.

If the Bulls are out too we can sing loud and that makes us feel better.

One last push to get it right. Eyes shut and get on with it. Only we'll have to keep our eyes open when we're on stage.

'Are we going to get into trouble?' says Janey.

'It's just a song.'

But we know it isn't.

It isn't raining so we've brought Melly to the playing fields. She likes to ride the little red pony on the giant spring. There's also a black motorcycle, which Janey's sitting on, so I'm left with the train, only I can't quite get my legs inside – which is odd because we used to fit two of us in here.

The train reminds me – I've had this idea to start off our song with a rap. These are the words:

Christmas is coming like a red-and-white train.
If you carry out your plan you're going to cause a lot of pain
If you don't do nothing then it will get to you
that you're just too scared to do what you've got to do.

'I don't know,' says Janey now. 'It might be a bit...'

'Too much?'

'No.'

'Stupid?'

'No.'

Pause. 'What then?'

'No, you go on,' she says. 'Read my mind.'

I was hoping she wanted to say brilliant. It's a bit brilliant.

'Weird,' says Janey. 'I was going to say weird.'

Whinnying, Melly reins in her pony. 'Merry-go-round?' she says, needing us to push.

She sits on top and holds on. Janey and I push from opposite sides. We bend low and push hard, faster and faster until we're nearly running.

We've already had the dress rehearsal. We made up our own costumes. Kind of a street kid look from the old days. The music teacher wanted Janey to wear a long dress but we said no, that's not our vision. Anyway, what we have was much easier to find and much better for running away. We'll probably mess with our collars so we look like a couple of drunks. We think that will be more funny. We could just put our caps on backwards or sideways for the rap.

We're going so fast now. I jump on, then Janey. 'Woh!' Everything flies round, the swings with their basket seats, the trees, the grass and hedges, the football pitch, the shelter that smells of wee.

As we're slowing down Melly says, 'Again.'

'It'll be like a mash-up,' I say. 'Anyway you said it was good before.'

'Yeh,' says Janey, 'but is it standing-up-in-front-of-hundreds-of-people good?'

'Yeh, you're right.' I jump off. 'We won't do it.' I feel suddenly lighter. Almost happy. I think I've just been scaring myself about doing the rapping bit so that actually singing the song will seem easy. It kind of works for Janey too: she looks relieved. And we push the merry-go-round again.

Relief doesn't last. All the last week before the Show, I have this horrible feeling of dread stalking me like a monster silent cat. By Thursday, even Nan is getting nervous. She lies awake in the night listening to the cricket: England are in Nagpur. Captain Cook's out for 1 run from 28 balls. On the other side of the world it's another tough day at the crease.

Friday morning: the Show's tonight. Frost crackles the windows and I'm so tired at breakfast. Nan is in a funny mood, flying round the kitchen as if we're late. 'I had one of those anxiety dreams. They needed me to open the batting. Play was meant to start at 12 and I had an hour to get dressed and get from the hotel to the ground, but I couldn't check into my room to get my kit. Then there was only twenty minutes to go and I still hadn't booked into my room. On each floor there was a reception desk but not the right one. Then I was miles away down a country lane trying to get a friend to hurry up. It was Irma. I don't know why I called for her because you could never get her to run.'

She liked to sing and dance though. I have Irma's wooden spoon in my school bag. Got it from under Nan's bed. The firebox was under there too. She must have taken it down from the high cupboard. Now she can easily grab the important stuff if the house is on fire. Only she should have told me too. But I can't say anything or she'll know I was looking under her bed.

'Then I made it back to the hotel and it was many storeys high, a mansion, with a great staircase I would have to climb to get to the main door, but when I got to the stairs there were steps missing. A workman told me I could do it: if I climbed over the chairs they'd left in the gaps I'd get to the top. I was doing it and I thought, well, no, I'm not opening the batting, I'm going in at number four. So that will be all right, as long as they don't lose any quick wickets. But I just couldn't get there and then I thought, why is it so hard? And I woke up. I wanted to go back to sleep and fix it, and climb the stairs and get there on time. But I knew if I went back into the dream it wouldn't work out, no matter how hard I tried. And now I don't feel like I've really woken up and I can't shake off the feeling. It's like I'm not really here, that the dream was more real than this. Here's your porridge.' Her hands are shaking, blurring the big brown freckles on her skin.

'It's OK, Nan. It was just a dream.'

'A horrible dream,' says Nan.

I push the bowl away. 'I feel sick.' I can hardly breathe. How can you sing if you can't breathe?

She puts her hand on my forehead. 'It's just nerves,' she says. 'Don't you think?'

'There's something wrong with my tum.' I keep going to the toilet. Maybe I'll be too ill to do the Show.

'You'll be all right,' says Nan. 'We'll all be there to watch. Eat something. You'll feel better.'

She sees me off, handing me my bag. 'Take care on the way to school in case it's slippery.'

If only I could really break a leg.

Eleven hours later, we're waiting in the wings. The hall is full and the people are using up all the oxygen. I'm stewing inside my jacket. Janey's better off in her shirt and waistcoat but she says she feels kind of dizzy. We both feel sick. The music teacher says, 'Not you two, too.'

So far, Bully's only been on to move props but even he went to the toilet three times before the Show began and the boy with the trumpet has been throwing up so much he's passed out, hit his face on the toilet bowl and chipped a tooth.

Now the trumpet player is out the first half will end with the girl who's on after us. She's only plonking out a Girls

Aloud number on a keyboard and singing out of tune at the top of her voice. Her act is not even proper Old Time Music Hall but the teacher's making her wear a big feathered hat. That's it. That's what's closing the first half. Does that mean we're worse than that? I'm leaking confidence.

We've practised our routine so many times and I know our only hope is to do it like we mean it but all the words are jumbling in my mind, and the moves: we put in some they didn't know in the old days of Music Hall and now at the last minute, Janey says maybe we should take them out again. I don't think we should change anything and as she thought up most of that strange stuff she'll go on and do it if I have to push her.

Spying through the side curtain, Janey's anxious to see her mum arrive. Then she spots Nan sitting by herself.

'That's it,' Janey says. 'Mum's broken our deal: I'm not doing it.'

I grab her arm to stop her leaving. 'What about me?' I lower my voice and hiss. 'And *Irma*.'

She pushes out her bottom lip and looks grim.

'If you're only doing it for your mum, what's the point?'

But then, I'm mostly doing it for Irma. To make myself feel better. To feel I haven't let her down. All of a sudden it hits me just how much trouble we're going to make. My guts start working like a washing machine.

Janey tucks her stick under her arm. 'You're right. Mum can do one.'

'Your mum can do me,' says Bully, sneaking up behind us so close I feel hot breath on my neck. The music teacher frowns at him but she doesn't want to say anything to undermine his confidence now he seems to have got his courage back from somewhere. He's been on and offstage a few times and nobody's booed so he's feeling pretty almighty. Like it's all so easy.

Janey closes her eyes but that doesn't make him go away. He looks through the curtain. 'She's out there with your little sister.'

'What?' says Janey, darting to see. 'Yes! They're here. She must have driven herself.' Now Janey is even more pleased.

I go and take a peek too. Brilliant. But why are they sitting down with the Bulls?

You can't miss *them*: Shawn Bull's bald head; Mrs Bull's blondeness. Janey's mum and Melly are getting wedged in right next to them, in the very middle of the row. It will make it harder for them to get out and run away. I don't say anything to Janey. I don't want her to think about it.

Nan's further back right at the end of her row on the side nearest the door.

The magic act before us finishes with a bang, a puff of smoke and a smell like sparklers. The audience goes, 'Ooh', some people laugh, someone says 'Hurray' and everyone claps. I feel like I'm at the top of the slide about to dive down it headfirst.

'This is it,' I say, and grip the wooden spoon. Don't think about it flying out of your sweaty hand. Just look Shawn Bull in the eye and do the song.

'Wait,' says the music teacher. 'You two will have to carry that easel on yourselves.'

Where's Bully gone? That's his job. We're just psyching ourselves up to be our artistic best-that-we-can-be and now she wants us to move the furniture.

The stage is like a dark cavern that opens up and there are hundreds of faces looking at us. It almost stops my breath. The lights at the front of the stage feel hot and bright. I've put the wooden spoon under my arm and Janey has hold of her cane too: it's still in her hand. We didn't want to put them down, so neither of us has a very good grip on the easel, and the board with the words of the chorus might fall off and the cloth covering the boards is slipping. We shuffle stage left and as soon as we're more or less in the right place we drop the easel with a bump. There's a murmur and a chirrupy laugh from the audience. We steady the easel, turn it round the right way and pull the cloth straight. Janey doesn't look at me or the audience. Everyone can see that my hands are shaking but some of them won't notice because here comes Bully, stomping across the stage to hold up a note for the MC. Someone laughs and Bully looks around, surprised and pleased with himself.

Now he goes off doing a funny walk, a kind of swagger. Just before he disappears into the wings he turns and walks backwards making the sign of the Loser. That gets another laugh. He doesn't even carry off the conjuror's table so we have to do that too.

We both feel flustered but so annoyed at Bully we forget to be quite so scared. We bounce on again, and take our places side by side, front and centre, big and tall as we can. I remember to grin at Nan, and Melly and Janey's mum. My heart is jumping in my throat (I'm so glad we're not doing the rap). I raise the dry wooden spoon to my nose and sniff and say clearly, not shouting, 'Just wanted to make sure...' My mike's not turned up. I glare at Golden Boy up in the balcony and he raises a hand to say sorry and then flaps it to say try again. 'Just wanted to make sure it doesn't still smell of soup.' That gets a couple of chuckles and a murmur like puzzled bees.

We wait: it is a big thing, trusting Golden Boy to get this right. At the side of the hall, Nan has a hand over her mouth. There's Bully's dad, arms folded in a show-me-what-you've-got pose. Mrs Bull straight-mouthed. Melly sitting on Janey's mum's lap. Janey's mum smiling at us, right from the centre of the audience.

And here's the intro. We draw breath and start to sing.

'Jeremiah Jones, a lady's man was he.

'Every pretty girl he loved to *spoon*.'

We each throw out an arm to the side in a big welcome.

'Till he found a wife and down by the sea.

'Went to Weymouth for the honeymoon.'

It should be Margate, but we want people to think closer to home.

'But when he strolled along the promenade…'

Arm in arm we go across the stage.

'With his little wife just newly wed.

'He got an awful scare

'When someone strolling there

'Came up to him and winked and said…'

We turn and point directly at the Bulls, first Shawn and then Mrs, Janey with her stick and me with Irma's spoon, as we hit the chorus:

'Hello! Hello! Who's your lady friend?

'Who's the little girlie by your side?'

Some people think we're just singing a song. They have no idea how brave we are. Other people notice we keep pointing at the Bulls. Janey's mum's smile drops a bit. But we carry on: we have to now.

We do the 'stir the pot' move:

'I've seen you, with a girl or two

'Oh. Oh. Oh, I am surprised at you!'

Quarter turn. Back to back. Hands to our mouths, standing sideways on, whispering now to bring the audience to us:

'Hello, hello. Stop your little games

'Don't you think your ways you ought to mend?'

Jump away, face front, arms out wide, loud and brassy:

'It isn't the girl I saw you with last *Christ*mas.'

Wagging stick and spoon.

'Who, who, who's your lady friend?'

We changed 'at Brighton' for 'last Christmas' because we want to be sure Shawn Bull gets it. His face: the blinds have come down. He's just staring straight ahead. Mrs Bull keeps looking from us to him as if to say, 'Am I hearing this right?' Maybe she doesn't know Irma liked to sing this song, but she knows we're talking about her.

In case there's any doubt, when it comes to the second chorus we bend our knees in turn and do a 'hello hello hello' like we're a couple of Old Time Music Hall coppers. Shawn Bull goes red from the neck up, until by the end of the song it looks as if his head's been boiled. In a minute steam will come out of his nose and ears.

The last verse is a good one:

'Jeremiah now has settled down in life
'Said goodbye to frills and furbelows.
'Never thinks of girls except his darling *wife*.
'Always takes her everywhere he goes.
'By Jove, why THERE HE IS! You naughty boy
'With a lady too. You're rather free
'Of course you'll stake your life
'The lady is your wife
'But tell me on the strict Q.T....'

Janey whips the cloth off the board. We stand on either side of it and point to the words of the chorus. A few people get it. Frantically, we say up up with our hands and then enough people sing with us that – to our relief – we can ride a wave of sound to the very end, arms spread wide, as the miracle happens and everyone – now it feels like everyone – joins in. I am shouting the words, letting out all the air. Here's the Big Finish:

'Hello! Hello! What's your little game?
'Don't you think your ways you ought to mend?
'It isn't the girl I saw you with last *Christ*mas.
'WHO, WHO, WHO's your lady?
'WHO, WHO, WHO's your lady?
'WHO, WHO, WHO's your lady friend?'

Great applause. We take a bow, then another. Shawn Bull is

leaning forwards as if he wants to talk to Janey's mum. She's busy helping Melly to clap. I waggle the wooden spoon at the Bulls one last time, squint and nod – and we run off.

The teacher looks a little bit puzzled but remembers to say, 'Well done, you two.' The MC is already announcing that there will be just one more act before the interval.

'I've lost George though,' says the teacher. 'He's disappeared.' Bully's supposed to be helping her bring on the keyboard.

We run out through the back door to the cold hallway behind the stage. 'We did it!' says Janey. 'Did you see my mum?' Her eyes are shining.

'Did you see Bully's dad?' I'm jumping up and down. This is the best feeling. Now it's over, I want to go back and do it again. Without thinking, we give each other a wonderful hug.

Then she looks up at something, someone behind me. I already know: if Shawn Bull comes I'm going to run back on stage so he'll leave Janey and have to follow. If he tries to grab me I will shout in front of everyone, 'Get off! Get off, YOU FUCKING MURDERER!'

Too late. A hand drops on my shoulder.

III

ON THE RUN

I twist away. It's Nan!

'Michael! You're coming with me.' She pulls my arm and I drop the wooden spoon. Barely stopping to say, 'Well done, Jane, very nice,' Nan hurries me out to the car. 'Get in,' she says, pushing me into the passenger seat. 'Quickly now.'

She fires up the engine, turns left out of the school and drives straight on, out of town. As the street lights end, Nan changes gear and accelerates. I hold on to the door handle.

'I had a bad feeling about you and your song. It'll all be kicking off back there.'

'What about Janey? We have to go back!' I think of Shawn Bull steaming towards her. Janey's mum will be upset and think she should have stayed at home.

Nan searches ahead on full beam and the hedges stream towards us.

'Janey will be all right,' she says. 'It isn't about Janey.'

'But where are we going?'

'I can't talk now, Michael. I have to drive. You've caused a lot of trouble. That's all I can say.'

I'm only twelve: no one can lock me up for just singing a song. And what about Janey? Why do we have to go on the run? Unless Nan knows something: it isn't safe.

Neither is her driving. She's going so fast – I don't dare open the door, though I see myself doing it, over and over, falling out, hitting the ground, rolling, leaving a trail of broken body parts and blood. Soon we cross the border into Somerset. I listen to the noise of the engine, the wheels drumming, the shifts of gear as we bend through the lanes. Something flutters inside the dashboard: maybe the car will break down and we'll have to get towed home. Then I can make sure Janey's all right.

What is she doing? Is she OK? If only I had my own mobile phone!

I cool off quickly until I'm shivering in my sweaty shirt inside my jacket – my bare knees are chunks of ice, my hands too. I'd tuck them under my arms but it's better to hold on to something the way Nan is sliding the car round the bends. I reach to turn up the heating, switch on the fan and open the vents at the front. Pieces of leaf blow into our faces. Nan spits something out of her mouth and says, 'Thanks.' On and on through the dark lanes. I try to notice signposts, landmarks. Anything so I will be able to find my way home again. But Nan knows all the back roads and I soon feel lost. Suddenly there are streetlights, the glare of a roundabout, and Nan takes the long straight road towards Taunton and the M5.

'Are we going to Scotland?' I ask. That's the furthest away I can think of.

'No,' says Nan. 'We're going to Cardiff.'

'What for? To watch a game?'

'You'll see.'

But somehow I don't think it's a treat.

'I'm tired.'

'Then go to sleep,' she says.

'But I'm hungry. And I want a drink. And I need the toilet.'

We stop at the first service station. Nan and I both use the toilets and she's waiting for me when I come out. Then we go to the shop and I get a drink and a pasty. I want it heated up. Nan is impatient because this takes two minutes.

She gets herself some coffee and some water. We sit in the car and she drinks her coffee before we leave. There are cameras here. We're being recorded. But maybe no one is looking for us yet.

'Can we go home now?'

'No, Michael. We can't.'

'Tomorrow then?'

'No. Not tomorrow.'

'When?'

Nan turns in her seat to look at me. 'Michael, what you did tonight. It really doesn't help. But, I'm not cross with you. You're not the only one who's done something that's…' She stops and faces forward again, pressing her lips together.

'What?'

She blinks. 'It'll have to wait,' she says. 'We can't stay here all night and I can't talk about it *and* drive. Do you want a blanket?' Maybe now is the time to open my door and run. But as soon as I touch the handle Nan pushes the button so I can't get out.

She reaches into the back seat and brings out the picnic blanket we usually keep in the cupboard under the stairs. 'Put this over you and try to go to sleep.'

'I haven't got a toothbrush.'

'I've packed your toothbrush.'

'I'm not even wearing proper trousers!'

'I packed all the important things.'

I don't ask any more. I don't want her to tell me we're never going home.

I pull the blanket over me and sniff it to see if it smells of our house but it only smells of the cupboard – like coal, though we don't keep coal in there. We don't even have a fire. Just a nice warm house. Nan speeds up on the slip road and launches us onto the motorway like we're going into orbit.

I wake up as we go through a checkpoint. The man in the booth isn't asking for passports though. Nan gives him some money and he gives her some change.

'Where are we?' The barrier lifts and we drive on, across a wide concrete apron. Luckily, there's no one to get in Nan's way as we funnel into the middle lane of the motorway.

'Wales,' she says. 'Didn't you notice the bridge?'

In half an hour or so we turn off and start to go more and more slowly as we come into Cardiff. Nan seems to know exactly where she's going, even without the sat nag. We stop at a massive 24-hour Tesco. The security guard gives us a good look as we come in through the sliding doors, but he doesn't say anything. He must wonder why I'm out so late in my shorts and cap. The clock in the store says five to eleven.

Nan tells me I'd better use the toilets because I might not get another chance. We walk all the way to the back, past tins of Christmas biscuits, decorations and bottles of wine. I spend a long time washing my hands with warm water and drying them in the hot air. She's waiting for me again when I come out and herds me back to the car, but we only drive a little way before she turns left down a dark road between tall trees. She stops and turns off the engine. It's very quiet. 'Climb into the back and lie down,' she says. I look out into the night and think I'd better stay with Nan until I can see where I'm going. I do as she says and she twists round to put the blanket over me.

'We'll be all right here. You don't need to worry. You can just go to sleep.'

She doesn't even tell me to brush my teeth, which feel like they're coated in gritty plastic. She locks the doors, tips back her seat, pulls her coat over her and shuts her eyes. I lie on my side with my face pressing into the seat cover and think: someone's bum's been here.

This is not what I expected at all when the day began. I turn over on my back and let out a big sigh. Nan doesn't say anything. Is she sleeping? Is she even breathing?

'Nan?'

'Yes, Michael?'

At least she's still alive.

'Why are we here?'

'I'm too tired now, Michael. I have to shut my eyes and go to sleep. Night night.'

I don't say anything. But even that doesn't worry her. In a few minutes I hear her breathing, deeper and deeper, until she starts snoring.

I put my fists over my ears.

Somehow I doze off and wake with gritty eyes to a grey light and a lurching feeling as if I was just about to fall out of bed only it's not bed it's the back seat of the car. It looks like we're on the edge of a park. Beyond the big trees are some playing fields. I don't know what we're doing here. It hurts in my guts to think I've left Janey on her own.

Nan's awake. She stretches, smiles at me and says, 'Morning,' as if this is some normal day.

'I need a pee,' I say, thinking she will have to let me out.

'Just climb over and strap yourself in,' she says.

'No, I need a pee now. I can go by a tree.'

'Just do as I say for once, Michael.'

I stay where I am. She sighs and starts the car. We go back to Tesco. The same security guard is still on duty. I give him a little wave. He nods. I hope he will remember me. In case I disappear.

We walk past the Christmas stuff again to use the loos. We should be getting our tree today, unpacking the decorations. I don't like it that things here already look so familiar.

There are cupboards for the trolleys outside the loos but we don't have a trolley. We're not like other people.

When I come out, Nan's not there. I don't know whether to run, or panic and look for her. Has she left me? Am I going to have to go up to that security guard and tell him I've been abandoned?

Nan comes out of the Ladies. 'Well done,' she says. 'Do you want breakfast here?' We look upstairs but the café isn't open yet.

We leave. The security guard says nothing. I wonder how

many times we can do this before he works out we're on the run, or homeless or whatever it is we are now.

Back in the car, we drive round the edge of the park and turn in, past another café that isn't open yet. We bump our way under some trees to a big open parking place and stop. Nan gets long wave on the car radio and we listen to the cricket on *TMS*. India v England. You can hear the heat.

Slowly the grass turns from grey to green as all the light and colour come back into the world.

There are early dog walkers now and a few Saturday runners.

I'm so tired I can't even speak.

Nan says, 'When it's a bit later I'm going to book us in to a B&B. Won't that be nice?'

It would be nice to lie down in a bed. And I never thought it would happen but I look forward so much to cleaning my teeth.

When the park café opens, we sit at a table outside and have breakfast baps with bacon, egg, sausage and tomato. Nan has coffee. I have orange juice. When she goes looking for the loo, I think, this could be my chance to escape. It would help if I had her mobile phone and maybe some cash. Or I could take plastic because I know her PIN. Only, where am I going to go, except home – or to Janey's? Maybe I could get a taxi.

But Nan has taken her bag with her. I might as well wait and see. I've never stayed in a Bed and Breakfast.

'Filming, is it?' says the man behind the counter. From the way he speaks, I know we are in a different country.

I swallow a mouthful of bap and say, 'Pardon?'

'Filming. What you doing? *Dr Who*?'

'Umm,' I say. 'No. It was Old Time Music Hall. We did a show last night.'

He looks puzzled.

'My name's Michael Davies.'

'OK,' he says. He doesn't tell me his name but that doesn't matter. I just want him to remember me.

Nan comes back, rubbing her tum. 'Ooh,' she says. 'That coffee sorted me out.' She sits down. 'Don't know about you but I'm knackered. One night in the car and I feel broken.' She takes a big bite of her breakfast bap and egg yolk runs over her fingers. She tuts and wipes them on the paper napkin. If we were at home she'd lick them and say, 'Don't tell anyone.'

'I didn't sleep. You were snoring.'

'I don't snore. And anyway, even if I did, you've kept me awake often enough, crying.'

'I don't cry.'

'You did. When you were a baby. Do you know this is where you were born?'

'Here?' I look around at the big trees and sweeping plains of grass, the row of terraced houses across the road, all the parked cars and the slowly building traffic.

'Not right here,' she says. 'I mean, in Cardiff.'

'Oh.' How could I know that? She never told me. 'I thought I came from Dorset.'

'I know,' she says. Her voice has changed, like she's copying the way the man behind the counter speaks. I hope he doesn't think she's doing that to be funny. 'We'll go to the B&B soon.' She looks up a number on her phone and makes a call. She gets up and walks away while she's talking.

'Come on,' she says, when she's done. 'You can have a good rest and a shower.'

'What about Janey? Can I call her?'

She holds the phone close to her chest. 'Not yet,' she says. 'I'm sure she'll be all right.'

'I'm not.'

'Michael, I'm too tired to argue.'

Well, whose fault is that?

The landlady says this is a family room. She let us in early because it was empty anyway.

'All I ever wanted was to keep you safe,' says Nan.

She's wearing her favourite purple jumper. We've both had a shower and changed our clothes and tried to have a little sleep and now we're sitting on our beds. I have a single and Nan a double. Across the river is the Millennium Stadium, like a giant space ship landed in the city. Or a great insect with its legs drawn up ready to hop. Or...

'Michael?'

'What?'

'Are you listening to me?'

'Hmm.'

She sighs.

On the table next to Nan's bed is the photograph of her and Grandad Michael with the wind blowing their clothes. 'That was taken here,' she says. 'Or near here. A day out at Barry Island.'

It's no good pretending now that we're just on holiday.

She knew we wouldn't be going home after the Show: she planned it. She even brought Ted, wrapped up in a carrier bag in the boot. Suffocating. I took him out and put him on my bed, where he could breathe. She packed a big suitcase for herself, a bag for me and she's brought her firebox with all her important papers.

I ask her, 'Was the house on fire?'

If she'd set fire to it, the house would've burned down while we were at the Show. Our house and Irma's house next door – the fire would spread because the houses are joined together.

'No,' she says. 'At least, not when I left it.'

I get up and look out of the window. There's a man across the road looking up at our B&B. He nods – as if he knows me.

Nan says, 'We have been happy together, haven't we, Michael?'

Apart from when I was bullied? Apart from Janey's dad? Apart from Irma – dying like that? Murdered? It's been OK, I s'pose. It would have been nice to have had a mum and dad. But at least I had Nan and Irma and Janey and her family.

Now it's just Nan. And I don't feel too sure about her.

Oh. Is she going to tell me that she's dying?

I don't want to hear that.

'I've done my best,' she says. 'I hope you'll realise. I've always done what I thought was right. What was best for you. I asked you not to push the Bulls too far. I knew what would happen if you did. I knew he'd tell you…'

I turn and look at her.

She shakes her head. 'It's not going to be easy to explain.'

'Whatever.' I lie down on my bed and put my arm over my eyes.

'All right,' she says. 'I've waited this long. Another five minutes won't hurt.' I hear her get up and I peek. She's putting on her make-up, sitting at the little dressing table. She keeps looking at me in the mirror.

This is weird: Nan colouring herself in like she's getting ready to go out – or face the end of the world.

I turn my back on her and curl up: there are things I don't want to think about, like how good Nan is with DIY. How she was cross with Irma. How she kept telling me not to make trouble. How scared she was of Shawn Bull. And Nan is never scared.

Her phone rings. 'OK,' she says. 'I'll be there now.'

She puts the phone in her handbag. Nods at the photo by her bed. 'You know your grandad? Grandad Mike?'

'Of course not,' I say. 'He's dead.'

'Well, there's the thing, Michael. He isn't. He's here. You're going to meet him.'

I turn and look at her to see if she's making it up.

'Just wait,' she says. She goes to the door and looks back at me. 'Another thing I have to tell you – he's not really your grandad.'

I sit up. She's quick out the room. I hear her going downstairs, then talking in the hall below. When she walks back up, she's followed by someone with heavy boots. She says, 'Michael, there's someone I want you to meet.'

Behind her is the man I saw looking up at me from the road. A tall man with not much hair. He's quite old but looks suddenly much younger when he sees me and smiles. His eyes look kindly at me. 'All right, but?' he says.

But what?

'Why is he staring at me like that?' says the man. 'Can he speak?'

'He thought you were his grandfather and he thought that you were dead,' says Nan, closing the door. 'It's a lot to take in.'

I look at the old photo of Nan and the tall thin man when they were young. And here he is. Like Nan: much older – and not dead. At least, not like Irma, only half-there. He's solid. Twice as big as he used to be. If he's a ghost then so is Nan. So am I. Maybe we're all dead. Right now, I don't feel real and yet there is my grandfather, my dead grandfather, in scuffed brown boots and jeans and a jumper with a big ragged hole in the shoulder, looking as real as anything. Only Nan says, he's not my grandfather. So – who is he? Why is he even here?

'Oh lovely,' says the man. 'It's all right, Michael, but. Think of it as a "This is Your Life" moment: "The grandfather you thought had died..." And here I am. Rejoice!' He speaks in a gravelly Welsh voice. I don't know what I expected, not ever expecting to hear him speak. Now I know why he never turned up under the bed, or in the cupboard under the stairs: he was never really dead.

'Oh,' I say.

'Then again I'm not your granpops either. Though if I'd

had the chance I'd have given it a bloody good go, but.' He pulls a sad face.

'It's a shock, I know,' says Nan, wringing her hands. She hasn't even told him off for swearing.

'Why does he keep saying "but" at the end of a sentence? But what?'

'Kids!' says the man who is not my grandfather. He looks pleased. 'You can't beat 'em.' He looks gloomy. 'Not nowadays.' His feelings chase over his face like clouds throwing shadows on a hillside.

'It's "butt", Michael,' says Nan. 'Or "butty". Like mate, friend. You know.'

'A butty is something you put chips in. Or jam.' That's what I know.

'It's an expression you hear in Wales,' says Nan. 'Please don't be difficult.'

I gasp. I can't even speak. *Me* difficult? How difficult does she think it is to have a man turn up who's supposed to be your dead grandfather? And isn't?

'He's got a point, Zene,' says the man called Michael. 'The boy won't know if he's coming or going.'

He sits down on Nan's bed. 'It's been a bit of a shock for me too, both of you turning up again. And finding out I've been dead all these years. How old are you?'

'Twelve.'

'Just,' says Nan.

'Still, a good age,' he says. 'Has it been that long, Zene?' He looks up at her face, then grins. 'You haven't changed.'

'You have,' she says.

'Let myself go. Well, why not? Nothing to keep myself together for, was there?'

'Drinking?' she says.

'No more than usual.' His eyes are warm and twinkly when he looks at me. 'I likes a pint. No harm.'

'Mmm,' says Nan.

'So are you going to tell me why you've come back? Have you come back?'

'I – I don't know,' says Nan.

I say. 'We've run away. There was a murder.'

'Oh?' He looks at Nan.

'He has this idea that our neighbour was murdered.'

'What makes you think that, Michael?'

'She was making chicken soup. And after that she was dead and there wasn't any.'

'Maybe the police ate it,' he says.

'Michael has an idea that she was killed by an electric shock,' says Nan. 'But the police don't agree.'

'No evidence?'

Nan shakes her head.

'It was taken away,' I say. 'I told you – the soup...'

'Oh.' He nods.

'He's obsessed,' says Nan.

'Obsessed? OK. But is he right?'

Nan says, 'You're not helping.'

'Oh, pardon me.'

'She didn't just die,' I tell Nan. 'And you know it.'

'Michael...'

She reaches out for me but I slip away from her, off the bed and into the bathroom. I lock the door.

'Michael?'

I look at myself in the mirror. Is she talking to me?

She's knocking. 'Michael? Are you all right? Michael?'

The lid of the loo is down, just like at home. It's the only place to sit. There isn't even a window. Just a fan that whirrs when you turn on the light. I don't turn on the light.

They are talking out there. Quietly. Things they don't want me to hear.

Where's Irma when I need her? Is she still at home under my bed, wondering where I've gone? A ghost ought to know better. Maybe she doesn't know that much after all.

I feel sad. I've just lost my grandad. OK. So he's not dead. I should be glad about that. All the times I have held his big hanky with the embroidered M and thought, I wish I could have met him. Now I have. But I don't know who he is.

I take some soap on my finger and write 'Help' on the mirror. Then 'Murder'. I want it to show up next time Nan has a shower and steams up the glass.

I hear him say, 'It's lucky for you I still drinks in the same pub!'

They're laughing!

It's gone quiet out there. I unlock the door and open it slowly, thinking they will be sitting in silence just waiting for me to appear. But they've gone. There's no one in the room. I'm all alone.

I sit on my bed and curl my arms around myself. It's when I reach for Ted that I find the other photo: four people standing in a doorway under a stone arch – Nan in a jacket and skirt; the man who isn't Grandad, not much thinner but with a bit more hair, wearing a suit; in front of them, a younger man and woman, leaning their heads towards each other. She has long brown hair and a flowery dress covering a big bump. One hand on the bump. He has brown hair too, down to his shoulders – and the sleeves of his suit hang down too long. Shoulder to shoulder they stand. Everyone is smiling – except Nan.

I turn the photo over. Aberystwyth, July 2000.

I look at it for a long time, at this man and woman side by side. They look so happy: it feels like they're smiling at me, like they knew I would hold this picture in my hands one day.

When I hear Nan coming, I slide the photo under my pillow.

'You left me,' I say.

'Mike's gone to move his car. And I thought you'd better have some time on your own. But I was only downstairs.'

'I didn't know.'

Her eyes are searching the bed. 'Did you see the picture?'

I shrug.

She sits down. 'Do you want to ask me anything about it?'

I don't know what to say to her. I sit Ted up against the pillow and lock my hands together in front of me. Nan concentrates on picking pills of fluff from her purple jumper.

'Who do you think it is?' she says.

I shrug.

'Mike's in the photo,' she says. 'Maybe you recognised him. I'm sorry about him not being your real grandad.'

'You told me he was dead.'

Her fingers rub the bits of purple wool into a ball. 'You were never going to see him.'

'But why?'

She looks down again. 'We disagreed about something very important.'

I wait. The ball of purple fluff falls to the floor. She looks at me and sticks out her chin in a way that reminds me, with a stab, of Janey. 'I did what I thought was best.'

The voice in my head screams, '*But it was a big fat lie!*'

As if she's heard me, Nan goes on: 'I was telling the truth when I said I was sad. I did miss him.'

My eyes feel hot and there's a strange fizzing in my nose like I'm going to sneeze. Like I'm allergic to Nan all of a sudden. 'But what about my *real* grandad? And how do I even know you're my real nan?'

'Oh, Michael,' she says. 'Your real grandad didn't want to know. And you are the most important thing in the world to me.'

'I'm not a *thing*,' I say, unlocking my hands so I can chop the air. 'I'm a *person*.'

She nods. 'The most important person in my life. You know that.'

'I don't know *any*thing.'

'That's why we're here,' she says. 'It's time I told you everything. I admit, perhaps I always hoped I wouldn't have to, but every time you pushed that man, that *police officer*, about Irma, he said I'd better keep you quiet or you'd find out everything she'd told him – and a few things besides. Everything was fine until she met *him*. And then I couldn't trust her any more.'

'You had a row.'

'Yes. We had a row. But she still cared about you.'

She cared about me so much she left me on my own, when she was supposed to be looking after me. 'She was making me soup,' I say, stubbornly.

Nan sighs. 'If she said she was going to make you soup, I'm sure she would do that.'

Was Nan very angry with Irma? How angry can Nan get?

Angry enough to murder her best friend? My heart pumps faster and faster. 'When are we going home?'

'I don't know,' she says. 'It all depends on you.'

I get up and Nan watches me walk towards the bathroom but she's too slow to catch me when I dart instead for the bedroom door. I thunder down the stairs and out of the house past the man who isn't my grandad, who turns and looks surprised. I don't know where I'm going, I just run, following the river to the main road. There are four lanes of traffic and I run along the pavement over the bridge to the traffic lights and push the button to cross. On the other side of the moving cars, people are going in and out of a big gate: a wide stone archway with studded wooden doors pulled back. For a wild second I think it's the same place as in the photo. Inside the gate is a wide path sloping down between tall trees. A woman in a car going by frowns at me: a boy on his own with no coat in winter. I push the button again three times. The man who isn't Grandad is just coming round the corner by the bridge now. He stops and puts his hand on his chest; looks around; sees me. As soon as the lights change, I run across the road and through the archway. Ahead of me a woman wearing a head-scarf, and a long black skirt under her coat, is walking next to a man pushing a buggy. They turn when I run past them. I jump down some steps to the right and hide behind a massive tree trunk. Peeping round, I see him, my not-grandad, puffing and stopping to ask where I've gone. Nan comes flying down the path too – she's got my coat in her hand but she isn't wearing hers. The couple with the buggy nod and point towards my tree. I run and run, turning to look behind, and don't see the slope open beneath my feet. Bang! I'm down, biting my tongue, rolling over and over until I crash into a damp bed of nettles and weeds. I lie still with my eyes shut, tasting iron.

'Michael?' calls Nan. I don't move. 'Michael?'

'He's fallen into the bloody moat,' says the man who isn't Grandad. 'Good job there's no water in it.'

'Feeder canal,' says Nan.

'This is no time to be right about everything,' he growls.

I've never heard anyone tell Nan off like that before.

I open my eyes and look up. There are the castle walls, tall towers, swirly spires and a clock with figures painted in red and blue and gold. Like in a storybook. Or have I travelled back in time?

Right now anything seems possible.

'Michael, can you hear us?' says Nan. 'Do I need to call an ambulance?'

I try to move my head. Although, if my neck is broken, it's better to stay still. 'Ow?' I offer.

'Go down and get him, can't you?' says Nan.

'How did you manage without me all these years?'

He comes swearing and stumbling down the slope, picking

up speed. He might crush me, unable to stop himself. He blocks out the light. 'Are you all right, butt?' he says. 'Can you move? Have you got any pain?'

He's looking at me as if he cares. Well, if he cares, where has he been all my life?

'I don't blame you for being angry, butt,' he says. 'I'm bloody furious with her myself.'

'Pardon?!' shouts Nan.

He ignores her and talks gently to me. 'Going off. Never a word. Turning up again. Bit of a shock. Bit of a shock for you too? Now be serious. Does it hurt anywhere? Can you wiggle your toes? Sit up? No, roll over on your side first, if you can. That's it, now push yourself up.'

'Is he all right?' calls Nan.

We both ignore her.

'Want a hand?' he says.

I give him my hand, and he puts his other hand under my elbow. I gather my feet under me, and feel how strong he is when I pull myself up.

'No bones broken? Right, now all we have to do is climb out of this bloody ditch.'

'Will you stop swearing?' says Nan. 'He's only twelve.'

'You've heard it all before, haven't you, Michael? Is that what they call you? Not Mikey. Not Micko?'

'Michael.'

'I'm Michael too.'

'Hello, Michael 2.' My voice sounds shaky.

'Are you coming back up?' says Nan, hands on hips.

'I don't want to go with her,' I say to Michael 2 in a low voice. 'I think she's done something bad.'

'Well, I told her that.'

How does he know about it? I back away from him and stumble. He reaches out and grabs me. I don't fall over. He doesn't let go.

I let him push me up the slope and out of the ditch. Nan fusses over me and I pretend I'm sorry. I'm scratched and stung – and muddy. As we walk out of the park again, people look at us but no one asks if I'm all right, walking between these two, who have a good hold of me. They make sure I stay between them so I can't run away again.

They would have walked me all the way back to the B&B like that if there hadn't been a police car at the traffic lights because for some reason that makes them both let go. I dart up to the police car away from Nan's reaching hands, and knock on the window. The startled woman in uniform turns and the window comes down. 'Is there a problem?'

'Yes,' I say, pointing at Nan first. 'I don't know who she is. And I don't know who he is, either.'

'He's just having a bad day,' says Nan. 'I'm his grandmother.'

'He's in a bit of a state,' says the police officer, looking me up and down. 'What happened?' She's asking me.

'Please can I sit in your car?' I say. 'I don't want to stay with them. She took me away from my home yesterday.'

'Our home,' says Nan. 'The home we share? It's called going on holiday. I'm really sorry, officers.' The police car moves through the lights and pulls up half on and half off the pavement. The traffic edges past, people staring from inside their cars.

'Now you've done it,' says Nan.

'What about what *you've* done?'

'Oh, Michael, I have been *trying* to explain.'

'You can't blame him for being pissed off, Zene.'

'Pissed off?' I roar. 'Of course I'm pissed off!'

'You see,' says Nan, talking over my head. 'He's only known you five minutes.'

'I knew him when he was a baby, remember?'

The police woman walks over. 'No need for anyone to shout. Right, first of all,' she says to me, 'can you tell me your name?'

A pause. 'I *think* I'm called Michael John Davies.'

'OK, Michael,' she says. 'And can you tell me what's happened to you?'

'He lost his footing and fell down a slope,' says Nan.

'I'd like to hear it from him,' says the officer.

She gets all our details written down – the names we go by, our addresses, here and at home. She asks me do my parents know where I am. I say, 'No,' and Nan says, 'That's irrelevant,' and she has the paperwork to prove it – back at our B&B.

'Do you always travel with these papers, Mrs Davies?' asks the officer.

'Ms,' says Nan. 'Not always. This is a special occasion.'

'So,' says the officer, turning to me again, 'you were running away from your nan and you fell. Can you tell me why you were running away?'

After a bit I shake my head. Nan is looking at me and I can't say, 'I think my nan is a murderer.' I don't even half believe it myself. I was just – I don't know. Maybe I just wanted to run away.

'The truth is, officer,' says Nan. 'I'm afraid to say my grandson has been making a nuisance of himself. He's got himself into trouble. He's been told to stop, but … he's been bullied himself in the past and he just doesn't want to face up to the fact that he's become a bit of a bully himself now.'

My mouth falls open.

'I've told him several times that he's doing wrong. On Friday night he just went too far. People were starting to get angry with him and I thought – a weekend away would calm things down.'

My mouth is still open as the police officer closes her notebook. 'Can't be too careful where children are concerned.' She turns to me. 'So, are you happy to go with your nan now?' and then, not waiting for an answer, she says to Nan. 'How long are you staying?'

'As long as it takes to get him to understand,' says Nan.

'He'll have school on Monday.'

'I know,' says Nan. 'I've been getting him to school on time for the last eight years.'

The police officer gives her a long look and gets back in the car.

We cross the road and go straight down the boardwalk between the stadium and the river.

A cold wind flicks the back of my neck.

'Here,' says Nan. 'Put your coat on.'

'No. I don't want to.'

'Don't be silly, Michael. You'll catch cold.'

'No!' I shout. 'I'm boiling!'

We get to the end of the boardwalk in silence. Nan puts a hand on my shoulder and I shake it off. 'Michael,' she says.

I pretend it can't be me she's talking to. Then she puts an arm round me and squashes me against her side. I don't hug her back and I don't struggle. 'Let's go and get you cleaned up,' she says.

We cross the bridge at the far end of the stadium. I can see trains coming into the station. We walk back round to the B&B and the other Michael says he'll wait for us in his car. Upstairs, I wash my face and hands and comb my hair with my fingers. There's not enough steam to make the words appear in the mirror.

When I come out of the bathroom, Nan's sitting on my bed with her firebox. She's put Ted aside, and the photo I hid under my pillow is in her hands. She pats the bed beside her and I sit – but not too close. 'I left this for you,' she says, 'because I thought you'd ask me about it. After all this time, it's hard to get started.' She angles the photo towards me and waits for me to help her out.

At last I say it: 'Is that my mum and dad?'

'Yes!' She sounds relieved. 'Can you tell? It's their wedding day.'

I nod. 'They look nice,' I say. 'Happy.'

'Well, they were getting married. Register Office, Aberystwyth. We had fish and chips on the beach after and a bottle of champagne. Mike brought the champagne. She didn't drink much of it of course: six months pregnant with you. Not that she'd every really deny herself anything she wanted.' She points to the photo. 'You see? You were there too. You're the bump.'

'Everyone looks happy. Except you.'

'I was worried. They were living in a bus in a muddy field at the time. I told them they could come and live with me in Cardiff and you came here to be born but after that they wanted to do their own thing. I said to them, "How are you going to manage all winter in a freezing cold van with a baby?" They just laughed. They said something would turn up. They talked about following the sun. Well, that's not good enough, is it?'

She stops. I'm still trying to take it in when she gathers herself again.

'Well, they ended up squatting in a dirty old house with no proper heating. Then other people moved in. And my brilliant son, the chemist, turned his talents to making drugs. Illegal of course. In the kitchen. You can see why I didn't want you to know! How could I explain? It was just a bit of fun, they said. They didn't think it was wrong! Didn't even try to hide it from me. But what kind of state were they in? And you? Oh, they thought it was all a great game. Until they were all arrested. I got a call in the middle of the night to drive up there to look after you. You were three months old.'

'But Mike said you did a bad thing so...'

'Did he?' She looks straight ahead as if she's staring down the tunnel of the past. 'After they were sentenced, we were all together at first, you and me and Mike, here in Cardiff. It's what your parents wanted. Don't forget – they agreed to sign the papers.'

She opens the firebox and takes out an envelope marked 'Birth Certificate'. Carefully, she unsticks the flap, slips out a folded paper, opens it flat and checks it, before handing it over to me. I see my name there: I am Michael John Davies, born 12 October 2000. Underneath that is Nan's name and an address in Cardiff.

'That's your *legal* birth certificate. We were given that when I adopted you.'

'I didn't know I was adopted!'

'It wasn't like I had to change your name or anything. I never pretended you were my son or tell you that your parents didn't exist! And don't forget – they wanted this. They knew they were going to prison. I said if they wanted me to look after you it was better I did it from the start and we agreed this was the best way. Then no one could interfere. I suppose they thought I'd love you and keep you safe and when they came out I'd just give you back. Or let them see you. But oh no. I wasn't having that. A fresh start, that's what we needed, and well away from them. Mike didn't agree. And when he wouldn't give me his support I decided that maybe we were better off without him, too. So we left. We didn't tell anyone where we were going. We didn't have to.' She sounds proud of herself, even when she adds, 'You cried all the way down the motorway.'

She tells me how we ended up in Dorset, how she met Irma in a queue in the supermarket, how Irma got me to stop crying by singing me one of her daft songs. How much Irma loved me, right from the start. We stayed with her until we moved into the house next door. It's the first time in ages Nan's talked about her.

'I told her everything,' says Nan. 'She was the one person I confided in. I suppose I needed to tell someone but I should have kept it to myself. Only, she was always so good with you.

And we were fine until she met *him* and then ... I couldn't believe she told him all about it. Things that weren't her business to say. She said, "If you haven't done anything wrong, why does it have to be a secret?" But he didn't want us to go on being friends. And then he threatened you, I mean, he threatened *me*, every time you made things difficult, talking about Irma being murdered. He said, keep that boy quiet or I'll tell him all there is to know. And after that show on Friday he would have told you – out of spite if nothing else. I had to get you away so I could tell you first.'

She waits. Raises her eyebrows. 'Aren't you going to ask me what?'

'There's *more*?'

'Well, maybe just that ... it could be that your parents have been out of prison for a while. Maybe the last eight or nine years?'

'What?!'

'Michael, it's not as if you ever asked about them.'

I can feel it coming – it's going to be all my fault! 'I did! You made me think they were – bad.'

She hesitates. 'They weren't evil, Michael, but they were selfish. They would never have put you first.'

We sit and think about this. I feel this bubble of anger rising up – I'm going to belch flames in a minute.

'Your dad was such a good little boy,' says Nan. 'I don't know what went wrong.'

I look down at the paper in my hands. It looks official but it also looks to me like another big fat lie. If I had lived all my life here in Cardiff, I'd have been a different person. I would have a different voice. I feel my fingers and thumbs holding my birth certificate by the edges left and right and I press: left–right–right–left. Right–left–left–right. Right–left–left–right. Left–right–right–left. So quickly you can hardly see my thumbs twitch. It's either that or screaming.

'I suppose you're going to say you want to see them now.'

I jerk my head up. 'Are they here?'

'Oh no,' she says. 'I have no idea. Officially, you can say you want to make contact once you turn eighteen.'

'Eighteen?!' Another six years.

'But if you really want to see them, we can try. I mean they might have left a message to say that if we want to get in touch, they'd like that too. And anyway, it's not that hard to find someone. Not if you really want to.'

She gives me a meaningful look and tries to put her arm around me but I open my mouth and shout, 'You took me away! They didn't know where to find me!'

She winces. 'No? Well…' She twists her lips like she does when she thinks she knows better. She fishes inside the firebox again and takes out a second envelope. 'I want you to understand, Michael, I don't have to show this to you.' And she hands me another piece of paper, this time without inspecting it herself. It says 'Birth Certificate' too but it's only a photocopy and this time there's a different address, somewhere in Ceredigion and Nan's name is nowhere. Instead, Father: Graham Davies, Mother: Sylvie Duval.

I look from one piece of paper to the other. The only thing filled in the same on both is my name and date of birth, so I suppose that part must be true. But I shake my head. 'I don't get it.'

'It's quite simple,' she says, taking back the photocopy, like she doesn't want me keeping hold of the wrong piece of paper. 'The one with my name on it is the real one now: the one that means something under the law. We were given a new document when I adopted you. You see, Michael, I haven't done anything wrong. I didn't steal you. Your parents signed the papers to give you away. All I decided to do was to make a clean break and start somewhere new.' She tips up her chin. 'I thought it was for the best.'

'But I didn't know … I thought they were in prison.'

'They were,' she says. 'For the first few years.'

'You could have found them any time you wanted.'

'But, Michael, I didn't want to find them, remember? And if you had wanted to then, when you were old enough – that would have been up to you.'

She breathes out and smiles like she's relieved now. Like it's all been said. It's all over and we can just move on. Her phone rings. Mike is hungry.

'Come on,' she says. 'We should go and eat something.'

I want to say, get lost but – I'm hungry too.

The three of us walk into town. It's blustery, with rain in the air. 'Did you tell him?' says Mike.

'Yes.'

'Everything?'

She doesn't answer at once. 'The main thing is whatever that Bull-fella wants to do, it will make no difference now.'

'Never get on the wrong side of the law,' says Mike. 'But you're doing the right thing at last.'

'Mmm,' says Nan. 'I did the right thing twelve years ago too.'

I make Nan buy me what I want: a burger and chips. Before we eat, Nan goes to the Ladies, leaving Mike between me and the door.

But why run away now? I *want* to see my mum and dad. I could try to find them myself. Or ask the police. That makes me think of Shawn Bull and my guts twist. He must be so angry. I left Janey in trouble. But that's not my fault: Nan took me away – again.

'Do *you* know where they are?' I ask.

'I could find out,' he says. 'But it's no good. Not unless your nan agrees. And they'd have to want it too.'

I shake my head.

'One thing about your nan,' says Mike. 'She did what she

thought was right, no matter what the cost to herself. She put you before everyone else: me, her own son. She left behind all her friends. Only, I told her at the time, it was a little bit selfish too. She always thinks she knows best, see?'

'I wish you were a grandad,' I say, after a bit of thought.

'If I were a grandad,' he says, 'someone else's, I wouldn't be sitting here with you.'

'Oh.'

'But I hope you'll get to see your family now.' He *sounds* hopeful and I'd like to believe him.

How am I going to tell Janey that I suddenly have parents of my own? A mum and a dad too. Only – maybe they don't want me. Never have.

Mike takes us back to the B&B and leaves us there.

That night, in the dark, the cricket comes to us again from sunny India. As England go into bat, Geoffrey Boycott says the thing is not to be negative. If we lose a couple of wickets then pressure comes: pressure does funny things to people. So – don't feel the pressure. That's the answer. How do you do that? Have character.

The crowd roars as an Indian bowler runs in.

When I turn over in bed, two envelopes crackle under my pillow. I'm keeping them. These are *my* birth certificates.

Sunday. We have our breakfast in the B&B and then wait for Mike. It's too windy to be out in the park, he says: branches are falling. 'Do you want to go to Winter Wonderland?'

It's a place where you can go skating. Outdoors. They do it every year in Cardiff.

'And maybe there's a Big Wheel as well. Come on. Your nan's paying!'

We go but I'm the only one who skates. They just watch. 'I don't like falling over,' says Mike. 'At my age, that could be a hip!'

I'm hanging on to the side most of the time. There's a girl who looks like Janey from the back. But it can't be. Nan and Mike stand next to each other as if they don't need to speak. I pull myself round to where they are.

'When are we going home?' I ask.

'Tomorrow,' says Nan.

Mike looks glum.

'You can come and visit us,' I say.

'Can I? Thanks.'

Nan says, 'Of course. Yes. That would be nice.'

'"Nice",' he says. 'The word of doom.'

'Don't start!'

'Ah, that's better. I always know where I am with you when you're biting my head off.'

We have a sleep in the afternoon, Nan and me. We're still so tired. Mike goes away. When he comes back he's still on his own. I try not to look disappointed. 'When am I going to see my mum and dad?'

'We have to find them first,' says Nan. 'They could be any-where. In France maybe? She's half French, you know.'

No, Nan. I didn't!

'They might have gone to *her* parents, I suppose. If they're still alive.'

Grandparents. In France. I feel like Nan has been digging a big hole right at my feet – and now she's pushed me in.

In the evening, I let her and Mike take me to see *Skyfall*. Sitting in the dark, deafened by explosions, watching James Bond wear himself out, it's all I'm good for. When we leave, the streets are wet but it's stopped raining. A train screeches steel, braking into the station. A short walk in the damp wind back to the B&B.

'Well,' says Nan. 'Thanks for looking after us this weekend. Don't forget now.'

'I'll do my best,' says Mike.

If I wasn't there – what would they do? Would they be kissing?

He holds out his hand to me. 'It was nice to meet you, Michael.'

I shake his hand: it's warm and dry and a bit rough.

'We'll find them,' he says. 'Don't worry.' He actually gets a tear in his eye.

He turns when he gets to the corner and I wave. Nan is already going in.

In the hallway, I ask her. 'Are we going to see him again?'

'Do you want to?'

I nod.

'Then we will.'

'How?'

'I've got his number. Now shush.' We're climbing the stairs.

'Did he give it to you today?'

She doesn't speak again until we're in our room.

'No,' she said. 'I've had it for a week or so.'

'Easy then. He was easy to find. Why can't we just stay here and find my mum and dad?'

'I thought you wanted to get back for Janey.'

'I thought you didn't care!'

'It's too late in the day to have this conversation,' says Nan.

'About twelve bloody years too late!'

'Don't swear, Michael.'

I glare at her. 'You're not my mum.' And she's not my dad. All this time, and they didn't know where I was. They will be so worried.

Our last night in the B&B. It's hard to sleep. I think now I'm twelve I should have a room of my own. In the morning, Nan rings school and tells them we had to go away on urgent family business and I'll be back in class tomorrow. She could have just lied a bit more and told them I was ill.

It's a long silent drive home. There isn't even any cricket to take the edge off things, because it's all over. Bell and Trott scored centuries. We drew the match and won the series. I should be happy about it but I can't be happy sitting next to Nan. We zoom past the giant wicker man walking south. Even though he has a bird sitting on his head, I say nothing. There's a camel looking over a hedge. Looks like it's made out of papier-mâché but then why doesn't it dissolve in the rain? I don't ask. Normally, Nan would point things out and give me little educational speeches. Her hands fidget on the wheel, gripping and letting go. Now and then she sighs.

When I see Janey – as soon as she's home from school – she says, 'What happened to you?' She isn't even angry.

I don't tell her everything straight away. I ask her how things went after I left the school hall.

'Oh. Georgie Bull disappeared. But his dad found him and took him home. His dad – wow. He lost it. He said he'd had enough of our bullshit. But Mum stood up for me. So it was OK. I've got your wooden spoon.'

'Thanks.'

'What happened to you? Your nan rang and said you'd gone to Cardiff.'

I tell her about my weekend, meeting Mike, the man who isn't my grandad, running away, the Bond film and last of all I tell her about what Nan did, and about my mum and dad. She looks at me in wonder. But she doesn't cry or anything.

'I don't know what they're like,' I say. 'I don't even know if they want to see me.'

'You might have brothers and sisters,' she says. 'Hey, I always knew your nan was fierce.'

'I could kill her,' I say.

'You could afford to,' she says. 'Now you've got a mum and dad.'

It's nearly Christmas. 'You know what feels good?' Nan says.

I don't answer. I don't think Nan has a right to feel good about anything.

She goes on anyway, like I'm interested. 'I don't have to be afraid of the Bulls any more. Now you know the worst – I mean now you know everything – there's nothing they can do to me.'

She sounds so cheerful about it. Lucky old Nan. 'Well,' I say. 'Every cloud...'

Nan has handed Irma's wooden spoon back to Mrs Bull. 'It belongs with the rest of Irma's things,' she said, 'so you'd better have it.' Mrs Bull looked at it like it's been up a cow's arse but Nan put it into her hands anyway. I expect it will turn up at a car boot sale or maybe they will just put it in the bin. Or burn it. Actually, I wouldn't mind that.

At school, Bully and I are made to sign a pact: no more bothering each other. My friends don't really get it. Felix says, 'What was the fuss about? Some stupid song?' And they think I was off school Monday because I was scared.

I say, 'No. My nan kidnapped me.' I tell them where we went but they don't ask a lot of questions and it's hard to start talking about everything that's happened. So I keep quiet and I feel I'm on the outside of everyone else's bubble.

Is this why Nan has no friends?

I'm glad Janey knows. I will always be able to talk to her. She will never let me down.

Janey and I have to go and say sorry to the Bulls for what we did in the Show. Nan and Janey's mum go with us in case there's any trouble. Shawn Bull sits quietly and stares at the carpet like he's been told not to speak. Bully fidgets. He keeps looking over at his dad. Mrs Bull says, very carefully, 'It's nice that you wanted to sing a song that reminded you of your friend but I hope you understand that the whole thing has been very painful for my husband and my son too.'

We have to say we do understand and that we are very sorry for making things more difficult.

Mrs Bull looks relieved. 'It's our first Christmas back together as a family,' she says, smoothing her dress. 'I hope we can enjoy it in a spirit of peace and goodwill.'

As we leave she says, 'We thought we'd have a party for the neighbours New Year's Eve. You must come.'

We have to say yes that would be lovely, thank you.

When we are away from the house and out in the windy dark, Nan says, 'That's so she can show everyone nothing's wrong.'

'I guess she's just trying to fit in,' says Janey's mum.

'Mmm. Well … we all deserve the benefit of the doubt sometime.' Nan looks at me.

'Can my mum and dad come for Christmas?'

'It's too short notice,' says Nan.

'For who? Or I could go there.'

'If and when they get in touch, we'll see,' says Nan. 'We don't even know where "there" is yet.'

'Good luck,' says Janey's mum, sympathetically, touching Nan's elbow.

'Thanks,' says Nan.

'You too,' says Janey, bumping my arm.

I'd rather go home with them, but, 'Harry's looking after Melissa,' says Janey's mum. 'He's remarkably patient for a teenager.' Just the mention of Golden Boy's name is enough to give Janey rosy cheeks. 'And Melly adores him,' says Janey's mum.

I give the gatepost a kick on my way through.

The Saturday before Christmas. It's me who answers the phone. A woman's voice says, 'Is that Michael? It's Mum.' She sounds so normal and not really French. How do I know it's not a trick? And I thought she'd be more upset. She says, 'I'm so happy to talk to you. How are you?'

'I'm OK. How are you?'

We are so very polite. It's weird. My mum says, 'I can't wait to come and give you a good big hug.' I don't know what it would feel like to have a cuddle from my mum. Do they even remember that I'm twelve?

'You don't sound very French.'

'No,' she says, with a laugh. 'I don't. Hey, I've got your dad on speakerphone.'

My dad calls out, 'Hello, Michael, it's your dad.'

'Hello.' I have never had a dad of my own and I don't know what to say. What would I say to Janey's dad? I'd talk about chess or the football or the cricket. By now, Nan is waiting anxiously. She motions for me to put my mum on speakerphone. I ignore her.

'Are you coming for Christmas?' I ask.

There's a pause before my mum says, 'We'd love to, but…' Nan tries to take the phone and I won't let go. While we're struggling, I hear my mum's voice, but can't make out what she's saying. Nan twists the phone until she gets it out of my hand and says, 'He's a bit overwhelmed…'

'Nan!' I shout. I'd like to kick her but instead I just walk out. I'll leave it to my mum and dad. They're going to be so angry with her: it won't just be me any more. Somehow I feel taller, stronger. Every step pushes me a little higher off the ground.

I go round to Janey's and we help Melly make Christmas cards with too much glue and too much glitter. I've decided I'll stay here until Nan comes looking for me. Janey's mum is looking well. She's wearing jeans and a red Christmas jumper. They all went out together to buy a tree. 'I pick-ted it,' says Melly. 'It was the biggest.'

'We had to cut the top off,' says Janey. 'Have you got a tree?'

I shake my head.

'You can have the top of ours if you want.'

'Doesn't your nan always get you a tree from work?' says her mum.

'Yeh. It'll just be something scabby left over that no one else wants.'

When it gets dark, Janey's mum says, 'Shall we all walk Michael home?'

Janey smiles and they all put their coats on. I came out without one. We take the top of the tree with us. At least it will smell a bit more like Christmas with that in the house.

We all cram through the front door and stop as Nan comes out of the living room. Her eyes are red – and her nose. Then she laughs, a weird sort of gulping laugh.

'We thought we'd better just pop Michael home and see if you're all right,' says Janey's mum.

It suddenly comes to Nan: you can see it in her face, how different things are now. I bet she'd like to go back in time to when Janey's mum was being hopeless and Nan was all in charge.

'Michael's mum and dad are coming for Christmas,' Nan says. 'And his brothers and sister.' Before this can sink into my brain, her voice rises. 'I've got *four* grandchildren!'

I can't get my breath. The hall carpet is sponge under my feet.

Everyone is looking at me: Janey, Melly, their mum, my nan.

'Congratulations, Michael,' says Janey's mum. 'You're a real big brother now.'

For Christmas, I get two chess sets and a whole new family. The first chess set is from Janey's mum. Nan lets me open this one on Christmas morning, before my mum and dad arrive. I can't believe it's mine: the set that belonged to Janey's dad, all cleaned up and back in the box. I'm so happy to have it, but sad too because the game we were playing has gone forever. Nan gives me bath stuff. Another hint about washing. Nothing else. Well – she's giving me my family, I suppose. But they were always mine.

And here they are: it's a real crowd in the hallway, all eyes and arms, mouths talking about the very early start and the state of the roads. Mum still has long hair and wears velvet. Dad is thin and tall and his hair covers his ears. Their children are round their feet like that's the safest place. Nan says there might not be enough turkey but Dad say that's all right because they're still vegan and they've brought some special nut roast to pop into the oven. My mum and dad hug me, and ask, would I show my two brothers and my little sister where they will be sleeping and maybe the garden while they 'talk' to Nan?

Talking is what they do. At least – I don't hear any shouting. Afterwards, Mum and Dad look happy and Nan looks stubborn. She picked the wrong team when she chose me: now she's only got one child to play against their three.

My mum keeps hugging me. She doesn't even care if I feel shy. But it's OK. It's nice. She says, 'There'll be plenty of time for talking. Let's get to know each other and have a lovely Christmas.' Dad doesn't hug me much. He doesn't look at me much. He knows what to say to the others, but not to me. He doesn't know me.

'Do you like cricket?' I ask him.

'Can't stand it,' he says, cheerfully.

So that's the end of that.

It's very busy having everyone in the house. There's always something going on. It's like a test to see how I will manage. Everything is different. I have to share my room with my two brothers. They have an airbed on the floor. My little sister, Bella, who is nearly two, sleeps with Mum and Dad in the spare room. Mum and Dad. Mum and Dad. It's weird that these words belong to me now too.

My youngest brother, Fred, who is only four, sees Ted up on his shelf and he wants him. He climbs on my bed, pulls Ted down and after that he won't let him go. I say, 'Fred. You can hold him, but Ted lives at my house, OK?'

'Good luck getting that back,' says Terry, who's already sitting on my bed and inspecting my room and stuff. He's eight.

I worked it out: my mum wasn't in prison as long as my dad but when he got out they must have decided on replacing me straight away. Until now, Terry's been like the oldest. I ask him, 'Did you know about me?'

He thinks about it. 'Never talked about you much,' he says. 'Only yesterday, when Mam says, you know you've got a brother? And there's a photo of a baby that Mam and Dad said was you. But no.' He looks at me from the corner of his eye. 'It was more like you'd died.'

Funny: to them I am a ghost. The little ones aren't scared of me though. I thought Terry would be like a younger me, but he isn't. He's more – sturdy. Nothing seems to worry him. And if I thought I was going to get all their respect just for being older – think again. I have to try hard to get them to even like me. They just don't seem that bothered – like this is normal but a bit of a pain. Terry just keeps grumbling that it was a bloody long drive on Christmas Day.

I show him all the toys and things of mine that I liked when I was eight. I even get things out from under the bed. I offer Fred the Action Man but he pounces on the dinosaurs. He makes them fight each other while Ted looks down from the bed, like a giant, like a god.

Terry is harder to impress until he finds Squawky the T. Rex. Nan gives us new batteries but every time my little sister, Bella, comes into my room, Terry makes the T. Rex roar and lunge towards her so she runs away screaming. I say, 'Look, Bella,' and knock the dinosaur over. Squawky lies on her side, legs pedalling, her mouth opening and closing, doing that tinny little roar. 'Don't put your finger in there, Bella!' More tears.

Nan says we ought to have a gate at the top of the stairs before Bella takes a tumble. 'I suppose we need one at the bottom, too, really. I had them for Michael.'

'No, Mother,' says my dad. 'We've seen enough bars.'

Terry's favourite sport is rrrrugby. He ripples the r.

'We play rugby at my school,' I say. 'I'm not very good at it.' I try to roll my r too but I can't.

'We play it at my school and I'm brilliant,' says Terry. They start young in Wales. He plays football as well. And cricket. He breaks 'cricket' and 'football' like this: crick-et; foot-ball. He sounds all the 't's.

'Why do you talk like that?'

'Like what?'

'I sound more like Mum and Dad than you do.'

'I talk like my friends,' he says. He speaks Welsh to his little brother and sister and I don't understand anything except when a word pops out, like 'deinosor'.

I want him to teach me. Then I can talk to people in Wales. 'They speak English too,' says Terry.

'Well, I know that,' I say. 'I've been to Cardiff.'

'Oh Cardiff,' he says. 'Not as good as Aberystwyth.' He grins. 'Mam and Dad have nooo idea what I'm saying. But they can't make me speak English if I don't want to.'

'It would be good to have a secret language.'

'No!' he says. 'It's not a secret. Millions of people speak it. Even in miles-away places like South America.'

'I mean, a secret language from Mum and Dad. And Nan.' Especially Nan.

'Oh!' He nods, a light in his eye. But he isn't ready to teach me anything yet.

We do presents next. I went into town on Christmas Eve: I never had so many people to buy for. Nan said she would use her staff discount at the DIY store and I said no thanks. I use my own birthday money and get something for everyone in Bits n Bobs.

Nan sits on one of the hard chairs and I get ready to give out the presents, kneeling by our tiny tree. Nan said it would do after all, but now it's just embarrassing. 'We cut a real tree in the forest and drag it home,' says my dad.

'Is that allowed?' says Nan.

Terry comes in with Ted under his arm, followed by Fred, who is trying to get the bear back.

'Oh my,' says Dad. 'That's Ted! He was mine, then I gave him to you, Michael, when you were born.'

'I should have been next,' says Terry. 'So it's my turn. Then Fred.'

'I want Ted!' Fred shouts.

Bella looks as if she is going to have her say in a minute. I hope she will like the doll I got her for a pound. Nan said I didn't have to think girl = doll but I said, 'It was Melly's idea.'

'Ted's mine,' I say. 'I said they could play with him.' I mean them to understand: I'm not giving him away.

Nan gives me a funny lopsided smile. 'You'll have to learn to share now.'

Mum says, 'All right, you two. He belongs to Michael, so give him back.'

'It's OK,' I say. 'You can take turns. Only don't hurt him. He's getting old.'

'He's at least as old as I am,' says my dad.

Terry soon forgets and then Ted is back in Fred's arms.

My new family take up all the comfy seats and we get started. Mum and Dad give me two presents. The first one I open is – a chess set. 'I've already got one of these,' I say.

'Michael!' says Nan.

'It's OK,' says my dad. 'We didn't know. I mean, we thought you didn't have one.'

'I only got it today,' I say. 'I – thank you. I really like it.'

'And it's a travelling chess set,' says my mum, 'so you can take it with you on a journey.' She smiles at me.

'Do you play chess?' I ask her.

'It's not my thing,' she says, 'but your dad does.'

'Oh.'

And for once my dad looks at me and smiles and nods.

The other present they give me is a book of photographs, snapshots of the life I've been missing. They gather round me now to point things out: pine trees, old stone barns and sheep; my whole family standing next to a big pond. Ducklings!

'So you still live in a field,' says Nan, who can't even see from where she's sitting.

'That's not a field,' scoffs Terry. 'That's the back garden.'

Pictures of ducks and geese and hens and my brothers and sister feeding them or just looking surprised. 'That goose was biting the back of my leg,' says Terry.

Sunsets. Me as a baby. Then Terry, Fred and Bella. Photos of all of them growing up. Ducks on a tin roof, looking down at the camera.

I say thank you.

'Your mum's been making that for a long time,' says my dad. 'Your whole life.' We don't have time to look at them all.

I got Mum and Dad a calendar with pictures of dogs. 'We've got a dog of our own,' says Terry. I had thought about giving them the stick blender I bought from Mrs Rogers at the car boot sale but in the end I still give it to Nan. She's lucky to get anything and then she looks at it funny when she takes it out of the paper.

I say, 'I'm sorry it isn't new.'

'Oh, but that's a lovely present,' says my mum.

'Yes, it is. Thank you, Michael.' Nan scrunches it back up into the paper and puts it down.

She's very quiet, but it doesn't matter because Terry and

Fred and Bella make a lot of noise. Mum and Dad smile as if everything is lovely. Just like in their wedding photograph.

At Christmas dinner, Mum eats me up with her eyes. She beams at me and says, 'I'm too happy with what I've got right now to be sad about what I've missed.'

Nan looks at the ceiling. I don't know why we're making it so easy for her: I thought Mum might pin Nan against the wall and shout in her face. That would make me feel better.

They're not like that though. They're kind of wafty, my mum and dad.

Nan and I eat sausages wrapped in bacon with our turkey. Terry wants to try one but he's not allowed. I try their nut roast. It's all right. I like the crunchy edges.

We have two kinds of gravy. Nan's comes out lumpy.

'You can blitz it with your lovely present,' says my mum.

'No, I'll just pass it through a sieve,' says Nan.

My mum looks at me to see if I mind Nan not using the stick blender.

'Our gran in France makes good gravy,' says Terry.

'Good vegan gravy,' says my dad.

'Where do they live?' asks Nan.

'Mum's still in France,' says my mum. 'Where they always were.'

'We did go and see them,' says Terry.

'Do you speak French?' my mum asks me.

I know how to say, 'Un peu.'

'Ah bon! But I'm sorry to say that my dad died last year. So – you missed him. Mum might come and live with us but she hasn't decided.'

In one go I lose my grandad and the possibility of future holidays in France. I don't know how Nan is ever going to make this up to me.

Later, Mum will show me a photo of me with my French

grandad. 'They came over to see you when you were born,' she says. 'A special trip.'

Nan says, 'More nut roast anyone?'

I say, 'I wonder what Mike is doing?'

'I expect he has plans,' says Nan.

'No he doesn't,' I say. 'He doesn't have any family. We should have asked him to come.'

'There's hardly enough room!' says Nan. 'Where would we have put him?'

'He could have stayed in with you.'

Nan nearly chokes. Mum and Dad start laughing. We all join in, except Nan.

After dinner they are all so tired from the long drive that they cuddle up like puppies and go to sleep in the living room, while Nan and I wash up. You'd think she'd do it on her own for once. But no. Mum yawns and says it's good I help Nan out so much: we really are a team.

Nan doesn't say a lot and the washing-up takes forever: all those plates and saucepans and the big greasy tins. All the food we didn't eat to put into bowls and boxes.

'Don't you like your present?' I ask her, while I'm drying up and on my second tea towel.

'It's lovely. It's just ... I know where it came from, Michael.'

'Oh.'

'I suppose we'll have to take that back as well.'

'Why?'

'You can't just go taking things. You know that.'

'I didn't!'

'But...'

'I bought it from Mrs Rogers! At the car boot sale.'

'Oh!' she says. 'I see.'

'And I bought a new plug.'

'Why?'

Duh! 'Because it didn't have one!'

'Oh. I wondered why it didn't have a sealed plug on it. So who wired the plug?'

'I did.' The new plug had a diagram so that part was easy. The hard bit was peeling back the plastic of the outer cable – it had just been cut off straight – so I could strip the wires. You'd think she'd be proud of me.

'Why was it like that?' says Nan. 'But really, it could be dangerous. And besides, that blender has a very sharp blade!'

She puts the stick blender on one side. I know she'll take the plug apart to check I did it properly.

Funny isn't it that *she* doesn't trust *me*. Does she think I'm trying to give her an electric shock so I can live with my mum and dad?

By the time we've finished, everyone has woken up and wants a cup of tea. My brothers and sister want to watch the telly. Mum says to me, 'Shall we go upstairs and have a little talk? I haven't seen your room yet.'

Nan looks worried but she can't stop us. And Bella wants Nan to help her dress her doll.

Mum says she likes my room. There are still dinosaurs all over the floor. 'It's usually more tidier,' I say. Then I get embarrassed in case she thinks I'm complaining about having them there.

'You should see our house,' says Mum, sitting all the way back on the bed and leaning against the wall. I stand and look at her, then sit down too, facing away.

'Are you all right?' asks Mum.

I pick at the duvet. 'Why don't you get angry?'

'Oh!' says Mum. 'I'm *beyond* angry.'

My anger is so fierce I feel it could burn me from the inside out but she seems quite cool about it.

'Why didn't you want to find me?'

'Oh! We did. We always had messages about you. We always

knew you were all right. Only, we weren't allowed to know where you were.'

'Because of Nan.'

'She doesn't make the rules,' Mum says. 'But she knows how to use them.' She sighs as if she's said too much. 'Is there anything else you want to ask me?'

'Do you believe in ghosts?'

I can tell she wasn't expecting that, but she covers it up, like I could say anything and it would be all right.

'Anything's possible,' she says. 'But if you've got one bothering you, I know someone who could do an exorcism.'

I tell her about Irma.

'Is she under your bed now?'

'No. I don't think so.'

'If she is she's very quiet.'

'Yep. But that's worse.'

'I see. And why do you think she's under your bed? I mean, not under someone else's?'

'I don't know.'

'Do you think it's your fault somehow? I don't mean that it *is* your fault. But, sometimes we feel guilty about things even when there was nothing we could have done.'

'Mmm.'

'Have you tried telling her to shut up?'

'Yes!'

'Good for you.'

'But then I felt bad. She doesn't want to be forgotten. And I really did think she was telling me that the policeman next door was a murderer.'

'A policeman next door,' says Mum. 'Your grandmother would not have liked that.'

I look at her: she sits there smiling as if everything is fine.

'Why didn't you look for me?' I say.

She raises her eyebrows. 'Did you ever ask about us?'

Wait. Is she saying it's my fault? Like, finding my family just gives me a whole new set of things to get wrong? I turn away again. I feel like I'm choking.

She strokes my back. 'We said we'd see you, yes, if we were ever allowed. We said we wanted you. But you know … your nan had her reasons. It's funny, for years I've dreamed of my little boy, of being able to hold you. But you can't go back to being a baby. We have to start from where we are now.' She doesn't say, 'Please come and live with us.' She says, 'You'll be able to visit us next, I hope.'

'Do you have room?'

'Oh yes. Maybe at half term? You've got school here and friends. You don't want to make a lot of changes all at once. You are who you are.'

I don't know what to say.

She tries again. 'You're not a baby but just knowing we exist: this is a new life for you. So start with baby steps.'

After a bit, I say, 'OK.'

'There we are then,' says Mum. We go downstairs to be with everyone else again.

When it's time to go to sleep, Terry and Fred bounce on the airbed. Even when they're lying down at last they keep jiggling and laughing. I say Ted had better come in with me and Fred says no and I say well then settle down. Fred is too wound up to sleep. He wants to play I-spy. 'I spy with my little eye, something beginning with Guh,' he says. After two seconds he says, 'Give up? It's goose!' He means he's seen one on my wallpaper.

'We've got real geese at home,' says Terry.

For two nights Wallpaper I-Spy is Fred's favourite game and whatever it is – pig, dog, donkey, tractor – Terry says they have a real one at home. I look for things he might not have but they've got it all: shed, barn, grass, hay bale, even an old milk churn. 'Why have you got a pig if you don't eat meat?' I say.

'Rescue pig,' says Terry.

He's probably making it up. I don't mind. 'Think of all that bacon,' I say. I'd like to see a real pig but I don't want to have to kill one.

Boxing Day morning and the house is littered with bodies. They rise up one by one. Nan is busy making tea and coffee and then breakfast. 'We'd better get on if we want to see the Boxing Day Swim,' says Nan. It takes ages before everyone is ready. It must be like this every school day.

We have to take two cars to the Bay. They all get into their car and that leaves me with Nan. 'We're going through your milk,' she says. 'They could have brought some with them.' We have to park in the car park and pay because Mum doesn't want to walk miles with Bella and Fred, and all the spaces where we could have parked for free are taken. 'We should have been here earlier,' says Nan.

'It was always going to be hard to find free parking for both cars,' says my dad. We walk round the harbour. On the coast the wind is cruel and I'm freezing even in my big coat. Both piers are crowded. Mum holds on to Bella and Dad holds on to Fred so they don't get pushed in. At the top of the slipway over a hundred half-naked people are dancing to keep warm, waiting for the signal to dash into the harbour. For once, wearing fancy dress looks sensible: you can keep more clothes on.

'They used to do this on the beach,' Nan explains, 'but it can be dangerous.'

The water is grey-grim and sloshy. They only have to swim to a buoy in the harbour and back – not out to sea – but I wouldn't do it. There's a boat in case anyone needs help. Someone is making a speech but the wind tears the words up before they reach us. I see Janey and her mum and Melly: they have a good view from the other pier near the huddle of swimmers. Golden Boy is there in his swimming trunks. Still they are waiting. Then Parp! Some people run down the slipway and dive into the water – swim quickly round the buoy and get out. Golden Boy makes a race of it. Janey jigs up and down. Not everyone can get into the water at once. Some people feel how cold it is on their feet and turn and run. Some people get in slowly and then stay in for ages. It feels like we should wait until everyone has been in and out, but not if they're enjoying it.

The collectors come round and we put some money in a charity bucket. It's like you owe something to the swimmers for watching their pain. Bella doesn't want to give up the 10p coin Mum puts in her hand. Mum has to shake it over the bucket to make her let go.

When we are walking back to the car, Mum says to Terry, 'Did you know they call this the Jurassic Coast?' Looking at Fred's face, you'd think a T. Rex is about to drop its head down on us and roar, or the seagulls turn into pterodactyls. Next time they come we are going to Charmouth or Lyme Regis to look for fossils.

'I expect you do that all the time,' says my dad.

'Err no. Not really.'

Nan sniffs and says, 'Fred will be disappointed if he finds nothing bigger than an ammonite.'

'Actually, ammonites can be quite large,' says my dad.

In the afternoon we go round to Janey's house. I say thank you very much for the chess set.

Janey's mum has given herself a present of a treasure chest. She's going to use it for all the things she really wants to keep. She seems to like talking to my mum and dad.

Janey has a whole new football kit, and boots and two new footballs and some mini goals with nets that we set up out in The Middle. She plays against me and Terry. Fred tries to join in: he's already tired of Melly bossing him about.

Melly is so proud to be an older one at last. She takes charge of Bella. 'Look at your little sister,' says my mum to Terry and me when we go back in. 'She's following Melissa round like a duckling.' Melly loves it, being Mumma Duck. It's all about the quacking for a while.

In the evening of Boxing Day when we are back at ours, my dad says, 'This other chess set. I hear it's kind of special. I'd love to see it.'

So I show him the box. 'Shall we have a game?' he says.

'OK. But I'm not very good. I was only learning.'

'That's all right,' says my dad. 'Let's play anyway.'

We sit at the dining-room table, just the two of us. Mum's upstairs putting Fred and Bella to bed. She told Dad she didn't need help and he should stay and talk to me; they're going home tomorrow. Nan and Terry are on the sofa watching *That Dog can Dance*. Terry is telling Nan about the dog they have at home. 'I wish we could have brung him,' says Terry.

'Maybe next time,' says Nan. She doesn't even like dogs much: she says pets are messy.

Dad spills the pieces onto the board. I can smell polish. 'Black or white?' says Dad.

Last time I played I was black and Janey's dad was white. White goes first. I don't know which I should be now.

Dad picks up a white pawn and a black pawn and puts his hands behind his back. He brings out his two fists and rests them on the table. 'Choose.'

With Janey's dad I would tap the back of his hand. With my dad, I point.

He shows me. 'Black for you,' he says.

'That's what I was last time.'

'Do you remember how to set up the pieces?'

I turn the board so that there is a white corner on my right. The pawns are easy: all the same at the front. At the back, the rooks go on the outside. I remember that because they're like castles – like towers. Then the knights – the horses – go next

to the castles. Then the bishops next to the knights. Then –
you put the White Queen on a white square, the Black Queen
on a black. The King gets what's left. But I can't remember,
when I look at the pieces, which is the King and which is the
Queen. Dad's nearly finished setting up his but he waits to see
what I will do.

'The King,' says Dad, 'is this tall one with the cross on his
head. He's the most important. The Queen is this one, with
the crown. She's the most powerful. It's good to remember
that. Are there any rules in the box?'

'We didn't need them,' I say. 'Janey's dad knew everything.'

'Let's see,' says Dad. 'There's a piece of paper.' He takes it
out. 'It's always handy if you can check things when I'm not
here.'

He opens the folded paper. 'Oh,' he says. 'This is a game.'

He shows me. It's a drawing of the chessboard with the
pieces laid out. The game has already been started.

I know what it is. It's the game I was playing with Janey's
dad. Janey's mum must have drawn it for me.

'OK,' says Dad. 'Do you want to set it up like that?'

'No,' I say. 'I don't think so. Not this time.' My throat closes
up and it feels sore to speak.

'You know you could start the game at that point and carry
on, and it wouldn't always turn out the same. It would all
depend on what you did next. Or the other player.'

'Yeh,' I say. 'I get it.'

'Well,' he says. 'When you're ready.'

And we play one game. He wins.

They leave the next morning, my new family. Mum is crying.
She's not cried before. 'We've only just found you,' she says,
'and it's such a long way.'

Fred is crying too but only because he has to say goodbye

to Ted. 'You can see him next time,' I say. I don't want to be mean but I'm not letting him go off to Wales. I don't even know exactly where they live yet. Dad smiles at me. He gives me a hug but it feels awkward. 'Let's start a new game of chess,' he says. 'You can make the first move.'

'I'll have to be white then,' I say. 'White always begins.'

'If you like,' he says. 'We don't *have* to stick to that rule.'

'But...'

'But OK. Text me what you decide. And your first move.'

'Oh,' I say, embarrassed. 'I don't have my own phone.'

'Then just call me on the landline,' he says. 'Is that OK?' He looks at Nan.

'I expect you'll have your own mobile soon,' says Mum.

Nan says, 'We'll see.'

'Bye, Mum,' says my dad. He doesn't try to hug her.

They shut the doors and wave and off they go.

If they wanted to take me with them they'd need a bigger car.

'You'll be glad to have your room back,' says Nan, hopefully.

When we go into the house and it's just the two of us, it is so quiet. 'I'm going round to Janey's,' I say.

'All right,' says Nan. 'I love you.'

She never says that, so she can't be surprised when I don't say it back.

Janey's mum says, 'It was so nice to meet your family, Michael.'

'You look like your dad,' says Janey.

'Do I?'

'I don't mean you look exactly like him,' says Janey. 'More like you in a bendy mirror or something.'

'He doesn't have cow's milk either,' I say. 'None of them do.'

'Is that how your Nan knew what to do?' says Janey's mum. 'Because you're the same?'

'I don't know if he's allergic. They just don't like hurting animals.' When I think about it, neither do I. Maybe I should become a vegan.

'Are you going to live with them?' says Janey.

'Mmm. I don't know.'

'Your nan must feel so bad,' says Janey. 'You could get her to do anything you want now.'

'I don't think so.'

'No,' says Janey, sighing. 'Neither do I.'

I stay for hours – and Nan doesn't come to fetch me. I wonder if she's gone away. I could just live at Janey's until – what? Until I can go and live in Wales? I can't go anywhere without Nan's permission. And I wouldn't know anyone there. Only them.

'Are you sure your nan's all right?' says Janey's mum. 'I'd ask you to stay for tea but...'

'It's OK,' I say. 'I'd better go.' I remember what else I had to say about the chess set. 'Thank you for making the drawing. I didn't see it at first. My dad found it.' I feel bad saying that: my dad.

'I hope you don't mind,' she says. She sounds relieved. 'I thought you might want to remember that last game.'

'I did. I do.'

'Nice that your dad plays too.'

I go back to our house. A full moon behind the clouds. Nan is watching TV with the sound low. She hardly moves when I come in. I go upstairs. Without all the stuff, without my brothers, my room feels empty.

I sit with Ted in my arms. I could almost wish that Irma was here to talk to but, like Mum said, maybe I should let her go. Maybe me thinking about her all the time was keeping her here. I thought that was what she wanted.

It kind of feels like Nan's died too. If she really was dead – would I miss her?

I wonder what's for tea.

I hear Nan coming up the stairs and my heart clenches like

a fist. I think she will come and knock and ask if I'm all right, do I want something to eat? But she goes to her room and shuts the door. The house is quiet.

Then the phone rings in the hall and I run downstairs to get it. 'Michael?' It's my mum. 'We're home!' The dog is barking, so she has to shout. 'We've just got him back from the neighbour. He's excited.'

'I wish I could meet him.'

'Seven hours!' says Mum. 'We had to stop three times. You can never get them to all go to the loo at once. And then there was the shopping.' She says something about dinner – not to me. Maybe to my dad. 'Well I won't keep you now. Just wanted to let you know we'd made it.' Her voice sounds like she's smiling. 'It was lovely to see you, Michael. It really was. I hope you and your nan will be OK.'

'Tell Dad I'm thinking about my first move.'

'You do that,' says Mum. 'Love you.'

'Love you too, Mum.' I trip over my tongue because I've never said it before. It makes me feel light-headed. Something seems to give in my chest, like those pictures of ice floes breaking up because of global warming. I'm even smiling when I put the phone down.

The silence creeps back in. I sit at the dining-room table and study the chessboard. There's no sound from upstairs. No radio. I push a pawn forwards two spaces and write down my opening move. I could ring Dad now. I walk to the phone but – they sounded busy. Don't want to spoil things.

I make tea: a mug for me and one for Nan.

I carry Nan's tea upstairs and knock on the door; she doesn't answer.

'Nan?' I could open the door. There'll be a hump in the bed, not even the top of Nan's head showing, like those fake bodies made out of pillows. I'll go in and call again: 'Nan?' The hump will be breathing. I'll put the mug on the coaster on her bedside table and stand there, wondering whether to try and pull the covers back. Just enough to see her face. She has hold of it and won't let go. I'll pull harder.

'What?' she'll say, crossly, pushing back the covers. Her hair is sticking out like Einstein.

'They got home all right.'

'Oh good for them.'

'Are you hiding? I brought you some tea.'

'Thank you. You're a good boy.'

'Most of the time.'

'I love you, Michael.'

'I love you too, Nan.'

It could go like that. But I don't go in. Instead, I put the mug down outside her room, rap on the door three times and shout, 'Tea!' Then I go downstairs.

I have Christmas cake and sheep's milk cheese with my tea and study the chessboard. I don't touch the pieces. I have to wait for Dad to make his move. And anyway, I wouldn't while my hands are sticky. When I've finished I wash up my plate and mug and dry my hands. On the worktop by the side door, tucked behind the kitchen roll, there's Nan's pouch of tobacco. She said she'd give up – but when?

I put the pouch in the fridge behind the milk and go back and sit looking at the chessboard, thinking what move my dad will make and what I will do next and on and on, until I notice that my hands are tapping on my knees: left-right-right-left; right-left-left-right; right-left-left-right left-right-right-left; left-right-right-left right-left-left-right right-left-left-right left-right-right-left; right-left-left-right left-right-right-left left-right-right-left right-left-left-right...

We're lost in that no-man's land between Boxing Day and New Year. The fairy lights are all off in our house. It should be cosy and Christmassy but instead it's dark and dead.

Nan's like a chess piece, made of wood. I feel she's hiding from me: only it isn't a game.

I think I can tell Janey about it. I try.

'You've got to pull her out of it right now,' says Janey. 'Or she'll be stuck, like Mum was.'

How am I going to do that? I don't even want to speak to Nan. I wish I wasn't there. All that's left in our house is an ache.

'Can I come and live with you?' I ask.

'You can't leave your nan on her own,' says Janey. 'You've got to start being normal.'

'Yeh. Maybe with a cricket bat and some golf balls?'

'No. Copycat.'

At least I can speak to my dad on the phone every day because of the chess. I always have my next move ready. Sometimes they're quite busy at the other end and Mum takes a message and Dad rings me back. If Terry takes a message I think he sometimes forgets to pass it on. I wait and wait, wondering when my dad's going to call – or should I try one more time? I think of them all sitting at the table with the phone ringing. 'Oh. It's *him* again.'

It would be easier if I could just text my dad. Our game is going very slowly. Sometimes I have all day to think about my move and Dad works out his in the five minutes when me and Mum are talking. Then I have another whole day to think about mine.

'Do you think I could learn Welsh?' I ask Mum.

'You could. It's easy for our three. Terry started at primary school and he's teaching the others.'

'Are you going to learn?'

'I know more than Terry thinks I do. But for some reason he gets upset if I speak Welsh. He doesn't mind me speaking French though.'

'Does he speak French?'

'Not much.'

'So you could teach me French and that would be our secret language.'

She laughs and says, 'Peut-être.' When she speaks French she really sounds French too – like a different person.

Me and Nan: a horrible silence has clamped down on us. She hardly even looks at me. I feel like shouting at her: 'I don't know why *you're* cross. I haven't done anything wrong!' In my head I'm shouting it over and over.

I ask Nan, 'Why can't we go to Aberystwyth?'

'I don't feel like going anywhere,' Nan says.

'You could put me on the train.' If I could be with my mum and dad, I wouldn't have to go to the party the Bulls are having in Irma's house.

'You're too young to travel alone.'

'So what about New Year's Eve?'

'So what?' she says. 'So what about it?'

'Do we still have to go?'

'I think we do. What do you think?' I think what's the point in being good and helpful if you still feel like you're bad? I stop doing the washing up. Nan stops too. And she hasn't cooked since Christmas Day. The plates and mugs pile up. There are no clean knives or spoons. We've finished the turkey and are eating cheese and crackers, pickled onions, mince pies, chocolate, Christmas cake, nuts, little oranges and cereal. I don't know what will happen when the party food runs out.

Monday morning: 31 December 2012. I wake Nan with my T. Rex by walking her into the bedroom door over and over until Nan opens it. Squawky has a note stuck to her forehead: it says, 'Downstairs', not in my writing. Nan rips the note off Squawky's head and squints at it. Sniffs: the smell of coffee, and of bacon frying. With one foot Nan topples the mighty dinosaur and is already backing into her room when she looks right at me, peeping from mine. Our eyes lock for a second or two before she shuts her door. If she looks out of the window, she'll see Mike's car, in what Mrs Bull likes to think of as her parking space.

I tiptoe past Nan's room and down to the kitchen where Mike is stirring and scraping pans: we're having bacon and eggs, mushrooms, toast and beans. I pour orange juice into three glasses. Mike has done some of the washing up, with too many suds. Froth is popping, sliding down the clean plates in the rack. It's warm and the windows are steaming up. Nan acts very surprised to see him when she comes down in her dressing gown but she's combed her hair and coloured herself in just a little. And I bet she's brushed her teeth.

'Oh, look at those plates,' she says. 'They need rinsing.'

'I'll do it,' I say. 'You sit down.'

'Oh, torture for your nan, not to be in charge,' says Mike.

'Oh stop,' says Nan. And sits down to prove that she can do it.

'Pour the coffee then, love,' says Mike.

She pours and stirs, taps with the spoon on the edge of a mug. There's a pattern. I stop rinsing to listen.

'Morse code,' says Mike, stirring the beans. 'Your nan's sending out an SOS.' He takes a dripping plate from me. 'That's good: nice and warm.'

'I'll dry them,' says Nan. She hops up and gets a clean tea towel. 'That's usually Michael's job. I wash and he dries.'

'Only you've both been on strike.'

Between us we get everything on to the plates and sit down.

'Wow,' I say, happily. 'This is huge.'

'Mike has a rule, don't you, Mike?' says Nan.

'Oh yes. "Never eat anything bigger than your own head".'

I check the size of my breakfast. It's just about OK.

'You must have had an early start,' says Nan.

'Oh. 7-ish,' says Mike. 'I can always have a lie down this afternoon.'

'Ready for the party,' I say. Because we're all going to be up until tomorrow.

'You're staying here, are you?' says Nan.

'Michael invited me.'

'It was a surprise,' I say, pushing my beans away from my egg. I give her a quick look. 'To cheer you up.'

She takes a sip of coffee and I think she smiles but she hides it behind the cup.

'You've got a good one there, Zene,' says Mike. 'He's a credit to you.'

'I don't know about that,' says Nan. 'I didn't give him permission to use my phone. But thanks anyway.'

After breakfast, Nan says she will have to take some food to the party and what would I like.

'Crisps I can eat and sausages.'

'All right,' she says. 'And I'm going to make some hummus.'

'Hummus?' says Mike, winking at me. 'Isn't that something you put on the garden?'

'Ha ha,' says Nan. 'I need to practise my vegan recipes. I'd better get changed and get to the shops. Can't spend all day in my dressing gown.'

Mike's interested in my game of chess with Dad. He doesn't play chess but I could teach him with the other set. I could play two games at once.

It's good having Mike here. He acts like everything is all right. He gets Nan talking and there isn't that horrible silence. Even going to the Bulls tonight will be better now he's around.

He has a snooze on the sofa in the afternoon. I want to go to sleep in the armchair but Mike snores, so I go and see how

Nan is doing. She shuts the kitchen door.

'I had to buy tinned chick peas,' she says. 'No time for soaking and boiling. Don't tell your mother.'

'I don't want to have any secrets.'

'It's only hummus,' says Nan. 'Anyway, I was joking.'

In the washing-up bowl is the jug blender. She still isn't using the one I gave her.

'Maybe next time,' she says.

Later, we are all sitting at the table having tea and Christmas cake so that we don't turn up next door hungry like wolves. 'Are you going to be all right at this party?' Nan wants to know.

'Oh,' says Mike. 'I'll be all right.'

'Yes,' says Nan. 'I know *you*'ll be fine: I was talking to Michael. Mrs Bull wants to show the neighbours that Michael's given up worrying about Irma's chicken soup. We're supposed to be on our best behaviour.'

'You'll get no trouble from me,' says Mike.

I shrug. 'But nobody ever explained what happened to it. It didn't just disappear.'

'Easiest thing in the world,' says Mike, 'making food disappear.' And he takes a big bite of cake.

'But remember, the police didn't find any signs,' says Nan. 'No evidence of cookery at all.'

'There was the spoon,' I say. 'Upside down. You wouldn't let me tell the police about that.'

'You were in there before the police came,' says Nan. 'They wouldn't have believed you.'

'Seems to me, Zene,' says Mike, 'that you've got to make up your mind. Do *you* believe Michael?'

'You don't understand,' says Nan. 'Michael found her. Well, George Bull found her first and then Michael went in there too.'

Even now, when I think about Irma lying on the floor, my fists clench, all by themselves.

'I'm sorry to hear that, butt.' says Mike. 'You shouldn't have seen that. It's a hell of a thing to have in your head.'

We eat our cake and drink our tea.

'So, yes,' I say. '*George* was there before the police came too: think of all the things *he* could have messed with.'

'Could you have done that, Michael?' asks Nan. 'If you were in his place? With Irma right there?'

I don't know. I remember I wanted to get out of that kitchen *fast*.

'OK,' says Nan. 'So where would you have put the soup?'

Easy. 'In the freezer. And then I'd wash up.'

Mike chips in too. 'But if you think the dad had something to do with it, do you think he'd leave her like that for his son to find? You'd have to be a hard bastard to do that.'

'He *is* a hard bastard,' I say, not catching Nan's eye. And so is Bully. Or – he used to be.

'What *I* thought,' Nan says, 'is that, because that boy was bullying you, not that you'd made it up, exactly, but that you *wanted* his father to have done something really bad. Or maybe that you couldn't accept losing Irma so soon after Janey's dad.'

'Janey's dad had cancer! He couldn't help it.'

'Well, Irma couldn't help it.'

'No, but…' I want to say, it *can't* just happen like that. Just when you're getting used to the idea of one person leaving you another one goes. But I don't say it because I know it could happen – just like that.

Nan insists on it. 'It's a horrible fact of life that people die – people we love and don't want to lose.'

'But this is *different*,' I say. 'It didn't have to happen.'

'*I* feel really cross with her sometimes,' says Nan. 'She should have been here looking after you. Not spending half the day next door.'

'She didn't want to make a mess in your kitchen.'

'Worried about *him* coming back more like.'

I thought of the way Irma kept running back next door. Those two faces through the window.

'Maybe she was just trying to keep everyone happy,' says Mike.

'Oh yes,' says Nan. 'She was that sort of person. And they knew just how to take advantage of her. But she let them! Just think of all the things she did for that horrible boy.'

Only, that day, she was supposed to be looking after *me*. Why didn't she come back with the soup? 'She left me on my own for *hours*.'

'Did she?' says Nan.

'Didn't you wonder where she was?' asks Mike.

'I didn't know! I was asleep. And she left the door unlocked. And when I rang her, she didn't even pick up the phone!'

'Maybe she couldn't,' says Mike. 'Not if she was already … you know.'

I shake my head. 'I *saw* her through the window.'

'I thought that was at lunchtime,' says Nan.

'No. There were two of them then. This was after. And don't say it's my fault if you didn't know. You told me to shut up. Remember?'

Mike looks at Nan and shakes his head.

'When was that, Michael?' says Nan. 'I mean, when did you see her?'

I think about it. 'After Lunch and before Tea.'

'That narrows it down,' says Mike.

'You mean in the cricket?'

I nod.

'So before 3 o'clock? Something like that?'

'Yes. I rang her number and she didn't answer and I didn't leave a message. But if she looked at the phone she'd know it was me, wouldn't she?'

'And then she came round?'

'No. I just saw her through the window.'

'Our kitchen window?' says Nan. 'Are you *sure* it was her?'

'Come on, Zene,' says Mike. 'His eyes must be better than yours.'

'But anyone can make a mistake,' says Nan.

'Even you?' says Mike.

I fold my arms. 'She was wearing her blue smock, remember?'

'Same colour as a policeman's uniform?' says Nan.

I shake my head. 'When *he* comes home he always takes off his jacket. And it's a white shirt.'

'And maybe for once he didn't and it wasn't Irma you saw.'

Suddenly I get the taste of banana and coconut milk in my mouth. I rang her number from upstairs. I thought she was just ignoring me. But what if I'd taken the phone downstairs and rung Irma from our kitchen? What if I'd *seen* that blue shape stop and listen to the phone and decide *not to pick it up*?

'So, are we still going to this party?' says Mike.

It's open house next door from 8 o'clock. I have to go and act like everything's normal. Nan says I should trust her. She says, 'Irma was my best friend. Do you really think I'd let them get away with murder?'

I think she'd like me not to make any trouble. But... 'I'm no good at pretending,' I remind her, which is not quite true, because I haven't told her my other worry, that it was Irma's ghost I saw through the window, puzzling over her own dead body. I don't think a ghost could answer the phone.

Mike seems to find it easy. It's all new for him, next door: everything and everyone. He shakes hands with Shawn Bull and Bully and Golden Boy and then starts giving out kisses, to Mrs Bull and Janey and her mum, not leaving out Golden Boy's mum and Mrs Rogers either, though he doesn't know who they are. None of them *look* as if they mind. When he swamps Melly with a big hug, Nan frowns, like he's not supposed to do that – but Melly is in love with him already.

For me and Nan it's hard being here: this is a house where we used to feel right at home. Some things look different: the furniture's been moved around, but that's OK. It's the things that haven't changed that don't seem to belong, like Irma's ukulele hanging on the wall. A shadow passes over its glossy green face: Bully.

He doesn't say anything. He just takes the ukulele down and starts twanging it, pulling so hard on the out-of-tune strings and making faces, like he's trying to bend it in two and break it. I turn away. Though it burns in my throat I'm not going to say anything. I have to be nice to him but – give me a minute.

Nan puts her arm round my shoulders and steers me to the crowded kitchen to get a drink. Apparently, the plan is to mill about first then eat and play games and maybe watch Jules Holland. Or switch over to see the fireworks at midnight. Nice and normal. 'The new normal,' says Janey's mum, raising her glass. She looks like she's determined to have a good time. She's brought champagne to open at midnight, if Melly lasts that long.

'Oh we've got plenty of fizz,' says Mrs Bull. 'And we can always put your little girl to bed if she gets tired.'

'So let's open Vi's bottle now,' says Nan. 'And we'll drink to absent friends.'

I wander back into the living room but there aren't enough chairs and I end up sitting on the floor, only people keep walking round me. So I stand up again. I don't know where to settle. If I liked Bully – if he liked me, we could have helped each other out. As it is, every time he comes into the room I think about leaving it. Hallway, living room, kitchen, we go round and round.

Neighbours come and go. Mrs Rogers stays: I feel her watching me and Nan and the Bulls to see how we're getting on.

Mrs Bull tries, I suppose. She asks me how I like my new family and isn't it funny my brothers and sister are Welsh?

I say, 'I'm Welsh too, aren't I, Nan?'

'Georgie?' says Mrs Bull. 'Did you know Michael is Welsh?'

'No,' he says. 'He's rubbish at rugby.'

'Ha ha,' I say. 'Ha ha. True!'

Nan takes a deep breath and smiles and asks Mrs Bull how the job hunting's going.

'Oh, I've got plenty to do being a homemaker.' Mrs Bull's sweeping arm includes the whole house, like she built it or something. 'I'm not looking for *more* work.'

Yeh, and they don't need the money, do they? Because they've got Irma's house and everything. Everyone's thinking it. Especially Mrs Rogers.

To help Mrs Bull out, Nan says, 'It's really nice to be invited. We've had so many happy times here in the past.'

I wonder if Irma will come to the party. Everyone must be thinking about her, even the few people who never met her when she was alive. Golden Boy's mum only saw her when she was dead. I don't know what I'm supposed to call Golden Boy's mum on her night off, but Nan says the police are never off duty, so I'll call her Detective Inspector Dunbar. There doesn't seem to be a Mr Dunbar.

'I didn't know you'd be here,' says Nan. 'Don't get me wrong. I'm glad to see you.'

'Shawn and his wife asked me ages ago,' the inspector explains. 'I'd have been happy with a quiet night in, only then Violet asked me too. And when you're asked twice. Well it would be rude to say no!' She clinks glasses with Janey's mum and nods towards Janey and Golden Boy ignoring us all in a corner. 'Those two. It's quite sweet, isn't it?'

Bully scowls so I smile. The way Janey and Golden Boy

look at each other – it makes me think of my parents. When I ring my family in Wales tomorrow (which is also next year), I'll ask Mum and Dad how old they were when they first met.

Janey and Golden Boy want to go into town to see their friends but they have to be back before midnight. So, no hanging round the Town Hall in fancy dress. Not this year anyway. 'And no drinking,' says Inspector Dunbar, holding up her wine glass and raising a warning finger.

'Janey doesn't drink,' I say. 'She's an athlete.'

Janey blushes because everyone laughs as if I've said something funny. 'I was joking, Michael,' says Inspector Dunbar.

'Janey's much too young for that,' says her mum.

It's not me who needs reminding.

Mrs Bull says they can see themselves out. 'Isn't this nice?' she asks everyone. 'It's *lovely* to get to know our neighbours at last. And we can all look forward to better things in 2013.'

It feels like a very long way to midnight.

All the food is laid out on the kitchen table. There are the sausages and the crisps that I can eat and Nan's hummus. There are quiches and pies and dips and cheese. So many things I can't eat unless I ask Mrs Bull what's in them. If this was Irma's party she'd take me round the table and show me: I wouldn't have to ask.

I go out of the kitchen door and stand on the doorstep, looking down the path into the dark garden. Here we are in her house and no one is talking about her. We're trampling all over her. All over her kitchen anyway, although Nan did raise her glass and say, 'Absent friends!'

She's been gulping down the wine. At least, if she falls over, Mike's here to pick her up. She and Janey's mum had tears but they brushed them away. I hear Janey's mum laughing now.

Nan comes out. 'Are you all right, Michael?'

I try to go past her, back indoors. I expect she just wants a smoke.

'No, wait,' says Nan, putting a hand on my arm.

I stop – but she doesn't say anything and then I hear someone eating crisps in the kitchen. Only Bully can chomp that loud. I bet he's eating my crisps: the only ones I can have. I push past Nan. I was right. He looks at me and grabs another massive handful from the bowl.

'They're mine,' I say.

'No,' he says, pointing to the food on the table. 'See this? All mine.'

'But I can't eat the others.'

He goes for some more and I grab his hand. Not that I want them if they've been in his sweaty paw.

'Get off me, gay boy,' he says. 'I don't wanna hold your hand.'

'Hello!' says Nan, coming in and making Bully jump. 'That's not very nice, is it, George?' I let him go and he backs away from us still feeding crisps into his mouth.

'Why don't you try some of my hummus?' Nan says, offering him the bowl.

He shakes his head.

Mrs Bull comes in. 'Everything all right? Michael, do help yourself. Don't be shy.'

'I thought George might like to try my hummus,' says Nan.

'Oh!' Mrs Bull says, peering at it and pulling a face. 'It's a bit lumpy for him. You don't like anything with bits in it, do you?' Bully shakes his head again, not taking his eyes off Nan.

'That's what I thought,' says Nan. Bully gets behind his mum and shuffles out of the kitchen.

I eye the dips of doom and ask Mrs Bull which ones I can have but she says, 'Err, umm,' and I say, 'It doesn't matter.' So we know she didn't make them even though they're all turned out in Irma's little bowls.

Nan pats me on the shoulder and gives me the rest of the

packet of crisps we brought, which she hid behind the spoon pot for emergencies. She follows Mrs Bull back into the living room. I stay in the kitchen and eat a sausage dipped in hummus and then in the broken crisps at the bottom of the packet. When I've finished I stand in the doorway watching everyone. I need to wake up to things. I need to take more notice of what's really happening instead of looking inside my own head all the time. But the back of my neck tingles as if Irma got up from the floor and is breathing on me. I shake my head and Nan glances over but she goes on chatting to Mrs Bull. She's asking her about her kitchen appliances. Mrs Bull is saying how she's felt really so much more settled now she's made space for some of her own stuff. Nan sounds like she really is interested. Bully keeps near his dad, who's talking to Mike. Janey's mum and Inspector Dunbar are chatting away, probably planning the wedding. Melly's asleep in a chair. It's only 9 o'clock. I think she just got bored. Mrs Rogers' sharp eyes are drilling into Nan and Mrs Bull.

I hear Nan say, over the top of everyone else, 'You could have used Irma's old one. It only needed a new plug.'

Bully's dad falters in his story. He says 'Umm' and loses his place.

Nan's telling Mrs Bull about the Christmas present I got her from the car boot sale.

Mrs Bull looks down her nose.

Mrs Rogers looks worried.

'Yes,' says Mrs Bull. 'I *did* get rid of a few old things from under the stairs. I thought it had all gone to be recycled or to the charity shop. How funny that it ended up at a … a "car boot sale".'

'I wonder why it needed a plug?' says Nan. 'It wasn't very old and I'm sure it would have had a sealed plug on it before. I'm sure it did. She hadn't had it very long.'

'I don't know,' says Mrs Bull, frowning. 'Only, you can't be too careful with electricals. Shawn did rather tell me off for passing it on. But I thought, *someone* might have a use for it.'

Mrs Rogers looks as if she wishes she'd gone home half an hour ago, but so far no one's mentioned her name, and if she leaves now, everyone will notice and start talking about her.

'Michael put a new plug on it,' says Nan. 'Is your George interested in things like that? Not that it's something for children to play with. You can't be too careful where electricity's concerned. Did Shawn ever tell you about the time Irma got a belt off the cooker? It was probably like that for ages, an accident waiting to happen. Then one day, the wires touched and – Bang!'

Mrs Bull's smile is fixed now. And everyone is kind of listening to what Nan's saying even though they're still talking. Then Nan calls across the room. 'Shawn? You know that blender that used to belong to Irma. Was there something wrong with it? Only I've ended up with it now...'

'I don't know,' he says. 'Not really my area of expertise.' He chuckles and looks sideways at Mike for support.

Mike says nothing and Nan carries on. 'No, I mean, I'm sure Irma must have used it quite a lot.' She looks past Shawn Bull to his son and puts her head on one side. 'Isn't that right, George? Because you like *your* food nice and smooth. And Irma was so *kind*, wasn't she? She'd always try to give you what you wanted. So I'm sure *you'd* remember when it stopped working?'

Bully shakes his head. Nan sounds so friendly. Like she's just having a chat. But Bully looks at the floor.

'She was so nice to you wasn't she, George? I'm sure you must miss her too.'

'Mum?' he says.

'It's all right, Georgie,' says his mum, looking icicles at Nan.

I turn back into the kitchen and open the tall freezer, pull out a drawer and start taking out boxes and packets: fish fingers, peas. There's no room on the table or the worktop so I just drop them on the floor. Ice cream. Mixed berries. A pizza.

Ice cubes. Half a loaf of bread.

Mrs Bull comes in. 'What on *earth* do you think you're doing?' She starts picking things up again. 'It's a good thing I washed this floor.'

I've got an unmarked white tub in my hand. 'What's in here?'

'I don't know, but you can't just go throwing things about.' She stands up with her arms full of frozen food. 'I'm *sorry* we haven't catered to your dietary needs but in future if there's something you would like you only have to ask.'

'I'm looking for the chicken soup,' I say.

'You're letting all the cold out.' She starts stuffing things back into the freezer. I'm trying to get the lid off the tub and it's frozen so tight shut that it cracks. She snatches the tub from me, shoves it back in the drawer, squashing the bread. She pushes me out of the way so she can close the freezer door. 'I'll have to get your grandmother.'

Nan's already here.

'Oh,' says Mrs Bull. 'This is just too much. You'd better take him home.'

'He's not hungry,' says Nan. 'He's looking for evidence.'

'Shawn!' Mrs Bull forgets she's such a lady and bellows like a cow.

Bully's dad comes wearily into the kitchen. He tries to close the door to the other room, but Mike has followed him and he's so big, you can't shut the door on him.

'You OK, Zene?' says Mike.

'Yes, thank you, Mike.'

'Michael?'

I nod.

'Michael's worked something out,' says Nan. 'Because little Georgie Bull doesn't like bits in his soup.'

Detective Inspector Dunbar, Janey's mum and Mrs Rogers are all trying to get into the kitchen. Mike lets them in.

'This again,' says Mrs Bull.

'What would Irma do?' Nan asks me.

'She'd use her blender,' I say. 'Make the soup all nice and smooth.'

Janey's mum nods. *She* knows what Irma was like. She hasn't forgotten.

'Yep,' says Nan. 'Sooner or later, that's what she'd do. And get the shock of her life. Maybe not enough to show but enough to make her heart…'

'Shake like a jelly,' I say.

'Fibrillate,' says Nan. 'And without help, she died, right here on this kitchen floor.'

'That's enough,' says Bully's mum. 'How dare you come into *my* house…'

'It isn't your house!' Nan says, her eyes flaring. 'You shouldn't even be here!'

At last. That's what I've been *saying*.

'I think you'd better leave,' says Mrs Bull, pointing to the kitchen door.

'No,' says Nan.

'Shawn?'

He hasn't said a word so far.

'You people,' says Mrs Bull. 'We've tried to get on with you. Have you any idea how traumatic it was for my boy? Well, I'm not having it.' She looks at her husband and at Detective Inspector Dunbar. 'You must be able to do something!'

Inspector Dunbar clears her throat – and then looks round. 'Where is he, anyway?'

Everyone turns to look. We all pile back into the other room. Bully's not there.

'Well thank goodness,' says Mrs Bull, with a sigh. 'Maybe he didn't hear it.'

'But where's Melly?' says Janey's mum. The armchair where she was sleeping – it's empty.

We look and we call but Melly doesn't answer. Her mum is first out of the house: she runs down the path in the glistening dark. 'Melly!'

'Mu-um?' Melly's voice, quavering down from upstairs.

'Vi!' shouts Nan. 'She's here.'

Janey's mum rushes back in looking around wildly.

'George will have taken her to the bathroom,' says Mrs Bull, still sounding peeved.

Janey's mum runs upstairs, tries the bathroom door and when it won't open, raps on the wood. 'Melly? Are you all right? Oh, sweetheart! You're not stuck are you? You haven't locked yourself in?'

Melly starts to cry.

'It's all right, darling, just stay calm. Mummy's here.'

Mrs Bull is climbing the stairs. 'There's really no need to make such a fuss.'

I'm still down in the hallway between Nan and Mike. I feel safer there: Bully's dad looks like he really could murder someone right now.

'Georgie?' says Mrs Bull. She goes out of sight, maybe to check his room, and comes back without him.

'Mum!' Melly shouts.

Then we hear Bully's voice, clear and low from inside the bathroom. 'Shut. Up.'

'All right,' says Janey's mum, trying to sound calm. 'Now, George, you don't need to have the door locked, do you? Can you open it for me?'

'I expect it was an emergency,' says Mrs Bull. 'He was just keeping an eye on her.' She taps on the door. 'Georgie? It's Mummy. Is everything all right? I expect Melissa's mummy can help her now. George? Can you open the door please?'

'Go away!' he shouts.

I want to go up the stairs. Nan holds on tight to my arm. She says to Shawn Bull, 'Let's not have anyone else getting hurt now. Can't you put a stop to this?'

Bully's dad – his eyes so pale and angry – doesn't say a word.

The inspector says, 'Shawn, perhaps we should concentrate on getting your lad to open the door? Melissa sounds frightened and we don't want this to escalate.'

Mrs Rogers looks glad now that she didn't go home before. She'll be putting this in a newsletter.

'Open the door, please, Georgie,' says his mum. She knocks again. 'George!'

Bully's dad pushes past us and climbs the stairs, slowly. He steers his wife to one side. 'It's all right, Son,' he calls through the bathroom door. 'Your dad's here.'

Inspector Dunbar is looking at me and Nan and she shakes her head a little, as if to say, what have you done?

Nan says to her, quietly, while we all watch what's going on at the top of the stairs, 'As soon as Melly's safe, we're going home. I need you to come round.'

'I can't just leave.' The inspector keeps her voice low too.

'You must,' says Nan. 'Please. We'll be waiting.'

'I don't know what good you think it will do.'

'Don't you see? It was the blender. Something to cause another electrical "accident", like the one Irma had with the cooker.'

'Yes what was that? What accident?' says the inspector. 'What were you talking about?'

'Didn't you know?' says Nan.

'I don't recall anyone mentioning it at the time,' says the inspector, giving Nan a hard look. Then she glances up the stairs and says, 'And a motive?'

'Isn't that obvious?' whispers Nan.

'But he's a police officer,' says Mrs Rogers.

'Not him,' says Nan. 'The boy.'

Silence. Then Mike says, 'But he's only a child.'

'And I suppose he's up there playing hide-and-seek right

now,' says Nan. 'That boy just wanted his real mum back.'

They all look at me, as if to say, either Nan's wrong or maybe I could be a murderer too. Nan squeezes my shoulder.

'Could be he's hiding from *you*,' says Inspector Dunbar.

Nan shakes her head. 'Maybe he thought, if only Irma had died that first time. And then he messed with the blender and half-forgot about it. An accident waiting to happen.'

That's still murder, isn't it? I remember how Bully looked when he came to the door. Crying. So upset. He wasn't pretending.

'But there was no indication,' says the inspector.

'And if you'd found her lying on the floor and a pan of soup on the stove and an electrical appliance she'd obviously been using? I'm just saying, you'd have looked at things differently, wouldn't you? If *someone* hadn't covered things up. Like Michael said all along.'

'But there was a post-mortem,' says Mrs Rogers.

'Yes,' says Nan, 'but what were they looking for? Maybe there weren't any marks.'

'I'm sure there weren't,' says the inspector.

'There weren't the first time,' says Nan. 'But she felt it just the same.'

'But internally,' says the inspector. 'If they checked...'

'If,' says Nan. 'And then she was cremated. And that isn't what *she* wanted.'

The inspector is silent.

'Tissue samples,' says Nan.

The inspector looks at her.

'If the pathologist kept tissue samples from her organs,' Nan says, 'if she had a shock you might be able to trace a pathway from those.'

The inspector doesn't answer.

I say, 'How do you...?'

Nan says, 'Michael. You're not the only one who knows

how to use the internet.' To the inspector she says, 'Please. I know it will be hard. But please come and talk to us. Apart from all that, you have to listen to what Michael has to say.' She leans in. 'It's all about *timing.*'

'You've changed your mind then,' says the inspector. 'You thought he was making things up.'

'I know,' says Nan. She looks at me. 'I'm sorry, Michael. I didn't want to believe it could be true.'

Didn't want to believe. I think Nan could be in trouble now. Maybe she'll have to go to prison. And if that happens…

'Do you think we should batter the door in?' asks Mike.

'Then they *could* get hurt,' says the inspector.

Nan squeezes my shoulder again. 'I think George will do what his dad says.'

At the top of the stairs, Bully's dad is talking. 'Son? There's nothing to worry about. Just open the door.' Janey's mum is biting her knuckles. Bully's dad puts a finger to his lips and then motions the two mothers away along the landing.

'It's just me, Son,' says Bully's dad. 'Everyone else has gone. So just come over to the door. There's a good lad.'

I shut my eyes for a moment. Please let Melly be all right. I don't even mind if they get away with it as long as nothing bad happens to Melly. You understand don't you, Irma? Bully's dad says, 'George, Melissa's mummy just wants to take her home now. It'd be good if you could open the door.'

He puts a hand gently on the wood. I think, any minute now he'll snap and bang his fist. But he doesn't. He stays calm. He waits. 'George,' he says quietly. 'Georgie.' He bows his baldy head like he's very tired and leans it against the door.

Nan gives the inspector a long look.

Are there scissors in there? Could he drown Melly in the bath? Why is it so quiet?

Shawn Bull looks up. The key turns and slowly the door opens. He takes one step so his foot will stop it closing again.

The door swings wider; he shields his boy as Melly is pounced on by her mum. Shawn Bull gives his son room to get out from behind him, and pushes him out of the bathroom.

Bully's face doesn't have any expression. His mum crouches and hugs him. His dad looks down on them both and says, 'No harm done.'

I call up the stairs, 'Is Melly OK?' I want to go and see.

Nan puts a hand on my arm again.

The inspector says, 'If this is all some fairy-tale…'

'Irma was my friend. I should have been the one sticking up for her.' Nan is looking at me. 'I'm so sorry, Michael.'

'What a party,' says the inspector, gazing into her empty wine glass.

Melly is coming down carried by her mum and hiding her face against her mum's shoulder.

'Is she all right?' says Nan.

I touch Melly's leg – she pulls away. Her mum stops to give Nan a good long stare. 'Fat lot you care, Miss Marple,' she says with tight lips. She holds Melly closer. 'She was *frightened.*'

'I'm sorry,' says Nan. 'I didn't think…'

Melly's mum doesn't let her finish that sentence and sweeps out through the open door.

'Shit,' says Nan.

Mike looks at me and his eyebrows go up.

'I'll see to them,' says Inspector Dunbar. She hands Mrs Rogers her empty wine glass. 'Where are their coats?' She takes them and her own and is gone.

Nan pushes me out the door too. 'Mike, get our things will you?'

He answers with a military salute.

'I think I'll just follow you,' says Mrs Rogers.

She would love to stay with us and hear what happens next, when Inspector Dunbar comes round, but once we're out of the gate, Nan stops and goes, 'Goodnight, Mrs Rogers. See you next year.' Disappointed, Mrs Rogers says goodnight too and cuts across The Middle, heading for her neighbour's house, where the lights are on for another party. Halfway there she hesitates, probably getting her story straight – how she just popped in over at the Bulls to make them feel welcome and you'll never guess...

That leaves us, standing outside Irma's house in the last hours of the old year. Last New Year's Eve, we were missing Janey's dad, we didn't know how great we'd be in the Olympics and Irma was still alive. I remember, with the same old kick in the guts, how she danced on the pavement here and sang a song, the day before she died. Just one New Year's Eve before that, we didn't even know that Janey's dad was ill. How much will things have changed when 2013 is old? Where will I be?

We move towards our own gate but Nan stops again and says, 'I'm so sorry, Michael,' as if she needs to sort this out before we go in. That's three times now she's apologised to me. Maybe she means it.

'All right then,' I say. 'But what's going to happen now?'

'There are things the inspector can check,' says Nan. 'We'll show her the blender. And you can tell her what you saw through the window. If Irma was already ... then it seems to me that George's dad was there after and covered things up. There's always the chance George and his dad will tell the truth if they're questioned. And I can tell her why I didn't want to listen to you before.'

'Not a bad offer, butt,' says Mike. I wonder where he's going to sleep tonight.

A movement at the upstairs window next door makes me look up. From Irma's old bedroom, Bully's looking down at us. Behind him, someone is nodding and smiling.

Irma puts her hand on Bully's shoulder and pulls him deeper into the room, their heads floating backwards like two pale balloons.

'Did you see that?' But Nan and Mike are both looking at me, like they're waiting for an answer.

'Can I go and see if Melly's all right?' I say.

'No,' says Nan. 'You're not going anywhere on your own. The inspector will tell us when she comes round.'

'Good job I'm here though,' says Mike.

'Why's that?' says Nan.

Mike waits until we're all safely inside our house and the front door closed before he says: 'Because of Baldy-Boy knowing Michael could be a witness.'

'I think you're forgetting something,' Nan says. 'According to my theory, Shawn Bull isn't a murderer.' She looks sideways at me as if half-expecting me to say I'm sorry too, for picking the wrong suspect.

We wait for the inspector. If she comes soon that will be a good sign because Melly will be OK. I know I can't build my whole life around living next door but one from Janey but however long it takes I will make things right with Janey's mum – and Melly. I don't want to lose anyone else.

I also really want the inspector to come before midnight because she's too blonde and we need someone dark for first-footing. I asked Mike to do it. There hasn't been anyone for that since Janey's dad died. Mike could go round to their house too, and bring them luck.

When the inspector comes we'll tell her everything and then – it won't be up to me any more. If I get my silver lining, the Bulls will soon be gone, sent away or put off by Mrs Rogers' gossip machine. Irma's house will be empty and ready for a new family to move in. Maybe someone we'd like. Or, maybe, because it's all possible now…

What if it could be mine?

Acknowledgements

I dedicate this novel to my late husband, Michael George Street, who loved me and was always proud of me.

Very special thanks to Melissa Roberta Ledwidge for reading drafts of the novel and for her invaluable support and advice.

Thanks to Danny Wallace for his kindness and encouragement. Also to Peggy Hughes and all at the Dundee International Book Prize for being such generous and fabulous hosts.

Special thanks to Penny Byrne, Aneko Campbell, Vicky Joyce, Sarah Klenbort, Holly Müller, Siân Price, Becky Shaw and Cath Sleigh – all busy women who gave me their time. To Alan Bliss and Melanie Byfield for their thoughts and for telling me to 'get on with it'. To Alf and Jo for the continuing support and inspiration.

Thanks to Jonathan Agnew and all at *Test Match Special* for bringing comfort through some difficult years and for unwittingly helping to anchor this novel in real time.

I am indebted to Penny Thomas, friend, editor and lifeline, and to all at Seren.

Thanks to Eric Goulden for making Irma's favourite album of the 1970s, *The Wonderful World of Wreckless Eric*. Lyrics from 'The Final Taxi' are included by kind permission of Eric Goulden (Wreckless Eric) and Imagem London Ltd, an Imagem company.

Finally, to Theo Bakhuizen for his generosity, love and support, and for the gift of speaking with me in Dutch.

About the Author

Maria Donovan is a native of Dorset and has strong connections with Wales and Holland. Past career choices include training as a nurse in the Netherlands, busking with music and fire around Europe and nine years as a lecturer in Creative Writing at the University of Glamorgan.

Among her publications are: *Tea for Mr Dead*, flash fiction (Leaf, 2006) and *Pumping Up Napoleon and other stories* (Seren, 2007). Further short stories appear in anthologies: 'The House Demon' in *Sing, Sorrow, Sorrow* (Seren, 2010), 'The Wish Dog' in *The Wish Dog and other stories* (Honno, 2014) and 'Learning to Say До Свидания' in *New Welsh Short Stories* (Seren, 2015). She draws on her experiences of place and of crossing borders, for instance in 'Slaughterhouse Field', commissioned for *New Welsh Review*, and set amongst caravan people in Holland. Her fiction is often offbeat, exploring uneasy relationships, mind and body: 'My Own CVA' was a prizewinner in a competition run by *The Lancet*; 'My Cousin's Breasts' was shortlisted for the Fish Short Story Prize. Her flash fiction story 'Chess' won the Dorset Award in the Bridport Prize 2015.

The Chicken Soup Murder is Maria's debut novel and was a finalist for the Dundee International Book Prize.

She can be found online at www.mariadonovan.com and on twitter @mestreet